Readers love

ME, HIM, THEM, AND IT

"Deftly captures the emotional complexities of teenage pregnancy. . . . For readers looking for genres that express the stark realities of life with all their highs and lows, this book will be one to recommend." —*VOYA*

"Very honest. Carter delves into all sides of the issue and captures the isolation, guilt, and complex boyfriend/friend/family dynamics surrounding teen pregnancy in well-drawn Evelyn. The popular subject matter should resonate with, and interest, many YAs." —*Booklist*

"Carter doesn't sugarcoat the pain and complications that result from Evelyn's choice. If anything, readers are left to ponder whether there are such things as 'right' decisions for girls in Evelyn's situation." —*Publishers Weekly*

"Characters feel true, and the pregnancy time line helps propel readers through a difficult but rewarding journey as Evelyn's life utterly transforms. A poignant tale that is likely to appeal even to reluctant readers." —*SLJ*

"Breathtaking, brutal and beautifully real, Carter's debut is stunning. She unflinchingly explores the intricate, difficult choices a pregnant teen mu

BOOKS BY CAELA CARTER

Me, Him, Them, and It
My Best Friend, Maybe

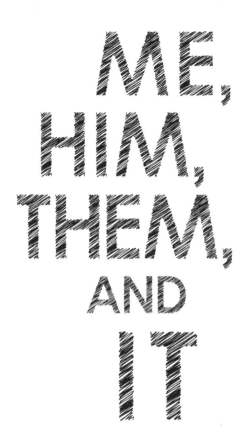

ME, HIM, THEM, AND IT

CAELA CARTER

BLOOMSBURY

NEW YORK   LONDON   NEW DELHI   SYDNEY

First published in the United States of America in February 2013
by Bloomsbury Children's Books
Paperback edition published in June 2014
www.bloomsbury.com

Bloomsbury is a registered trademark of Bloomsbury Publishing Plc

For information about permission to reproduce selections from this book, write to
Permissions, Bloomsbury Children's Books, 1385 Broadway, New York, New York 10018
Bloomsbury books may be purchased for business or promotional use. For information on bulk
purchases please contact Macmillan Corporate and Premium Sales Department at
specialmarkets@macmillan.com

The Library of Congress has cataloged the hardcover edition as follows:
Carter, Caela.
Me, him, them, and it / by Caela Carter. — 1st U.S. ed.
p.   cm.
Summary: Playing the "bad girl" at school to get back at her feuding parents,
sixteen-year-old Evelyn becomes pregnant and faces a difficult decision.
ISBN 978-1-59990-958-5 (hardcover)
[1. Pregnancy—Fiction. 2. Family problems—Fiction. 3. Emotional problems—Fiction.] I. Title.
PZ7.C24273Me 2013   [Fic]—dc23   2012014331

ISBN 978-1-61963-186-1 (paperback)

Book design by Regina Flath
Typeset by Westchester Book Composition
Printed and bound in the U.S.A. by Thomson-Shore Inc., Dexter, Michigan
2 4 6 8 10 9 7 5 3 1

All papers used by Bloomsbury Publishing, Inc., are natural, recyclable products
made from wood grown in well-managed forests. The manufacturing processes
conform to the environmental regulations of the country of origin.

For Mom and Dad

ME,
HIM,
THEM,
AND
IT

39 Days to Decide

This is a complete crock, but I shut my eyes like this squeaky counselor asked.

"Imagine it's just you. You are the only person in the universe. Now, what do you want to do?"

She is a bonehead. My whole freaking life it has been only me. This is the first time that what I do will matter to *someone else*. I open my eyes and survey the brochures on the coffee table that separates me from the Planned Parenthood lackey: *Choosing Abortion*, *The Biology of Abortion*, *Choosing Adoption*, *Teenaged Parenting*. An endless list of bad ideas.

"Anything?" she asks.

I open my mouth, and she scoots her oval face onto her hands, her pointy elbows perched on her tiny knees.

"I just want to disappear myself."

It's true. I don't want to have to make this decision. I don't want to have to face my parents or the nuns or Todd or anyone. I want to abort myself.

She sighs impatiently and tells me I am welcome to come back the next day. I walk out the door toward my Jeep, gripping *The Biology of Abortion* in one hand and *Teenaged Parenting* in the other. My hands are sweating like armpits. I won't be able to read these things anyway because by the time I get home, the little glossy flaps will be all crinkled and stuck together.

That night, I have a dream. I am standing, barefoot and naked, on my chemistry textbook, which is suspended in midair like a little space-aged platform. Everything is dark except an eerie blue ring that shines lengthwise around my body, head to toe. This is some kind of opposite halo; my chemistry book and I are both being flung into hell. Which seems fine, really. But then I hear the *whoosh* of a machine and I realize that I am standing in the middle of an enormous vacuum. The absence of air yanks my arms to their wingspan and my legs almost into a full split. My hair leaps to the top of my head like a troll's. I feel nothing but relief: I will disappear; the baby will disappear; it will be over. My fingernails and toenails are the first to detach and fly into the fluorescent-blue vacuum. It doesn't hurt. Instead, I feel strangely light, like I just had a back massage, or a painkiller, or an orgasm. When I am bald and nailless, the machine peels off my scalp and I feel it stealing each of the twenty-seven bones in my hand one by one. By the time my calf muscles skirt away and the blue light sucks up my brain like a long noodle of spaghetti, my heart feels like it must when you hear someone say "I love you." And I don't even care that it's about to be splattered all over this blue machine.

But then I wake up.

38 Days to Decide

After school, I trudge back to Planned Parenthood and barge into Mary's office. She manages to look happy to see me. Faker.

I start to tell her about my dream, but she shoves a *Suicide Prevention* pamphlet in my face, so she has me all wrong. I don't want to kill myself; I want to be erased. If I kill myself there is a whole big mess, and everyone will find out my business. She looks so worried; her brown eyes are twitching, and that annoys me because, come on, she doesn't even know me. She can't care that much. Maybe she would get in big trouble if I killed myself, since she counseled me the past few days and all.

But I'm not going to kill myself, so I say, "I think I need some more information." I remember the reading that this Planned Parenthood minion gave me for "homework," which is still buried in the back of my bathroom cabinets, hidden from my parents' prying eyes—in case they decide to come out of their caves long enough to pry. "I'm not getting anything from those pamphlets," I add, to cover my ass.

"It's okay if you didn't read them, Evelyn."

I guess all girls who come here are too worked up to read about the various machines that will be shoved up their vaginas in the next few months, no matter which option they choose.

"Let's get the basics on the table, okay?"

"Okay." I use my palms to pull my red frizz into a ponytail.

"You are sixteen, correct? Just beginning your junior year at St. Mary's?"

"Yeah." I wonder how she knows what school I go to until I remember the pleated plaid skirt that is shifting around my mid-thigh—our whole city knows what that skirt means. Even though this building is only a few blocks from my school, maybe three miles from my house, it feels a million miles away.

"So I imagine you have been taught by some pro-life folks in your school. Are you Catholic yourself?"

"My parents are." Here it comes. The nuns at school always paint Planned Parenthood as an abortion factory—taking in a girl and a baby, turning out a girl and a corpse. I didn't think anyone here would be as monstrous as they say, but I thought Mary might push the agenda harder than she has. I guess she was just waiting for the right moment. But then, it's hard to imagine this tiny woman with the twitching brown eyes and phony commiserating frown pushing me into anything.

Here's how I ended up on her dusty couch: a few weeks

ago, I was at the beach with Lizzie complaining as usual about the cavernous gap below my shoulders where God forgot to put my boobs. Lizzie said, "Yeah, I would've thought you'd fill that bikini out a little better now that you're on the pill," and when I told her I wasn't, she freaked. I wanted a chest, so when she said I could go to Planned Parenthood and get a prescription without telling my parents—and that it could move me up a full bra size—I did. I was having sex with Todd anyway, so it seemed like a good idea. On the way home from the first day of school, I just drove myself over here, whistling out the window of my car like a freaking idiot while visions of C-cups bounced in my brain. When I got here, they made me take a blood test, and it said I was already pregnant. The thought had not even occurred to me. That's how much of a dumbass I am.

I got drunk later that night. Todd's friend Sean was having some people over so I convinced Lizzie to go. We got shitfaced. We stripped down and went swimming in our underwear in Sean's pool. Later, once everyone was too wasted to notice, Todd pulled me aside, whispered how beautiful I looked, wrapped me in a towel, and tugged me behind the row of hedges that separates Sean's yard from the highway. We had sex right on the grass with the traffic swinging by. I wasn't sure if sex would hurt the baby, but I knew drinking would, so I figured screw it, and tried to enjoy myself. But that was Friday. I haven't drunk anything or smoked anything or even spoken to Todd since (not that he noticed) and now it's Tuesday and I don't know what to do.

"I didn't ask about your parents," Mary is saying, "I asked about you. Are you Catholic?"

I snap my gum and drum my sparkly blue fingernails on her coffee-table-slash-encyclopedia-of-teen-pregnancy. "Why does that matter?"

"It matters because if you are Catholic, or if your religion in any way precludes you from considering abortion, we'll skip talking about that option. But I want to know about your beliefs because, as I tried to emphasize to you yesterday, this is your decision. Not your parents' decision."

"Oh." Boy, do the nuns have these people wrong. "No. I'm not Catholic. I don't believe in God."

It's the truth. But every time I say it out loud, it has the metallic taste of a lie in my mouth.

"Okay. Basically, you have three options: you could abort, you could parent, or you could go the adoption route. There are advantages and disadvantages to each choice. Does one of them appeal to you more than the others at this point?"

"They all sound pretty shitty."

Mary laughs. I threw that curse in just to test her. She isn't grading me, though, so I can just be honest.

"And why is that?" she asks.

"Well, adoption is . . . like being an anonymous kidney donor. I take something out of my body and just give it away. Why would I do that? I always thought those anonymous donor people were creeps. Not just creeps, lonely creeps."

"Okay . . ." Her tiny hand scribbles tinier curlicues while I speak. I don't give a crap what she writes down, but I wonder what I could possibly be saying that merits notetaking. I imagine her writing her memoirs, not paying attention to me at all. She's in her own world while pretending to be concerned that I might run home and off myself tonight.

"And what makes the other options shitty, as you say?"

I almost giggle. She has such a hard time saying shitty, like she's trying to say it while simultaneously spitting gum out of her mouth.

"I would be a crappy parent. And I don't even like this thing," I say, tapping my abdomen.

"You don't like what thing? The fetus?"

"I don't like the baby. I know it's not the baby's fault, but it showed up and everything sucks. Now, I can't drink, I can't smoke weed, I can't have sex, I think there are kinds of food I'm not supposed to eat, and there must be other stuff. I can't even think since this baby latched on. It doesn't leave my head. Like some really annoying person at school that you just can't avoid even though you don't care about them at all. I didn't even get my homework done this weekend. And I'm always on top of school stuff."

She interjects, "I'm sure you are." Now I know she is lying. No one believes me when I say I work at school. Even the nuns look at me wide-eyed when they hand me my final grade, as if it never occurred to them that I was about to ace their class.

"I just don't like it. I don't like most people; it's a person. I don't like it. It's not Annie Maranski's fault that her voice is too high and she walks with a permanent limp to the left for no apparent reason, but I don't like her either. It's like that. I don't blame the baby, but I don't like it."

"And abortion?" Now I know she isn't listening. What kind of counselor, what kind of adult, would listen to that rant and just let it go? It's the truth, but not the kind of truth you are supposed to say out loud.

"Well . . ." It's not just that I think the thing inside me might be a person. It's not just that I don't want a vacuum stuck up my nether regions. It's not just that it's kind of Todd inside of me . . . that's not it at all. It's not just that it would be very interesting to see my parents' reaction to this little tidbit. It would be so easy to just get an abortion.

Finally, I say, "I don't want to kill Annie Maranski either."

When I leave that afternoon, I get a warning that soon there will only be two options.

37 Days to Decide

Before last period, I am crouching at my locker switching my chemistry book for my English anthology. Remarkably, the periodic table is running through my head like it's a day from last year when I could actually focus on school. I shove my chemistry book into my hanging backpack and lean over to hoist the million-pound *Anthology of British Literature* onto my hip.

When I am bent over, I feel a hand snake up my hamstring beneath my skirt and palm my butt cheek. I'm pissed. Not because he grabbed my ass; I live for that. Because he woke the baby that has been sleeping in my brain. I take the anthology and bash it into his forearm, knocking his hand off me and picturing his new bruise. "I told you not to be so grabby in school," I snap.

Todd tilts his head into my hair so he's speaking into the crook of my neck instead of my face. "Woah, feisty," he breathes. "I like it, E. You look so hot today. Can you hang out after school, before practice?" He licks my ear.

Half of my heart is melting into a pathetic mush, and the other half is growing digits and making a fist so it can punch Todd in the groin and not have to wait for my body to listen. "I have something to do after school today."

I slam my locker and book it down the hallway, but he follows like a puppy. Sometimes I deny sex just to watch him follow me. It's funny: his green eyes sad, his broad shoulders slumped, his crew-cutted head hanging to the side. But I don't do it too much or for too long; if I do, he'll just find it somewhere else.

He puts his fingers on my hip, swinging me around. "Come on, E! It's been, like, five days." *It's been five days since we talked, too, jerkface.*

"I can't after school, sorry." But I can't lose him. Now more than ever. "Sneak over after dinner tonight?"

The boys' bathroom door swings open and the sound of his last name—"Arnold!"—blasts us apart. Two of Todd's football cronies start to shake his shoulders, and he averts his eyes from my body.

"Yo," says Sean, "we're blowing off last period and going to Mickey D's since practice is late today and we are staaarving. You in?" He glances at me. "What up, Ev?" Sean offers his hand for a high five. I slap it and Greg's as well, as Todd says, "I'm in."

I watch the back of Todd's head as the three of them disappear down the hallway. He turns and winks at me. He'll come over tonight. What the hell do I do?

"I don't mean to pressure you," Mary is saying after school. "I truly don't. But your body is pressuring you. There is an urgency to this decision. While the law does allow for some wiggle room beyond the forty-day deadline I gave you for your decision, the sooner you decide, the more smoothly either option will proceed."

"Yeah, I know. But right now I have a more urgent question." I swing the sterling silver ring my mom gave me for my fifteenth birthday around my left index finger.

"Oh. Well, certainly, go ahead."

How do you have so much time for me? "Can I have sex?" I blurt.

I wait for the satisfaction I feel when shocking adults, but Mary's eyes fix themselves steadily on my face. "You mean, if you go ahead and decide to deliver the fetus, but you have sex in the meantime, will it hurt the child in the long run?"

"Kind of. I also mean, like, biologically. *Can* I have sex?"

"Well, no and yes." Mary sighs. "Married people have sex while they are pregnant all the time."

"Really?" I screech. It's hard to imagine. Then again, all the married people I know are adults, and I don't really believe adults have sex at all.

"Yes. But I would urge you to be very careful."

"What do you mean? Is there like . . . a bad position?" I mean, is there a place his thing isn't supposed to go, but I don't know how to ask that.

"No. Are we talking about the father, or another young man, or multiple partners?"

"The father," I say, wondering how much of a slut she thinks I am. "So that's okay? It won't hurt it?"

She pauses. "Well, although certain sexually transmitted diseases could factor into birth conditions, in general safe sex is not tremendously risky. However, you need to be careful. You need to protect your heart as well as your fetus."

"My heart?" I snort.

"If you are upset and become stressed or more emotionally strained than you already are, that could directly hurt the fetus through high blood pressure, irregular heartbeat, and so on. Also, it could interrupt your decision-making process, which needs to be at the forefront of your mind right now. If you are going to abort, you need to decide that very soon or it will be too late. If you are going to go ahead and deliver, you need to start taking care of yourself."

"Oh. I haven't been drinking."

"That's good but not what I mean. You'll need prenatal vitamins, a specialist, regular checkups and ultrasounds, a very nutritional diet." This is the kind of list my mom leaves for me when she goes out of town for some conference and expects me to run the household. I ignore Mary too.

"So . . . I can have sex?"

"I'd advise against it. Let's talk about the father. What does he know?"

I laugh. "He's kind of a dumbass."

Mary laughs too, that fake little squeak. "I mean, does he know you are pregnant? Does he know the baby is his?"

When it's mine, it's a fetus. When it's his, it's a baby. "No."

"Are you going to tell him?"

"I've . . . got to figure everything out."

"You don't want to tell him? Is he your boyfriend? Do you love him?"

"No!" I say. "He's some guy from school I use for sex."

Mary's tiny eyes and mouth form three wide Os like a bowling ball and I finally feel an ounce of success.

"Well, if you decide to deliver, he is probably going to find out."

I nod. I know that. The truth is I'm dying to tell him. The truth is I have a secret that I've kept bubbling in my stomach for much longer than this stupid baby: I am in love with Todd.

Somehow my tires roll me into Lizzie's driveway instead of taking me home. It's good though, I need to talk to someone who doesn't speak in riddles and write in curlicues.

In her house, my eardrums are immediately vibrating: Lizzie's door up the stairs jumps in rhythm with the rap playing behind it, the housecleaner runs a vacuum in the living room, her little sister is shouting at some cartoon in the family room, and her mother is yapping a story riddled with curse words into the phone in the kitchen. She looks at me, smiles, and blows me a kiss. My cheeks glow pink because it's embarrassing how mushy my heart gets from something so small. Mrs. Gates nods toward the stairs and I clomp up in my saddle shoes.

Lizzie is sprawled on her stomach, still in her uniform, her skirt barely covering her ass in this position. Her music blasts so she doesn't hear me open the door. In my house, you can hear someone open any door at any moment. She has her reading anthology open at the top of her head, but her face is buried in her plush carpet, her sleek hair spilling over the pages. I laugh. This is not how I study.

We've been best friends since sixth grade and she always does the talking. I know as soon as the littlest thing happens to her—she broke a nail, she shorted her skirt an inch, the hot lifeguard brought sunblock to her station, she bought new lipstick. And she tells me the big stuff too—all the juicy details of her quest to find her dad. It's not that I can't sneak a word in; the minute I start to talk, she stops. But talking doesn't come easily to me. I didn't get to have Mrs. Gates for a mother.

I pat Lizzie on the head and she jumps. I'm expecting her to laugh at the fact that she didn't even hear me come in, but as soon as she sees me she leaps to her feet and wraps her arms around my shoulders. I stiffen. I love Lizzie, but hugging isn't easy for me either.

"Oh my God. What's wrong?"

Can she tell that quickly? Is my stomach already sticking out?

I open my mouth to tell her. I came here to tell her. I came here because, even though she won't give me the best advice, probably won't even give me advice I would follow—when Bethany thought she was pregnant Lizzie told her to drink beer and eat sushi—she'll give me some actual advice. Unlike Mary.

But my words lock up. She sees the letters stuck in my eyes.

"Tell me now." She sits on her pink bedspread. I do too.

"Nothing's wrong, Lizzie. God."

She snaps her gum. "I'm not falling for that again. Tell me."

I want to, but I can't. "Doesn't it suck to be in school again?"

She sighs. "Not for me. Not for all the people who aren't Miss Goody Two-Shoes."

I scoff. She knows damn well I'm not anybody's good girl anymore.

She says, "School's just a party you have to get up early for. I like seeing everyone again. I missed flirting."

"Everyone is boring."

"That's because you're a nerd," she teases. "Hey, let's start scoping outfits for Real Friday. Sean said his parents are getting three kegs this year."

We lose the afternoon in trying on clothes and switching our makeup. Normally I find this routine so boring that Lizzie has to physically put the clothes on my body after an outfit or two, but today I pull on ten different shirts. I stare at my stomach in the mirror, imagining it swelling to the size of a balloon wrapped in each one. Every time I pull a shirt off, I check my middle for a little pouch, but my skin is flat and tight and pale as ever.

Finally, I say, "I have to go. Todd's coming over tonight. I gotta make sure the silent parents are in bed." Lizzie faces me wearing a pink skirt and a white bra. Her boobs perch on her tan chest, her stomach spreads into hips beneath her ribs. Her green eyes glow from within her heart-shaped face. I wish I looked like that.

"Todd's coming over?" Lizzie is the only one who knows about me and Todd.

"Yeah. Why?"

"I don't know. I figured you guys were fighting."

"We're not fighting. We never fight."

"I know." She pauses. "But then, what's bothering you? It's more than school."

I feel the story fizzing, but it's fizzing in the soles of my feet, and they are way too far away from my mouth for it to ever have a chance of escaping. I shrug.

Lizzie says, "Did your dad leave again?"

When my dad had an affair, I must have tried to tell her a dozen times. She would get mad at me over and over. She would yell about how I didn't trust her and how I would never feel better if I didn't just say something, but the words always got all locked in my lungs and when I tried to tell her, when I tried to say, "He fell in love with our slutty dentist and took off; he left me alone with the Ice Queen," I couldn't even breathe. Finally, she threatened never to talk to me again so I e-mailed her the story. By that point, he was back. Well, his body was back. But he wasn't my dad anymore.

"No," I say. "I'm fine. Really."

She shakes her head at me and turns back to the closet. I take that as permission to leave.

In our kitchen, chewing on their takeout, the Ice Queen and the Stranger sit across from me and the pack of cells inside me. The baby flips in circles in my brain and my abdomen. Will Chinese food somehow hurt the baby the way sushi does? Does that matter if I am going to kill it anyway? If I kill it by accident with Chinese food, is that still a sin?

We listen to the clock tick over our heads, the neighbor kids scream in their pool, the crickets chirp in the grass, the geckos patter on the outside of the kitchen windows. The walls are bare and pale. Mom said she was going to repaint the whole house the day after Dad left. She took down everything but he was back before she lifted a brush.

The Stranger's voice pulls my brain out of my uterus. "How was your day, Pumpkin?" I glare at him until he corrects it to "How was your day?"

I say, "Fine."

Not to be outdone, Mom says, "I trust you've gotten to your homework?"

I hate this stupid parent charade. I hate how they only ask about school and not about friends or boys or how I'm feeling. I have a freaking 3.9 GPA; they don't need to ask about homework. I hate that the ghost of the way we used to be hangs over this crazy table reminding us of everything we've lost. We used to play music during dinner. Dad used to pull me out of my seat for a dance. Dad used to laugh. Mom used to chuckle sometimes. But now they sit side by side like pillars, spitting out sitcom questions and competing to be parent of the year. I want to scream and rip the hair out of my dad's face and run away.

"I've started it. It'll get done."

Mom pushes buttons on her BlackBerry.

Wednesdays are the worst because they have their stupid marriage counseling meeting and the dumb shrink always says that we should all eat together afterward. Other days of the week, I eat with one of them while the other stays in its cave.

If there were a screaming baby at this table, the Stranger would make me nauseated being all kissy and lovey-dovey, but he would also be incompetent, bumbling with bottles and bibs and baby food and whatever else the monster would need. Mom would be carrying her BlackBerry into another room because of how embarrassed she is to be a grandmother in her forties. That would not fit into the picture-perfect life of the Jacksonville Catholic family we pretend to be for her.

I can't bring the baby here. I've got to get rid of it.

I shovel fried rice into my mouth and swallow an egg roll in two bites. Then I mumble something about homework and get the hell out of there. I dash up the stairs—the walls are still beige and mostly bare—and swing open the door to my room, which is directly at the top. Someone needs to tell me what to do.

I pick up my cell phone to call Aunt Linda. I trust her.

But when she answers after the first ring, practically shouting with joy, "Hello, little niece!" I know I won't tell her anything.

She doesn't know anything about me anymore: the mascara, the sex, the drinking, the weed, any of my new Bad Girl stuff. I can't tell her this. I can't stand to hear her voice fall with disappointment. She's the one adult who always sounds happy to hear from me.

"Hi, Aunt Linda," I say.

That's all it takes for her to know something is wrong. "Oh, Evie, what happened? Are they fighting again?"

I shrug. My parents aren't fighting right now and I can't lie to Aunt Linda, but I also can't have her ask me what's wrong again. Plus, somewhere in my brain and heart and reflexes, somewhere in both the past and future, Mom and Dad are always fighting.

She takes my pause as a yes. "I don't know why they do

this to you, Evie. But remember they love you. We all love you, okay? Even when they're fighting about you and hurting you and they're being so dumb, they love you."

I love that she gets mad at them for me. Just for hurting me.

"Okay," I say. There's no way I can tell her about it. She's the only person who ever talks to me like this. If I told her, she'd still love me. She's the one person I know would love me no matter what I do. I can't stand to disappoint her.

"Tell me what I can do for you," she says.

I suck in a shaky breath. "Tell me a story about my cousins."

A year ago my aunt and her girlfriend or wife or whatever adopted two little black girls. I still haven't met them because Aunt Linda moved all the way to Chicago when she left, but she tells great stories about them. She calls me at least once a week to tell me about something cute they said or did. And to tell me how much they want to meet me. If I could just get them to visit, if she could see what a mess everything is, then maybe I could tell her without shattering her image of me, her little niece. But Aunt Linda has her own life in Chicago, and she has Nora, and kids, and a social-worker job where she probably has her own pregnant teenagers to deal with. I can't tell her or anyone.

It's ten o'clock when I hang up, bedtime for the parents. A field of hardwood floor, beige walls, and silence stretches out on either side of me. I tiptoe down Dad's side first, past the Crucifix—one of two items that survived Mom's "cleansing" when he left—and check under his bedroom door to ensure that it's dark. I have to walk back past Jesus, and even though I don't believe in him, I hate crossing his path all pregnant and nonvirginal. I turn, stumbling over my socks, and pad back past my bedroom door, past the family picture where we three smile and pretend. I hate that picture. It's a reminder of why my mother even opened the door when the Stranger showed up again: so no one would know we had any problems. Two years later, no one does. Except Lizzie and Aunt Linda, both of whom I had to tell myself. We are like a happy, quiet, rich family and no one knows there's a war inside. Mom's bedroom is dark too.

I grab a highlighter, open my anthology to *The Canterbury Tales*, and sit by the window to wait for Todd to roll his bike into the yard. Usually, waiting like this, my blood is rushing with excitement. Today, my heart is pumping concrete.

How Life Got Shitty

Todd loved me first. Two years ago, in ninth grade, I used to catch him ogling me when I ran past the football field at the end of cross-country practice in a neon sports bra and gym shorts. We had art class together that year, and his knees knocked whenever he took the seat next to me. I found it entertaining, but I didn't really have an opinion about him. All of that was when I was just some goody-two-shoe, brainiac, string-bean virgin of a teenager. I was a kid. I was different back then, I really was. I was naive and callow, and the heaviest thing I had to carry around was my algebra book. I was stupid. I was happy.

By the time Todd asked me to be his date to the sophomore Christmas dance, the Stranger had left and come back with his eyes on his shoelaces, shivering in our kitchen, and Mom just let him in without a sound. I had been planning to go to the dance with Lizzie, and at this point I didn't want to go to some boring school dance at all, but I knew that sleeping with a football player was the fastest way to strip off the goody shoes and fulfill my goal. My goal was Bad Evelyn. Bad Evelyn would show my parents.

In the week Dad was gone, when I was still planning to go with Lizzie, Mom had taken me dress shopping and acted like everything was a big deal. I figured I would spend the night watching Lizzie grind with most of the male members of our class and sneaking cigarettes with her by the Dumpster while she debated which of them to hook up with next weekend. Of course, back then I didn't actually smoke cigarettes. Oh no, I was an athlete: the only sophomore on the varsity cross-country team; the top 800 runner in winter track. Mom took me to the mall and dragged me from store to store, practically pulling my wrist while I feigned disinterest. I should have cherished every second.

Even before, my mother was always busy, squeezing the moments with me in between clients, and rushing dinners before going back to work. She was busy, and she was stiff—she was no Dad—but she talked. That day, she had put me in her date book, scheduled me in on a Tuesday evening. I loved seeing my name in there, ever since I was a little kid and she would block out afternoons for Mommy/Evie days. I was embarrassed at how much it still touched me to see my name in her book like that, her time blocked out for me. Of course, there haven't been any Evie blocks since that day.

We finally found this red dress. It stretched across my pitiful chest, strapless, but it was bright enough that it didn't make me look like a total ghost and it cinched at the waist, creating the illusion that I had one. It made me look like a girl at least, and when I stepped out of the Macy's dressing room, it made Mom suck in her breath and her brown eyes got all wide and motherly. She talked about putting a straightener and then a hot iron through my awful hair and how she would give me these big, sleek curls. I've thought about that straightener every morning since while I wrestle a brush through the bush on my head, even after he got back.

When he got back, he was a stranger who wouldn't shut up: all these words filling up the whole empty house with nonsense, making every room crowded and claustrophobic, but in all those words, he only really talked to me once. "Mom's not the woman I married anymore. Of course I still love her, but you see her, Pumpkin . . . she's empty. And then when Dr. Alvarez smiled, it was just so hard to ignore." My jaw dropped but my tongue stayed still. Dr. Alvarez was our dentist. What kind of father runs away with the family dentist? He went on, "I just can't stand to be away from you." Like he could still be my dad after he left me. Really, he is a pair of handcuffs locking us all to my mom's crazy vision of the perfect family.

The night of the actual dance, I stood naked and freshly showered in front of the bathroom mirror and wondered what Todd would think when he saw the tiny swollen lumps of skin I called boobs and the spiderweb of pale-blue veins impossibly close to the surface right next to my peach nipples. I turned around and focused on my naked butt, or really, the place where my skinny back morphed into skinny legs. I didn't see what anyone would find attractive about all this paperwhite flesh. Todd could probably count my bones after I took my clothes off. I stood there until goose bumps cropped up across my stomach and chest. Then I counted to one hundred, just seeing if by some miracle she would remember and knock on the door armed with hair supplies.

In the end, I went to the dance with frizzy hair.

After about fifteen minutes of watching the drooling disgustingness of our classmates falling all over each other with their tongues hanging out, Todd reached for my hand and began to walk toward the dismal disco ball. I dropped his arm and held my breath. When he turned to face me, I stood on my tiptoes and kissed him on the ear. I'd never kissed anyone before, except in middle-school spin the bottle. He gasped.

"Let's get out of here," I said, like they do in stupid movies.

"Huh? Where?" He was still startled by the kiss. I didn't care. I ran through all the movie sex scenes I'd been watching in order to study up. I stretched again and pressed my half-open mouth into the space right behind his ear, running my fingers through his crew cut.

"The park? The Little League complex?" I suggested, reciting a few of the locations from Lizzie's list of conquests.

Todd's mouth dropped open like a dead fish. "Like, seriously?"

I just walked out of the school with him trailing a pace behind, puppy dog eyes blooming for the first time.

We went to the Little League complex and I sat in the corner of the back of his mom's old-school station wagon, shivering and watching him unwrap and break three of the condoms I stole from Lizzie. They snapped right over his junk. I felt ridiculously naked in the matching strapless and panties Lizzie had forced me to buy, and I didn't think he had noticed my underwear or even my skin in all his fumbling. The fourth one finally stayed on and I peeled my underwear down to my ankles. I had to lie on my back to try to tug my left foot out of them, and suddenly all of his football-player weight smashed into me. His thing tugged around down there while he tried to get it in and the condom pulled and yanked my skin in places it didn't want to go. His chest crushed into my shoulder and his chin kept banging my temple. Finally, he used his hand to push it in and it felt like an entire fist had forced its way into me, intent on stretching me out, filling me with solid parts from the inside. It hurt. Tears stung my eyes and I thought I would have to tell him to stop but then, suddenly, it was over.

Afterward, we were lying on our backs, side by side, as best we could. My feet were thrown over the bench backseat. Half of his back was pressed to the spare tire. My dress lay balled up by his left elbow. My panties hung from my right heel, and my bra was still on. He had on only a shirt and tie. He looked ridiculous. He asked, "So, does this mean that you're, like, my girlfriend?" He was nervous, but hopeful nervous, not uh-oh nervous. I told the butterfly flapping around in my throat to shut up.

"Please. Let's call this what it is."

"What do you mean?"

"Sex," I said. "Will you take me home?"

There was a long pause. Finally, he said, "Won't your parents be suspicious? It's only eight thirty."

We laughed. I didn't want to be laughing, but when I looked at him, I laughed harder.

"They won't notice."

"Mine will."

"Okay. We can kill some time." I slipped the rest of the way out of my bra and angled onto my elbow as best I could in the cramped backseat. I started to kiss him again and his pink penis peeked right up between the bottom wings of his button-down shirt. I started to giggle through the kisses. He started laugh-kissing too. I began unbuttoning all of his buttons, and he untied his tie and pulled his undershirt off. I pressed my pathetic chest to his. There was no way in hell I was going to have sex again, but Lizzie had taught me all about blow jobs. I reached for his thing between kisses, and my hand got sticky.

"I—" He stared at me, turning red. "I'm sorry, babe. I just got too excited." His stuff pasted his leg hair to his skin.

He pulled his undershirt out from behind the spare tire and I watched him wipe himself off. He'd called me babe even though I just told him I wasn't his girlfriend.

I stuttered, tightening my grasp on the control I had felt all night. But in the moment I paused, he grabbed my hand and my knees and managed to roll me up into a little ball on my side, like a puppy. Then he fit himself around me, curved like a comma. I was naked, but he ignored all my girly parts and just flung his arm over my middle. Every once in a while he would stroke the inside of my elbow with his thumb.

I told myself I was being dumb; I told myself to sit up and shift back into my clothes. This was the part where he spreads rumors about me. I wanted those rumors. Car-cuddling and laugh-kissing were not part of the plan. But my body kept listening to my elbow pit. Monday, the entire football team would know we did it in the Little League complex parking lot, but they wouldn't know about this part. Locker-room talk does not involve thumbs caressing the inside of elbows. I could feel his breath on the back of my neck and I wondered how my frizz was not crawling into his throat and making him hack like a cat. We ended up falling asleep like that. When we woke up, we started making out again, but he glanced at his watch and freaked. I got home to a sleeping house at 1:22 a.m.

The next morning my mother looked up from her Black-Berry and asked me if I had had a nice time. *She doesn't know. She can't tell*, I thought.

Monday morning, I steeled myself for school. I limped out of bed, my vadge still feeling bruised like a black eye, and I wondered why anyone had sex ever. I pulled on my uniform and practiced walking straight in front of the mirror. I said the things I knew I would hear throughout the day out loud to myself: "Easy," "Slut," "Whore," "Jersey chaser."

Then I said the things I knew I would hear in whispers, slithering up and down the hallway like serpents. I whispered into the mirror: "They did it in the Little League complex." "I heard it was all her idea." "She practically dragged him there."

I didn't care. It was what I wanted. I went to school.

But nothing happened. Other than the way I felt like hiding from the Crucifix in every classroom, nothing felt different. Not one nasty stare, not one ass slap by the other football players. Nothing. I heard plenty of lies about Lizzie, who told me that she'd actually just ditched the dance and gone home to stalk potential fathers online, but I was ghostly as always. When I got to practice, I was half disappointed. I trudged toward the track by myself, wearing my sneakers and a sports bra. I felt a hand on my ribs, and Todd said, "Hey, E!"

I yanked his hand off my waist and spun around, whipping my ponytail across his face. "What are you doing?" I asked.

"I've been dying to see you all day."

"I don't like PDA," I said.

He looked scorned but said, "Can you grab a coffee after practice?"

Instead of coffee, we had sex in the school parking lot.

As the months went by, when the rumors still didn't start and silence stole away more and more of the rooms in my house, I realized I would need a new plan to be Bad. I wanted my parents to see it and feel it. I wanted them to be mad at me, not just each other. Lizzie said, "You have to do more than just fuck Todd on the DL. You have to look the part. You have to get in trouble. Be a badass. Stop studying so much. Stop going to church. You didn't have to actually sleep with anyone, but I bet you're glad you did," and she nudged my ribs with her elbow. I followed all of her advice, except I kept studying.

I painted my eyelashes with mascara every morning and lined my lips in dark red, even just for school. I took my uniform skirt to a tailor and had him measure my leg and make it the shortest length that wouldn't land me in daily detention. I showed up in the locker room in my too-short skirt and told Coach I was quitting track. Her jaw dropped and emitted sounds about how I was throwing away a future and potential scholarships and all sorts of nonsense but I just spun around, hoping my skirt did not flare so much that she could see my panties, and walked out, ignoring the heaviness of tears that threatened to soak her words and my eyes. I hid my easel and paintbrushes in the very back of my closet and watched while the new paints the Stranger had bought for me streaked through the toilet water when I flushed them. I quit art club and French club and resigned as class treasurer. I got detention for chewing gum in class, for yanking my skirt too short, for talking back to the nuns, even for shouting at another girl in the hallway.

It works on Todd too. The badder I get, the more it drives him crazy. He finds me hotter by the second, but he also concedes that we have to keep everything secret. "If my friends found out about you, they'd warn me about diseases," he says sometimes. "If my parents find out, they'll ground me for a month." I ignore the way my heart bruises from banging into my rib cage when he says stuff like that.

Also, somehow I started liking sex. When I would lie down at night after suffering through another evening in household hell, sometimes hearing the shouts ricocheting down the hallway, and other times being obliterated by silence—which was worse—I would crave his attention. I would picture Todd propped on his elbows leaning over me, whispering questions about my life into my hair and chuckling and smiling and my elbow and stomach would get goose bumpy from memories of his flesh on mine, and I would literally shake with wanting him to show up.

So one night, I just called him.

"Come over?" I said.

He hesitated. "Now?"

"Yes."

"Okay." He sounded excited, which made me happy.

"Bring a condom."

"Oh . . . we can do that? What if your parents catch us?"

I laughed. I mean, really laughed. I knew it wasn't a joke but when you have just gone twenty-four hours without either of your parents, who are the only people you live with, saying a word to you, it sounds like a joke.

"Believe me. That won't be an issue."

He hesitated again. I don't know why. But he said, "Sweet." And hung up.

The problem with sex is the moment after. Your body is still buzzing with closeness and physical intimacy, and your mind gets all screwed up and forgets that it wasn't actual love that happened, just sex. So when Todd nuzzled into me like a hibernating bear and said, "So what's with your parents?" I stupidly answered.

"My mom is an idiot for being with my dad. He cheated on her. Now they both want to avoid each other, so they end up avoiding me."

He squeezed me and his head shot up so his eyes could meet mine. They are green with these gold flecks. And he has impossibly long, dark eyelashes. He looked like I'd just told him my parents were dead.

"Are you serious?" he said, his eyes steady on mine. When I didn't say anything else, he let his head fall and buried his nose next to my collarbone. "That sucks."

Gradually, after sex, he pulled the whole story out of me.

He joked with me. He tickled and teased me. He asked my opinion on things like whoever Lizzie was sleeping with at the moment or school lunch that day, and he listened to my answers. He started to hang out in my room with me for hours at a time, several days a week. We would have sex, but we would also talk. And joke. And sometimes even play games. But still, it was all about sex. In the part of my imagination that I store in the middle of my brain—farthest from my skull—I could see us holding hands, him putting his arms around me at parties. But it was too late for that. Plus, if I was his girlfriend, there's no way I could have held on to him for this long.

We run with the same crowd since I still hang out with some of the athletes at school, but he doesn't tell anyone about me, and I don't either. Except Lizzie, who keeps her mouth shut tight. We have sex in our cars after school, in the school bathroom, under the football bleachers. We sneak off from parties together, but we never get caught. Then we go back to the party and not exactly ignore each other, but just act like casual acquaintances. We are damn good. At school they started calling me slut anyway, because of how I dressed and talked and acted with the teachers. So it worked out okay.

I never did it with anyone else, but I let Todd think I might. And I don't think about him when he's not with me.

Still 37 Days

I'm almost finished with chapter three of *The Canterbury Tales* when my cell buzzes with a message that Todd can't get out of his house. I groan and grab my belly. "How the hell am I going to figure out what to do with you?" I put my fist directly on my uterus and shake it back and forth. I'm pretty sure that didn't hurt the thing—that it can't even feel yet—but my skin still tingles with guilt and I stop.

36 Days to Decide

"I just want you to think about why you are telling him," Mary says.

"Just to see what he says. What he would do."

"Are you sure you want to?"

"Yeah." I find a confidence that must have been buried someplace small, like my right pinky toe, because I can only find it when I am making ridiculous statements like this one. "What's the worst that could happen?"

"That's a good question. What is the worst that could happen?"

I swallow. It was rhetorical, damn it. Something about Mary and her fake smile makes me say things I never say. "He could stop having sex with me." The worst thing that could happen.

"Okay, true," Mary says. "There might be some other consequences. Are you sure you can't think of any more?"

"We would stop hanging out." I almost choke on the words.

"Or," Mary says, with that annoying air of I-am-the-adult-and-therefore-know-more-than-you-do-even-though-this-is-about-your-own-life. "He might convince you to have the baby when you really don't want to."

I laugh. "I really don't think so."

"He could tell your parents. Or his parents. He could tell his buddies at school and suddenly everyone will know."

I shake my head to each one of these as if none of them fazes me. I smile. I am a stupid fake just like Mary.

"Why do you want to tell him, anyway?" Mary asks. "I thought you didn't even like this guy."

"I don't dislike him," I qualify, and Mary gives this halfhearted little giggle. She actually laughs. What the hell? She's a freaking counselor; she's not supposed to laugh at me. That has to be seriously against her honor code or whatever. She has faked everything else; can't she just fake a stupid straight face?

But as I'm thinking this, my lips abandon me. Forcing myself not to smile is as strenuous as bench-pressing. I hate my mouth. Mary is still smiling. Like she thinks we are friends now or something.

She shakes her head at me and gets off the couch, moving toward the minifridge. "I know your life isn't funny right now, Evelyn, but I've just never met anyone who could sleep with someone with the frequency you describe for close to a year and still not feel some overwhelming emotion—love, hate, annoyance." She hands me a can of ginger ale without even asking me if I want it. I do want it, but she could have asked me, so I just pass it back from my left hand to my right and concentrate on keeping my lips in a straight line.

"You talk about Todd like he's an old couch in your living room or something."

Now, I actually let out a laugh. I hate myself sometimes.

Since I already hate myself, and Mary, I open the ginger ale. With the first sip, my stomach settles like a dog that has been running around the park, leaping with all four feet off the ground, and then just lies down to take a nap. I wonder how long the knots in my abdomen have been writhing and tightening.

Mary is saying something about Todd again, about why I want to tell him. It's not that I don't want to talk to her, even though she is crazy annoying today. I just don't really know.

"Aren't you the one who called it his baby?" I ask.

"It's only his baby if you decide to have it." She turns her head to peer at me out of the tiny corner of her minuscule eye because she thinks she just said something extremely wise.

"Says who?"

"The law."

I smile on purpose this time. "I actually break the law a lot. I'm not going to start following it as soon as it's on my side."

She squeaks that little laugh and I feel like talking, so I continue. "Besides, I just don't think I can really, fully decide until he knows. Until I know what he would say."

"In some ways you are very mature, Evelyn," Mary peeps. "It sounds like you have your mind made up about talking to him, though. So why are you here today? Do you want to practice?"

"Practice what?"

"Practice what you will say to him. Pretend I am him."

"No!"

"I'm sorry," she says. "Then why are you here?"

"I want to know if I have sex with him before I tell him, will it hurt the baby?" I've already had sex with him twice. I've already asked this idiotic question too. But I didn't understand her cryptic answer.

"I'm more worried about it hurting you, Evelyn," Mary coos her pretend concern.

"Will you just answer my question straight for once?" I shouldn't yell, but I don't want to hear about all the ways I'm hurting myself. I've been hurting myself one way or another my whole life and look at me, I'm still here, right? So I shouted at her. Whatever.

"No, Evelyn. Sex will not hurt the fetus. Just like I told you a few days ago." Even though she didn't actually say that.

"Thanks." I grab my bags in a huff.

"Will you come back tomorrow and let me know how it goes?"

"If I feel like it." I storm out of her office and leave my half-empty ginger ale can fizzing on her overly informative coffee table. I shouldn't have done that. I should have taken it with me and recycled it.

After dinner—chewing take-out tacos and answering the Stranger's questions monosyllabically while Mom eats in her office—I text Todd to come over. I say, *I'm horny. Come over.* But I'm not. Sex sounds less appealing to me right now than Chinese water torture, or a family vacation, or giving birth, even. But he responds with a smiley face, so when he gets here I lie on my back and let him do his thing. He brought a condom this time. Hilarious.

When it's over he holds me like always, and I try to just relax and enjoy it a little, but I can't because his hand is, like, directly on my uterus and I imagine that thing in there curling up into the crease of his palm the way I curl up into his body. And even though I know it's just a ball of nerves and cells right now, just a little blob—and even though I hate it—I kind of feel sorry for it, the way it's nudged between its father's fingers, and I'm about to kill it, maybe.

I sit up and look at him. I'm naked, but I don't really care. I've been naked so much with Todd, it almost feels weird to wear clothes around him.

"We need to talk." My words fall like bricks into the peaceful room.

"Uh-oh," he says. "Look, Evelyn—"

"No, Todd—" I cut him off but then he interrupts me again.

"Look, Evelyn, we always said this was just going to be about sex."

He swings an ax and hits my stomach.

"I mean, it's not that I don't like you." *Thunk*. "It's just, I mean, my friends." *Thunk*. "And my parents." *Thunk*.

"Stop!" I shout, too loudly. I never used to care if we got caught, but now I really don't want to. I lower my voice. "It's not about that."

"Oh . . . sorry. What then?"

"I'm pregnant." I said it. I swear I did. I just said it. But nothing came out of my mouth. My voice just ran away.

"What?" says Todd.

My lips move, but nothing happens.

"C'mon, what is it, Evelyn?"

"I'm—" There it goes again. No voice. Completely mute. I start to giggle. So does Todd. "I can't say it."

"So . . . act it out." He laughs.

"No, no." I take a deep breath to stop the laughing. "No. I'll just say it."

"Okay," he says, waiting.

"I'm—" Suddenly we are doubled over laughing again, but I can feel that it's almost over, that I am almost to the line where laughing at yourself morphs into stupid baby tears that leak all over your face.

So I take my hands and put them in front of my belly button, about a foot away from my actual stomach and make a convex motion. Damn, I hope I don't get this big.

Todd stops laughing instantly.

"No." A beat. Another one. I watch his eyes, which don't move from my bedspread. "Whose is it?"

This question should not be making my eyes sting. I'm ready for it. "It's yours. It has to be."

He sighs. Several minutes go by and then he says, "Wow. This is heavy," which is so boneheaded it makes me want to laugh again, but as soon as the first giggle escapes my lips he shoots me a look of stone and my mouth flattens straight.

"Do you know what this means?"

"Yes," I say, because I know more than he does even though I don't know anything.

"I'm going to have to pay child support for the rest of my life."

"Fuck you," I say.

"Huh?" Like he really doesn't know what's wrong with what he just said. He puts his hands behind his head and lies back down on top of my bedspread, his ribs poking out above his hip bones, his penis, soft and ridiculous, disappearing between his legs. Then he does something surprising. He puts up his arms and reaches for me. I collapse onto his chest. I am so grateful for this one thing, this feeling of skin and muscle and silky body hair under my cheek, that I tell him, "I'm not sure what I'm going to do yet."

"Oh," is all he says, but I feel something in his chest release beneath my right ear.

A long time passes. I keep waiting for the jerkface to ask me a question, to tell me what to do, or at least what not to do. Or maybe what he will do. He says jack. I mean, absolutely nothing. So finally I have to ask him.

"What do you think I should do?"

"I don't know. Whatever you want, I guess."

I sit up again. "Go home."

"What?"

"I said, go home." I've never kicked him out before.

"What the hell?"

"You're worse than my parents right now. Go home."

"I . . . uh . . . what . . ." He bumbles for a few seconds more before he says, "Fine," and pulls on his clothes like he's yanking apart a knot in a whole pile of jump ropes. When the door slams behind him, loneliness surrounds me, a fog so dense I can't see. I wish he hadn't left. I'm sinking in a vat of oil. I don't even hear the door swing back open, but I feel hands on either side of my shoulders where they lay on my bed. Todd's face comes into focus above me. "E. Hey, E!" he is saying. "E, we just had sex. We just had sex, E." *What is he talking about?*

"Yeah . . . ," I say when my voice comes back into my throat. "So?"

"So," he says, "do you think it hurt the baby? I mean, what if my dick, like, poked it?"

Suddenly I feel like smiling. "No."

"But what if I hurt it like . . . emotionally? Like, what if its first memory is its father's junk flying at its face?"

I laugh out loud. "It won't remember," I say, reaching up to touch his arms. "Besides, it's not a baby yet. It's a fetus. No face anyway."

"Oh. Yeah." He lies down next to me again.

"So what are you going to do?" he asks, and this time I don't mind.

"I really don't know." I search for my ceiling in the darkness. I can't find it. When I was little I always wanted a pack of those glow-in-the-dark stars just so I would know the ceiling was still there when I woke up in the middle of the night, but my mom called them tacky. It's so dark in my room. I know the ceiling is there now, obviously, but I wish I could see it.

"Man," Todd says. "How did this happen, anyway?"

What a boneheaded question.

How This Happened

At first, we always used condoms. I took a handful from Lizzie before the crazy dance, and then Todd kept buying more. He always brought the condom over. He would just roll over and put it on after I pulled off his boxers. We didn't even have to talk about it. It was almost freaking sweet or something.

But one day, last spring, he forgot. It was a really bad day, one of the worst explosions in the history of parents.

I came home and locked myself in my room with my homework as usual. Our house was so silent it was like no one was there, even though all of us were home. I took algebra 2 last year and I had this really rough teacher, Mr. Cattels. He made us do page after crazy-long page of problems every night. So there I am, sitting on my bed, still on the first page. To be honest, I didn't mind how much homework he gave us. I complained like everyone else because I didn't want them to think I was a freak, but all of that homework gave me an escape. And something else to think about since I quit running and painting.

And, okay, I actually like losing myself in math homework after bad days of school, and that day was the worst. Bethany had told me that Todd asked Amber Sallisbury to the prom in study hall. Bethany was chirping the news to all of us in that high, cutesy voice girls use to tell stories they wish were about themselves. I just smiled and *awww*-ed with the rest of the idiots at my lunch table, but for some reason the story made my stomach tie up in knots. Amber Sallisbury is one of those the perky, sweet, blond cheerleader types. I don't really have anything against her, and I didn't expect Todd to ask me or anything stupid like that, but I just kind of hoped he would blow it off like I was planning to and the two of us could go hide somewhere and screw until Sean's after-party where we could show up separately and no one would even suspect we had been together. But he asked this girl Amber, which was worse than just some flake because she was in honors classes with me and I actually kind of liked her, and for some reason when I found out that he asked her out, I just freaking hated her and that sucks. There aren't enough people I like for Todd to steal them away.

So I totally lost myself in my algebra. I do that sometimes. I don't know where the time goes or where my brain goes. It's bad, honestly bad, because a hurricane alarm could be screaming outside my window and I wouldn't notice or move out of the way. Eight o'clock, I'm still sitting on my bed surrounded by notebooks. Nine o'clock, I finally turn a page in the notebook and start the second set of problems. Nine fifteen: a dynamite explosion and I didn't miss that.

My brain was still flying through numbers when I heard my mother screaming shrilly in the kitchen. I tried to tune it out, but my dad was saying, "You know, Judy, she's your daughter, too."

"I was working, I'll have you know," my mother shouted.

"Yeah. And I was just twiddling my goddamn thumbs."

"Jim, you know perfectly well I ate with Evelyn last night, and you know I have a huge suit coming up, so of course I assumed you would take responsi—"

"Well maybe next time, instead of assuming, you should actually talk to your daughter!"

At that moment, divine providence, my stomach started to growl. It was 9:20 and I hadn't eaten since my stupid 11:15 a.m. lunch at school. You can never really eat lunch at school anyway. There are too many anorexic girls walking around with their noses to the ceiling for you to feel comfortable actually consuming a balanced meal. I hate them even more because I look like one of them with my skin stuck to my bones and my tiny, tiny boobs and my frizzy hair and my face as pale as paper, but those are just the good looks God blessed me with. Unlike most girls, I actually eat. Unless I forget.

And my parents are always arguing about who should be taking care of me—who should be feeding me, taking me to school, signing my report cards. It's like it never occurred to them that it was my own fault I hadn't eaten any dinner.

"Will you just make her some food and bring it up to her and apologize?" My mom was crying now, which was worse.

My dad sighed. "Of course I will bring her some dinner, Judy, but if I am apologizing, it is for your oversight."

"You jackass! You never take responsibility for anything! You are her father and you know that a father means something in this day and age. When will you learn—"

The sound of pots slamming into the stove and kitchen cabinets banging open interrupted their words too much for me to follow the conversation. I realized the Stranger was going to come up the stairs with some stupid home-cooked meal for me and pretend to be my father, and the last thing I wanted to see was his ugly face. So I snuck down the hallway, brushed my teeth, and padded back to my room. I shut off the lights just as I heard his loafers shifting up the stairs. He knocked on my door lightly, but I didn't answer. I slipped under my covers and pulled them up to my chin so he wouldn't be able to see that I was still wearing my peter-pan-collared uniform shirt.

"Hey," he called lightly at my door. I cringed. The door creaked open and I heard him put a tray on my desk. I kept my eyes shut, expecting to hear the door creak again, but it didn't. Instead, I felt his hand tracing a path through the muddled frizz on top of my head. "I'm sorry if you're hungry, Pumpkin baby," he said, so lightly he sounded like someone else. "Sleep well."

I lay like that for a long time. I pulled my knees all the way up to my chin and wrapped my arms around them, picturing myself as small as a jelly bean or a piece of chocolate edamame that Aunt Linda likes so much. *Why doesn't he ever talk like that when I'm awake? How often does he come talk to me in my sleep?* The words spun in my brain and I tried to sweep them out. I wished I could just go to bed for real, but it was only nine thirty and I wasn't even sleepy. And I was hungry as a starved animal.

When I finally opened my eyes, I saw Dad had taken the tray with him. I pulled my phone under my covers just in case one of my parents were standing at the door looking for ammo to judge the other one and noticed the eerie blue light filling my room when I opened my phone. So I texted Lizzie without really looking. "Parents exploded. Really bad. No dinner. Can you come with food?" I sent it to Lizzie. I really did. Like I said, I wasn't looking. I lay on my back, under my bedspread, sweating my ass off and listening for more signs of unraveling in my house. Everyone was pretending to sleep in their separate rooms. It was dead silent.

Lizzie has a key to my house, so I expected her to just come right in. Instead, I heard a tap at my window. Todd was throwing little pebbles like a scene out of some cheesy eighties movie. I looked down at him and he waved a brown paper bag.

"What are you doing here?" I hissed when I let him into the kitchen.

"I brought you food, like you said. Are you okay?"

"What do you mean, like I said?"

"You texted me and said your parents had some big fight and that you didn't get dinner. What happened anyway? Are you okay?"

"Oh my gosh." I put my hand over his mouth and we tip-toed through the inky blackness toward my bedroom. "I didn't mean to text you. I meant to text Lizzie."

A shadow crossed his face. I don't know if it was that he didn't believe me or that he wished he didn't believe me. He said, "Oh. Well, I brought you food."

We sat, fully clothed, facing each other on my bed while he pulled stuff out of the bag. "A turkey sandwich on white with mustard. A roast beef sandwich on rye with mayo. A ham sandwich on wheat with both. A cold but cooked hot dog that my brother left in the fridge with some ketchup packets from McDonald's. Some pasta salad my mom made. Some regular salad that I made myself. An apple. A banana. A bag of strawberries. And two brownies. One with nuts."

"Who do you think I am? The entire British army?"

He shrugged and he looked so cute. That puppy look was in his eyes and he wasn't even asking for sex, at least not right then. "I didn't know what you liked. It sounded like you had a rough night."

If I were at school, if there were other girls around, if we were anywhere in public, or if I even just gave a damn, I would have eaten the salad and left it at that. But I was freaking starving. I ate the turkey sandwich, the ham sandwich, half the pasta salad, and the brownie without nuts. With the first bite I thought I could feel the vitamins and nutrients attaching themselves to my blood vessels like cellular Legos. The day faded into fogginess. I felt like smiling.

"I was hungrier than I thought," I told Todd. He reached for the roast beef and peeled off the plastic wrap. "Did you skip dinner too?"

"No." He laughed. "But you make eating look like the best thing on earth."

So we ate together and my parents left my brain. He talked about spring football and asked about Lizzie, but not my parents. I fed him the last bite of my brownie, and soon we were making out, his hands running up and down my ribs and over my boobs, pulling at the stupid buttons on the uniform shirt I was still wearing, hiking up my skirt even shorter. As he traced his lips down my neck, I relaxed and began enjoying it. He whipped his head up suddenly.

"I forgot a condom." By now we were both in just underwear.

"Why?"

"Don't know," he said, sitting up. "I was so busy packing that food." He gestured to the remains in a semicircle next to my bed. "I guess I wasn't thinking about sex."

I was touched. It might be pathetic, but I was.

"We should stop then." I sat up next to him.

"We should." But his hand was still on my side, his thumb running over my hip bone and back in a goose-bump-producing rhythm. His eyes remained on the spot where my breasts should have been filling out my satin bra. So, in about a second, we were making out, devouring each other again. When he was on top of me, I said, "Screw it. One time won't matter." I said it. I am the idiot who said it. And we did.

The problem wasn't that one time, though. The problem was after that, every once in a while and then more and more he would put those pathetic droopy eyes on mine and say, "Can we do it without this time? Do you think it will be okay?" and I would usually, stupidly, say yes.

I never even knew what he meant. How am I supposed to know if it will be okay? What the hell does that even mean? But I always thought it would be okay. I know I'm a fool, but I never thought I could get pregnant. I'm a sack of bones with frizzy hair. I don't look like anything that could get pregnant. And I'm even more of an idiot, as Mary so kindly pointed out, because it's not like I knew for sure that Todd wasn't giving it to the cheerleaders, the field hockey players, and all the other run-of-the-mill sluts at school, so he could have easily had AIDS or herpes or any other nasty disease and I just kept letting him stick his thing directly in me. So stupid.

But it's my fault. "Screw it. One time won't matter." That's what I said. It's my fault.

Still 36 Days

After a long time, I turn so my face is completely pointed away from him and say, "It's my fault."

At first I'm pretty sure he doesn't hear me because he doesn't say anything. Finally, he buries his face in my neck and muffles the words into my skin so they tickle even in their nauseating truth. "It's mine. My fault, too. I'm sorry, Evelyn. And I don't mean to be a jerk or anything, but it is your problem. I can't decide what to do with it."

That doesn't make sense at all, but for some reason I'm nodding. I need a ginger ale.

He stands up. "I gotta go now. My mom will be pissed."

He just made a baby and he's still worried about his mommy grounding him. I'm laughing to myself as he walks out the door.

35 Days to Decide

"What does he want you to do?" Mary asks the next day.

"He couldn't care less."

I wait for her tiny eyes to twitch shock and judgment, but she stays calm. "So, what's next?"

"Can I have a ginger ale?"

"Sure," she says. She stands up and goes to the refrigerator. I shut my eyes tight, trying to erase the image that has begun to etch itself on the inside of my eyelids.

"So are you back to square one? Back to just you?"

Back to just me as in no more Todd? Or no more baby? I open my eyes to pop the top of my ginger ale. As it fizzes into my mouth, I squeeze them shut again. It does no good. My mother's face appears inside my brain like a bad omen.

"Do you feel ready to decide now?"

I open my eyes. Mary's tiny fingers shuffle through her endless display of informative pamphlets featuring smiling babies or relieved-looking teens in all sorts of angles.

I know Mary wants to hear me schedule the abortion. What would my mom want? Am I supposed to be the Catholic girl or the one who keeps up appearances? I shut them again.

"Evelyn? You here?" she asks.

I know she doesn't have all day. I don't know how she has fit in so much time with me to begin with. I have no idea what her life is like, but I'm sure I'm not the only girl in all of Jacksonville, Florida, who is knocked up and scared shitless.

"Evelyn?"

What is her life like anyway? She doesn't wear a wedding band. I picture her coming home from her dismal day counseling teens and poor people on abortion and birth control options. I picture her kicking off the stupid heels she wears in some one-room apartment where the lights are too bright and the beige carpets are so old they look dirty even when they're clean. She walks into the blindingly fluorescent bathroom and scrubs the sunny feelings off her face before microwaving Healthy Choice lasagna and sitting down in front of some small TV to watch reruns of *Teen Mom*. How depressing.

"Evelyn?"

I know I need to answer her. She doesn't have all day. There have to be other people here asking to see the lady who stores the hope of the world in her tiny face.

"Evelyn?"

But I can't even open my eyes. A stupid tear pinches the outer corner of my right eye. One dances in the well below my left. But I don't cry, ever. Instead, I start to shake. I try to raise the ginger ale can to my mouth again, but my hand is shaking so much I spill drops all over my skirt.

"Oh, Evelyn." Her voice sounds so sympathetic I almost believe her. She stands up and scurries over to the couch. She puts tissues on my lap and her hand on my shoulder, even though I'm not crying. I wish she would go away. Every nice thing she does makes the hidden tears heavier. Part of me wants to cry. Part of me wants to wail that kind of crying that you only hear from hungry toddlers or newly widowed women on TV. My head wants to plunk right onto Mary's shoulder and my back wants to sag into her arm and my huge hair wants to hide her entire face and I would let the tears stream down my cheeks until they spell out an answer on the floor. But I don't deserve to cry like that.

My shoulders shake so hard they hurt. My eyes are on fire. My face is dry. Mary's hand makes an oval pattern on my shoulder blade. I wish she would stop. I wish she would get up and go home. I hope she doesn't move. I have been here for an hour at least, I bet. It has to be past five. It has to be almost time for her to climb into her secondhand Camry or other gas-efficient vehicle and drive home to her microwave and TV. She is wasting her time. This is never going to end. I am going to shake silently like this for the rest of my life. I will have the baby in this room still waiting for my eyes to birth their first tear. I will grow old rocking on this couch. I will never have to open my eyes again. This is it. The end. I will never stop or start crying.

Then it stops. With a wobbly breath my body calms itself down like someone hit a switch. I take a tissue from the box on my lap and dab my face, even though it's dry. I should since Mary brought them over and all.

Mary leans back and points her pale blue eyes at me like lasers.

"If I have this baby," I whisper, "I'm going to need to tell my mom."

Mary nods. A baby is hard to hide. A pregnant teenager might be a problem that's just too visual for Mommy Stiff-Ass to ignore.

"And if I don't, does anyone need to know?"

Mary shakes her head. "Not necessarily." She pauses. "We would work everything out in a way that makes you comfortable."

"Schedule the ab—" I can't say it. "Make an appointment for me then. Please."

"Okay." I stand up to leave, but the words "Evelyn, sit back down. We have some details to discuss" float into the room. The damn decision is finally made. What else can there be?

"Details? What details?" I don't mean to shout at her but I need to get out of here before I lose it again.

"You need a consult with the doctor so he can go over the entire procedure with you. You need to decide if you want local or general anesthesia. We may need to speak with a judge to get you a waiver. You'll need someone to take you home. You'll be out of school for a few days." The words are wires; they wrap around my limbs and try to pull me back down to the couch. I don't sit.

"We'll talk details tomorrow," I say, even though she hasn't invited me back. And tomorrow is Saturday. I know PP is open but who knows if she even comes in on Saturday. Maybe she has some double life and Friday nights she highlights in a burlesque show and she'll show up to my session tomorrow with bloodshot eyes and thick mascara still staining her skin. Maybe she spends her Saturdays taking off that über-concerned mask and screaming at college football games. Maybe she throws sex parties in her living room for lonely people she meets online.

It doesn't matter. I'm sure she will show up.

When I get home my sneakers squeak over the kitchen tiles. A clock ticks in the hallway. Computers buzz in their offices over my head. I know both silent parents are home because their matching Beamers are snuggling in the garage. I look at my watch. It's six thirty. I am too tired but if I don't do something about dinner the dynamite will explode again. Silence sucks, but the shouting is worse. I wonder if it will be better when they shout at me instead of about me, when they find out how badly I fucked up. But they won't. I don't need to tell them anymore. I pause at the bottom of the stairs to enjoy the relief that should follow this realization, but it comes in a nauseating wave.

My room is directly in front of me. Their separate wings sprawl out on either side. I have to pull energy out of every blood vessel to yell loud enough for both of them to hear me. "I'm going out for dinner!" My voice bounces from the cream walls to the hardwood floors to the ceilings with automatic lights. Her words come echoing back at me, "Have fun, sweetie." The Stranger is probably mumbling into his phone or letting an iPod drone into his eardrums.

I don't actually have plans, but I will find some. This prospect is less exhausting than the Parent-Juggling Routine.

But first I press the back of my head into my purple bedspread, wiggling my butt so the blankets climb up my hips and almost surround me, and enjoy the *whoosh* of air-conditioning dancing on my skin. I'll close my eyes. Just for a minute.

Boom!

Something punches the inside of my stomach.

Boom! Boom! Boom!

Mary has told me it would not be possible for me to actually feel the baby—excuse me, the fetus—for months, but I feel it. It's pounding on my uterus. It's crashing and banging its little body-blob of cells into every wall it can find.

I am not actually feeling this.

Bang!

This is not really happening.

Crash!

Shitballs, I'm going insane.

I sit up and reach for my cell phone, which is buzzing on the little white table next to my bed. It's Lizzie.

"Where are you?" she asks. I hear rap in the background. The thing-baby inside me stops moving. I was dreaming.

"Home," I answer.

"Get your ass over here!" she says. "I have at least three different outfits I want you to see before we go."

"Huh?" The sound escapes my throat before the words she has said can break through the currents in my brain. It is the first Real Friday of school—the first Friday after surviving a week of classes. The football team's Real Friday kegger. How many times this week have I made, discussed, and reviewed this plan with Lizzie and now I don't even remember?

"Did you forget about Real Friday?" she asks.

"No, course not. I'll come over now. Do you have any food?"

"Yes." When she speaks again, the party has left her voice. She hushes and says extra vowels. She speaks like a grandmother. "Evelyn," she says, "everything is not all right with you. You've been weird this week."

"Yeah." I acknowledge the question but not the comment. Everything is okay now, I remind myself. You made a decision. This will be over soon. Things will go back to normal.

"You can tell me," Lizzie says.

I want to. The entire story bubbles in my esophagus like half-digested booze, ready to escape into a toilet and go away forever. "It's just . . . ," I start. But I don't want her to know. I want to say it and then erase her memory. If I tell her, she'll know forever. And what will she think of me? I can't tell anyone. ". . . school," I finish. "I hate being there again."

She sighs but says, "Okay. Get your butt over here." The party is back in her voice.

We arrive at Sean's two hours and approximately four and a half outfits later. I am wearing a black halter top tied tightly around my push-up bra, the bow disappearing in the orange animal I carry on my head, and a white miniskirt that flows off my hips with black strappy heels. I keep reminding myself that, actually, I can dress like this again for the next nine months. This is not my last hurrah. Everything is going back to freaking normal.

Lizzie has her blond hair swept up into a bun on the top of her head to show off the huge gold hoops that swing from her earlobes in the midst of all her gold studs. She is wearing a white sundress that sticks to her skin, darkened after a summer of lifeguarding on the beach. She looks sexy, but like it's accidental. She drives guys crazy.

Sean's parents talk constantly—to each other, to Sean, to anyone around. When we get there all of these words swarm in the air and make me itchy. They rub on my bare arms and make my body hair stand up straight. They swirl in my brain until they don't make sense anymore. They nudge my ribs and say see-what-you're-missing-in-your-silent-house?

We say "ma'am" and "sir" and answer questions about school and college and the St. Mary's football team and the weather. Then we hand over our keys. Talkative parents are the kind who buy their son three kegs and convince themselves it's okay as long as they collect all of our keys and only return them when we can prove we're sober at their door. Lizzie and I have been through this enough to know that by the time we leave Mr. Scott will be passed out on his own drunk ass and Mrs. Scott will be slurring her speech so badly that she would believe you if you said you were an alien, let alone sober.

We move into the backyard, swing our feet in the deep end of the pool. Lizzie talks about how she thinks she can find out her dad's name if she can get her hands on her birth certificate, and I struggle to listen. When something good happens to Lizzie, it feels like it's happening to me too. She talks to me all the time: at school, on the phone, texting, IMing, in the car, in my bedroom, in her bedroom, outside. Her voice is the solo soundtrack of my life. But I have barely heard a word she has said to me all week.

This blob-baby will take over my life. It's already putting Lizzie on mute. It will tie me to my silent house. It will light stick after stick of dynamite between my parents. It will scare Todd into another school district, or state, or planet. Or girl. It will tie up my legs and bring back my virginity. It will take a big eraser to my 3.9 GPA, my only ticket out of the state of Florida. It will cry and poop and pee and make me feel like a fool because I have no idea what else it will do.

Stop, Evelyn! This is over!

I accept the Solo cup that Sean is handing me. It doesn't matter if I drink now. It does matter if I do my homework. That is good.

But I don't drink it. I just carry it around with me, watching Lizzie get smashed off her ass. She starts to slur and stumble. Later, we join a bunch of jocks by the swing set. Lizzie and Sean share a swing: she's straddling him, her white skirt flying up her legs every time the swing takes them higher. I wonder if Sean's parents are also the kind who don't care if you screw their son on the swing set, as long as they have your keys.

A familiar sound buzzes into my ear. "Hey, E."

"Todd!" Lizzie shrieks, swinging her leg over Sean, hopping off the swing, and tripping over her feet. Todd catches her under her armpits and she drapes herself across him. "What's wrong with my friend Evelyn?" Todd looks appropriately confused for the masses watching this conversation, so I don't worry she's blowing our cover. "There's something wrong with my friend Evelyn. What is it, Todd?"

I lean over so I can stare into Lizzie's eyes, exaggerating for the crowd. "Yoo-hoo, Lizzie! I'm right here! Nothing's wrong!"

She shakes her head about a hundred times. "You're

not . . . you're still on your first beer," she says, providing explanation for her concern.

"What?" I explode into laughter like this is ridiculous, even though truthfully, I haven't had one sip of beer. Everyone starts laughing like I've been acting like a wasteoid all night.

"Whatever." Lizzie stumbles back over to Sean and lays a kiss right on his mouth. His hands come up to grab her around the waist. In the deafening "oohs" that result from this interaction, Todd and I disappear.

He's holding my wrist, not my hand. He pulls me to the basketball hoop and we sit on the driveway beneath it. People can see us, but they won't hear us. It doesn't matter. No one ever suspects Todd would screw an ugly string bean like me. He drops my wrist as soon as he realizes he doesn't need to drag me. There are two inches between us. Not even our clothes are touching. The baby took Lizzie's voice and Todd's hands. I could kill it.

"You shouldn't drink that." Todd points to the warm red cup I've been carrying for hours.

"It's okay," I say. "I'm . . . I'm taking care of it."

Todd nods. *Tell me not to. Tell me to stop and I will. Tell me you will love it, you will love me. Or just it. Even just it. Tell me it can live in your house where there are actual people and sometimes laughter. Tell me you'll hate me if I do this. Tell me you are leaving and you'll never speak to me again, but that I should still stop. Tell me and I'll have it.*

"I still don't think you should drink that," he says.

"I'm not, actually." I hold up the cup so he can feel how warm the beer is. Jacksonville August has turned it from frosty to hot chocolate He laughs and for a minute I think he's going to palm my knee, or put a piece of my hair between his thumb and finger. Or ask me to go behind the bushes.

He says, "I'm sorry. I suck at this. I just, I can't do better."

I let the crickets and the background buzz of our drunken classmates do the talking.

"I have a question, though."

"Shoot," I say. I feel calm for the first time all week. Sad, but calm. My heart is beating normally. No devil things are playing with a punching bag inside me. My blood is still flowing. My head is still connected to my neck. Everything will be back to normal soon.

"How do you know it's mine?"

Why didn't I know he would ask that again?

He sees the hurt dancing on my face or something because he says, "No, Evelyn. I didn't mean it like that. I believe you. Just . . . how do you know?"

Screw it. I'll tell him the truth. Todd and I are done with our pretend relationship anyway, so I'll spit it out. "I've never done it with anyone else."

"Unprotected, you mean?"

"No. At all."

He nods. "Me neither."

What? "You don't have to say that."

"I haven't."

"What about Am—"

"I haven't. Not anyone. I didn't even kiss her. It just never felt right."

Half my heart flies to the sky like it's finally allowed to fall in love, but the bigger half is being crushed beneath

Todd's practice cleats because this is actually a break-up disguised as a love song.

"I know there is a lot you could ask of me," he is saying, stumbling on the words. "I know I might have to pay or change diapers or . . . well, I know there's a lot. But I just can't do it. I can't tell my parents," he is saying. "It's not fair to you. It's not like it's all your fault. I guess if you decide to take me to court or something I'll do what they make me do and I shouldn't hate you or anything if you do that, but I might anyway, but I'm sorry if I do." He is rushing. "I know a good guy says he'll do whatever he can, whatever you need. But I guess I'm not a good guy."

He takes a breath and I shove my words into the empty space.

"You didn't hear me. I'm taking care of it. I'm having an . . . I'm getting rid of it."

"Oh."

Tell me not to.

He looks at me with relief in his eyes.

He puts his hand on mine. Finally. Like putting ice on a bumped head. "Then is there anything I can do to help you?" He laughs and I start to join him, but then my body resists. I don't feel like laughing. I don't feel like holding his hand. Wow: I'm pissed.

"Yes," I say, and he looks nervous.

"Shoot." His eyes stay on the pack of girls in short shorts playing drunken hopscotch at the end of the driveway.

"Drive me home."

"Your car is here. You're sober."

"Not tonight. Drive me home from the . . . from the

appointment. So I don't need to tell anyone else why I'm at a Planned Parenthood clinic."

He opens his mouth to object like a Good Catholic Boy, but the words to make him stop crawl into my windpipe from somewhere deep in my gut, somewhere where it is still two years ago and I am still worth something. The words latch hold of the back of my tongue and escape through the cage of my teeth.

"After that freaking asshole speech you just gave me, you owe me this. Pick me up three blocks from school, and drive me three miles home. You are doing it. You are not going to leave me stranded at the downtown Planned Parenthood after I just unpleasantly fixed a mistake that was at least fifty percent yours with no help from you at all. Also, if you bring a few hundred dollars to pay for it, I'll take it." I remove my hand from under his and stand up. "I'll text you to let you know when."

It feels good to be the one who walks away. I notice my blood running smooth as molasses, my breath coming in and out of my nose without effort, my knees swinging my feet out to walk without shaking. I'm sad but functional.

When I get home, I am finally able to shut my eyes, turn my brain to hibernate mode, and just fall asleep.

Decision

But then there I am, standing on that chemistry book, balancing in the middle of a blue ring. It's exactly like last time: the blue light glowing on my translucent skin, the nothingness creating goose bumps all over my naked body. Except the machine stays quiet. Then I notice that my hands are cupped in front of me, a black box with a red button resting in them. I know instinctively what it is: the on switch. I could press it. The machine would rattle to life and I would disappear into the blue light. It felt so good last time. I could do it again. I could disappear. One finger rests on the shiny red surface, rolling around. I could just press this button. It would be so easy. *Just press it*. But my finger stays still. *Press it*. Why won't I do it?

Boom! Boom! Boom! The baby crashes inside me, waking me up. I can tell that it's dancing, not punching, now. It's leaping and backflipping and spinning pirouettes. And it should. It just saved its own life.

I close my eyes to watch it all disappear again: Lizzie's voice, Todd's hands, my 3.9, the bed in my future dorm room, the promise of laughter in my ears one day. I sit up and pull my shirt up, speaking to my belly button. "I hate you," I say. "I really do."

It's still dancing.

"I'm not going to kill you, but I hate you."

I think it tries to high-five me. But it doesn't have hands yet, does it?

When I still can't sleep, I strip down in front of the long mirror. I turn on all the lights so it looks like noon in my room. It's three a.m. I look at the way my toes line up perfectly on the bottom of my feet. Ten little toes, each proportionally smaller than the next. The arches of my feet yawn toward the ground. I always thought they were my best feature. But I know from Mary's pamphlets that they are about to blow up like balloons. My bony ankles will probably break from my weight. I have always been too skinny. My knees and elbows look like they're jumping off my body, trying to escape. I hate that I look like a bag of bones by accident when I'm surrounded by so many brainless girls who are trying to achieve the sickly look on purpose. But too skinny is better than too fat. I see my arms and legs plumping, swallowing my kneecaps and elbows whole. I bring my hands up to my AA cups and push them toward my collarbone. The spiderweb of veins shifts beneath my skin. I imagine them growing but sagging, wrinkling with stretch marks, my nipples swelling to the size of Sacajawea dollars.

Finally, I push out my belly as far as it will go. I look pregnant: it's that easy. But I will be at least three times this size. I will be ugly. I already am ugly. I will be uglier.

It will be impossible to hide.

28 Days Till It's Too Late to Change My Mind

I'm in last-period British literature, trying to keep my eyes open while Sister Susan drones her way through a Shakespearean sonnet. We already studied the sonnets. We study them every year. I understand them. I actually like them, but it has been hard to sleep and hard to stay awake all week. And so, I mean honestly, I'm sick of them. I'm ready for the weekend; ready to go home, take a nap in the Empty House, eat in the Silent Kitchen, and study in my Locked Room. I've figured out that it will be April by the time this stupid thing is born, almost the end of the school year. If I get a 4.0 the first three quarters, I may not have to destroy my GPA completely until after junior year. I probably won't be valedictorian anymore, but I can still get into somewhere outside of Florida, maybe.

"Sister Susan?" the loudspeaker crackles, and half the class lurches to attention. I guess you don't need to be pregnant to get distracted in this class today.

"Yes?" She rolls her eyes at the loudspeaker so the class snickers.

"Would you send Evelyn Jones to the main office with her things, please? Her mother is here for early dismissal."

My heart bounces around in my chest, hitting every bone imaginable. I don't think Mom has set foot in this school since freshmen registration day, which was, of course, before the shit went down. She looks at my report cards, awkwardly pats my hand while telling me she's proud of me, and other than that, she butts the hell out. Someone must have died. Please, not Aunt Linda. My hands and arms move to gather my things off the floor. Holy crap, it's my dad. She's finally leaving my dad. Then my heart stops dancing, stops moving completely, and falls into my shoes. She knows. Oh God, oh shit. She knows.

I feel like a planet walking down the halls, like my slightly swollen abdomen is the size of a beach ball by the time I turn the corner. When I finally get to the office, a tiny voice squeaks, "Evelyn, honey, ready for the dentist?" It's coming from a mouth so far beneath my eyes it's out of my vision. Mary's arms stretch to hug my waist and I jump. *What the hell?* I ask with my eyes. She forms little words with her mouth: *trust me.*

I don't. She's going to tie my hands behind my back and force me to get an abortion. She's going to sit me down with my real mother, point a gun to my head, and warn me that if I don't spill my guts all over the floor, she will. Mary is insane.

But neither of these options seems all that bad. At least if I'm dead, I don't have to have a baby and I get to keep my 3.9. If she forces me to have the abortion, it won't be my fault. So

I follow the little woman, wondering how she doesn't melt into her gray blazer in this heat, thick as canola oil. A fresh wave of nausea lines my stomach when I choke the outside air into my lungs. I trail her footsteps toward her car and swing my bookbag into the space in the front seat. When I sit, she says, "You sure about this?"

This time, I try to make my eyes say *F you.*

"If you don't want to leave school, tell me now and I'll walk you back in and say we rescheduled the appointment."

I don't say anything.

"If you close the door, I'm starting the car and taking you to the park."

What the crap is at the park? I keep my hand steady on the car door handle. But then she flips open the glove compartment and pulls out a ginger ale, obviously cold from the way the condensation is beading the green surface. I shut the door and open the can.

We sit on a bench facing the playground. I hold the still-full can up to several places on my neck, making goose bumps break out among the pockets of sweat on my skin. The playground is crawling with kids: flying on the swing sets, digging in the sand, screaming on the seesaw, hanging on the monkey bars. There are so many of them, it almost looks disgusting. Like piles of ants writhing in your picnic basket.

"I was worried about you," she says, her voice dripping with phony sincerity so syrupy it adds a coat to my nausea. "What happened?"

I take a sip. It makes me feel like talking, which sucks. "What do you mean, what happened?"

"You scheduled the abortion. You claimed you were coming in to discuss details on Saturday. That was almost a week ago, Evelyn. Are you all right?"

" 'Course I'm all right." I hate myself when I lie.

"Then where have you been?"

"I changed my mind. People do that, you know."

Mary sighs. "Evelyn, I know you are going through something difficult now, but I want you to consider the position you put me in. You were seeing me almost every day. I came to care about you a great deal—"

I snort.

"And then you just stopped. I want to make sure you are okay, you are being careful, you are being cared for."

"Don't you have a pamphlet for that?" I spit.

"I suppose I deserve that," Mary says.

What a bonehead. What does that even mean? I down my ginger ale and move. I can walk back to school from here. It's only like a mile.

"Please, Evelyn," Mary says. "Don't you feel like talking?"

I do feel like talking but I don't want to feel like talking. I feel like talking to Aunt Linda, but I'm terrified to change her opinion of me, or to Lizzie, who jams up my words like traffic. But maybe I just feel like talking even to this nimwad sweating next to me on this burning metal bench. It's nice not to be in that creepy office with all of those pamphlets though. I'm still half poised to leave—one butt cheek leaning off the bench—when Mary reaches into her briefcase and pulls out another frigid can. That slumps my body back to the bench. Ginger ale is my new drug.

"So, I take it you decided against abortion?" Mary asks. She always knows where to start. This is exactly what I don't want to talk about. I know she wants me to decide that getting one is the easiest thing, but I won't. I can't. I wish I could, but I just can't.

I take a sip, nod my head.

"What are you going to do instead?"

My head shoots up. I slap my abdomen with more force than I thought I had in me and say, "I'm going to have this thing. No other choices."

"Evelyn, there are a million other choices. Not alternatives, but choices that come after that one."

"Like what?" But I know the answer.

"Like, how are you going to raise it? Where will it live? Where will you live? What do you expect from Todd? What do you expect from your parents? And more immediately, who will deliver the baby? Where will you go? Plus there are things you need to take into consid—"

"You see, this is exactly why I didn't want to talk to you. This thing is not going to be here for, like, eight months still. I don't really give a shit what else there is to do. I just want to keep my GPA up and stay skinny so no one knows. I don't want to think about anything else." I'm yelling, which isn't smart since we're outside and I don't want anyone to know.

"I see." Mary looks down at her own Diet Coke; her tiny fingers work the can in circles. She's hurt, the annoying fool.

"I didn't mean to yell at you," I say, even though I am Bad Evelyn now, and bad girls yell without feeling sorry.

"Okay, Evelyn." She sounds tired. We let the moisture buzzing in the air and the kids screaming their heads off do the talking for a while.

Directly in front of us, a blond boy tosses a rubber ball to a smaller boy who looks Cuban or Dominican. The blond kid has freckles and messy hair. He keeps wiping his nose on his bare wrist. He squeals his friend's name every time he drops the ball: "Carlos! Carlos!" Carlos stays quiet. His eyes are dark and serious, focused completely on the rubber ball. How old are these kids anyway? How can you tell that?

One of these is, like, inside my stomach right now. It might be a blob, but if it just keeps growing and I don't get rid of it, it will grow arms and legs and fingers. It might throw a ball one day. It might squeal and get covered in dirt or sand or snot. And I won't even be able to tell how old it is.

I breathe deep in an attempt to slow my heart.

"Evelyn?" Mary whispers. I almost forgot she was there.

"How do you have so much time for me?" I feel Mary's eyes move from the side of my face to the army of germs and screams swarming in front of us. For a few minutes, it seems like she's not going to answer.

Then, finally, she starts talking. "My mother was a teenager," she says.

I can't help it. I almost turn my head to look at her. I wonder if that's all she'll say, but after a minute the words come again.

"I don't think she ever wanted me, not really. She told me once that she only had me because my father promised to marry her, but he disappeared when I was still a toddler. My mother went after faraway jobs and complicated business plans and left me with different relatives in different schools almost every year." Mary turns and looks at me. "No, Evelyn. Don't think that. She wasn't a bad person, but she was a kid. She had no idea what she was doing. It just stayed like that our whole lives. You remind me of her, I guess. I wasn't there, obviously, but I imagine she felt and acted a lot like you when she was pregnant."

I'm so surprised by her honesty, I forget that it's time for me to speak. It's sort of a compliment to have an adult talk to me like I'm a real person who can understand life. Like I'm not a total idiot. But what she said doesn't make sense.

"I don't get it," I say. "If your mother was like me, why do you want me to have an abortion?"

"Evelyn." She puts a hand on my shoulder, and I finally meet her gaze. A fat raindrop falls from the sky, spreading through my hair like a raw egg. Mothers and nannies appear out of nowhere, ushering kids into cars with hand pulls and piggy-back rides and bribes of toys and desserts. But Mary stays still and so do I. "I don't necessarily want you to get an abortion. I want you to have a plan. A serious, well-developed plan, so that, should this fetus become a child, it will feel wanted."

But I don't want it. Out loud I say, "I don't know how to do that. How to make a plan."

"Well, let's take things one question at a time then, shall we?"

My heart speeds up. I don't want to think about any questions at all, let alone one after another. I say no, but I say it so quietly I don't think she hears me.

"Your parents. How are you going to tell them?"

"I'm not telling the Stranger anything."

"The Stranger?" Mary asks.

"Sorry, my dad. I'm not telling him."

"Do you always refer to your father as the Stranger?"

"Usually only in my head."

She sits her little body up like a beanpole. Her fingers twist the Diet Coke can with a newfound vigor.

"Does he hurt you? Neglect you? Why do you call him that?"

She's practically sitting on the edge of the bench. A chance to call Child Protective Services must be like a big break in the world of social workers.

"They hate each other, not me," I say. She is still buzzing with excitement, so to get her to stop, I agree. "I'll tell my mom. This week."

Her chin lowers toward her knees. "Okay. Then come back and let me know how it goes, all right?"

I've had enough. Anyway, now I have something else to work on besides the stupid sonnets. I stand up, ready to trudge the mile back to school. But she follows me, and drives me back to my Jeep.

When I wake up from my nap that afternoon, I clomp down the dark hallway and jump at the loud sound my hand makes when it knocks on Mom's office door.

"Evelyn?" she says. "That you?"

"Yeah." I walk in. She picks up her head, black eyes shining out from under black, shiny hair. She wears a brown suit. I wonder why brown doesn't clash with black when the black is your hair. I wonder why she wears a suit when she works at home. I wonder if she wore a suit when she was pregnant, then immediately shake the image from my brain. I wonder why she can't tell what's going on when to me it feels like the baby is a gleaming, bouncing bean in my abdomen. She should be able to look at me and just see it.

"Sweetie, do you want to see if Dad wants to have dinner with you? I'm swamped. I'll give you some money, though. What do you think, pizza or Mexican? Maybe sushi?"

I stand there for a minute, watching her hands shuffle through endless stacks of paper. They are normal, her hands, but her fingers look like sausages because I've been looking at Mary's all afternoon. *How am I ever going to tell you anything? You don't even wait for me to speak anymore. How am I supposed to become a mother when I can't even tell if my own mother loves me?*

"Mexican."

"Yup." She pauses her shuffling to smile at me. I turn to go. Then I stop.

"Mom." The word sounds funny in my mouth. It will sound funnier in my ears. "Can I get on your schedule sometime soon?"

27 Days Till It's Too Late to Change My Mind

It happens so quickly. The next afternoon, my mother and I are zipping down Atlantic Avenue, following the stream of cars racing toward the ocean. It's like a hundred degrees outside and I feel nauseated and exhausted, so I keep getting startled every time I see the shit-eating grin on Mom's face.

She yammers on and on next to me about lunch at La Sole and how they have the best fresh-squeezed lemonade. I nod, even though I want a ginger ale. She talks about lying in the sand and catching up and even going for a dip if the waves aren't too big after the tide comes in. Her words fill up the car like fleas, buzzing in every unwelcome direction, making me itch. I keep readjusting my bathing suit top under my coverup, but she doesn't get the hint and just keeps blah, blah, blahing. After years of silence, all this talking is just uncomfortable.

Plus, I know how quiet it will be on the car ride home. I don't know what she'll say. She doesn't show love like a normal mom—which is both a good and a bad thing. That disappointed look that would cover the faces of most moms when their daughters get knocked up will not cross hers. But I also don't know what she will do. Maybe she'll just zip her lips and walk back to the car, leaving me standing on the beach by myself. I just don't know.

The mariachi band in the restaurant makes the nerves jump in my gut, and my stomach sloshes close to puking. This is the last person I need to tell. I'll just spit it out and it will be over. We have a twenty-minute wait for a table, so we sidle up to the bar. She orders a Corona, which makes my jaw drop. She orders me a lemonade, but I shout over her, "No, a ginger ale."

"I didn't even know you liked ginger ale, sweetie," she says as the bartender turns to grab a Corona from the cooler.

"I didn't even know you liked beer," I mimic.

She looks bitten for a moment, but then she says, "I have a full afternoon to spend with my beautiful daughter." She takes my chin between her thumb and forefinger. I forgot how she used to do that. The warm and gooey feeling enhances my queasiness. "I'm celebrating."

The bile in my stomach feels gray and guilty. I chug the ginger ale and ask for more.

When we are at the table I order a third. Mom raises her eyebrows. "Are you sure you don't want to try the lemonade?" she asks. "It really is to die for."

She orders a glass for herself when I shake my head.

"I can't drink lemonade, Mom," I say when the waiter leaves. This was definitely not the line I planned to start with.

"Why not?" The Stiff-Ass looks curious. It's not like she would know if I had an allergy or anything.

"Because . . . I just can't stop drinking ginger ale." I look at her seriously because I know she'll know. Every female must suffer from ginger-ale addiction when they're preggo.

And Mom knows all about what it means to be pregnant. She has to know what this ginger ale means.

I wait for her eyes and mouth to widen into saucers while she says, "Oh no! You don't mean . . ." or something like that. My gaze is transfixed on her expression.

But she laughs like it's a joke. "I just never knew you were such a ginger-ale fanatic. I'll have to order some the next time I do the groceries."

She drops the menu to pat me on the hand. It starts tingling the way my chin did.

"Mom, I have to tell you something."

"Mm-hmm?" Her eyes stay on the menu. I should say it while there's a barrier between us. The words feel stuck in my nose somehow, like my brain is trying to force them out any way possible and my mouth has refused, so I'll have to tell my absent mother about my crappy situation through my nostrils. I sneeze.

"What is it, Evelyn?" She almost sounds like Mary, so sincere.

I try to picture her pregnant. Most memories from my toddlerhood involve her telling me that she was pregnant. She was pregnant four times, but I'm an only child. You do the math. It's hard to picture: not because she's a bag of bones like me, but because she's so stiff. Even sitting across from me in her tan one-piece and coverup, her hair is pulled into a suffocating bun, her black glasses perch on her nose so she can read the menu professionally, her neckline reaches her collarbone, obliterating any sense that she could possibly have boobs. She keeps smiling at me, but it's like she has to tell herself to do it. The pregnant women I see at grocery stores or beaches are all curves and softness: their stomachs, their huge breasts, their smiles, their eyes. Pregnancy just wasn't supposed to happen to her. Or me.

"I don't want to go walk on the beach," I say finally. "I want to go somewhere else after lunch."

"Where?" she says.

"It's a surprise."

Her eyebrows jump above the glasses. *And not a good one*, I add in my head.

"Oh, okay!" Mom says enthusiastically. "But I'll have to be home by dinnertime to get some work done." Typical.

Later, we're cruising back down Atlantic with the air-conditioning pumping so hard it makes goose bumps sprout along my limbs. I wonder if the baby can tell when I get cold. I pull my knees to my chin, curling up to keep it from getting goose bumps on its blobby body.

"Still the right way, Evelyn?" my mom keeps asking. The other words are gone. She thinks we're going somewhere fun and exciting. I don't care if I ruin her day; she's been half of the reason my past year was ruined. Well, less than half.

I direct Mom onto the highway and across the bridge toward downtown. She's silent now, back to her stony self, as if she knows it's not anything fun anymore.

When I give her the exit she says, "Are you in trouble?"

I squeak, "Yes."

"Are we going to your school?"

I squeak, "No." Minutes later we pull into the Planned Parenthood parking lot. Mom puts on her attorney face like a mask and follows me into the dark waiting room, flip-flops clapping on the creaky wooden floors.

Mary's door is open, so I march us right in there and plop on the dusty couch. My mother stands in the doorway, her lawyer face steeling her expression, looking strange on top of a body clad in beachwear.

"Evelyn," both the adults say in my direction.

I look at Mary. "Tell her," I say before I have time to wonder what they were each thinking when they uttered my name. "I can't."

If Mary is going to insist that I tell that woman, then let her be the one to bounce the words off her icy mask.

"Perhaps you'd like to sit down, Mrs. Jones," Mary stammers. I stare out the window.

When my mom sits without first correcting Mary to call her "Ms. Clark," I know she has figured it out.

"Evelyn is a very bright and talented young woman," Mary recites.

Mom puts her hand on my far shoulder and yanks it too hard so I face her. "You're pregnant?"

I don't answer. I don't even nod. I can't. I'm shaking. And besides, she already knows. I wait for the questions to fill the room: What will we tell everyone? What are you going to do with it? How pregnant are you? What will I tell my friends? Who is the father? Where will you live? What about your grades? What will we tell everyone?

But all she says is "You didn't tell me." Her eyes are dry and steady, but the words are a sob.

I stare at her for a minute, still waiting for the rest of the questions, the ones that have an answer. But she just holds my gaze. Then she starts repeating it over and over again. "Why didn't you tell me, Evelyn? Why didn't you tell me?"

That's all she says. For a second, she lets the attorney mask melt and just becomes my old mom. Mom from before Dad came back. Mom from before Dad left. Mom from before, before, before. That Mom when I was just a toddler and she thought she'd have four. She says it four times: "Why didn't you tell me?" Each time is like a staple fastening some kind of guilt to my heart. "Why didn't you tell me?" I almost double over in pain. "Why didn't you tell me?" Of all the things I should feel guilty for—having sex, having sex in her house while she was there, having unprotected sex, having sex with a boy who's not even my boyfriend, smoking pot, drinking, quitting cross-country, getting countless detentions, planning to run far away to college and never visit this stupid city again—why do I feel guilty for this? Keeping my life to myself?

Why would I tell you? You're a lawyer, not my mother.

I just shrug. Silence is in my genes.

I watch it happen. The mask descends onto her features and hardens. She stands. In an optical illusion her bathing-suit-and-coverup outfit morphs into a suit, her windblown hair winds itself into a sensible bun, her flip-flops grow to cover her toes and assume a small, reasonable heel. She extends her hand toward Mary, who is sitting behind her beat-up desk so quietly you would think she belongs in our house.

"Well, thank you for convincing my daughter to talk to me. Rest assured that her father and I will take care of things from here."

My father? Oh, hell no. He gets no say in what happens here.

Mary squeaks, "I'm sure you know, Mrs. Jo—"

"Ms. Clark." The Lawyer is back.

Mary's cheeks burn fuchsia. "I'm so sorry, Ms. Clark. I'm sure you know that Evelyn needs to get to a doctor ASAP and establish a birth plan and—"

My mom cuts her off again. "Thank you for your help, Mary. My husband and I are perfectly capable of dealing with this from here." She barely turns her head. "Evelyn?" she calls. She might as well say "heel." I follow a pace behind her to the car, ignoring the cheerful sound of our flip-flops. The sun is gone, hiding behind layers of gray in the sky. Heat lightning zigzags over our heads. If I could float into the clouds, would the lightning suck me up? And would it feel just like that dream?

When we get home, Lawyer Mom slaps her flip-flops down the hall and slams shut her office door. The Stranger waits until he hears the latch before coming to find me in the kitchen. I'm sitting at the kitchen counter, watching Discovery Channel lions chase each other on mute and downing a Sprite. We don't have any ginger ale. I doubt Mom will add it to the grocery list now.

"Did my girls have a nice day?" he asks.

No. It was awful. Your slut of a daughter is pregnant,

your shrew of a wife only cares that she wasn't the first to know, and neither of us are your girls because you're nothing more than a scared little boy.

I shrug, but I startle when I look up at him. Sometimes it's surprising to see his face and remember how much I used to love every time he came into a room—how he would cook dinner several times a week and it was so delicious, how he would dance with me in the kitchen and the hallways, how we would play that card game War for hours every night and the loser would have to do the dishes, and then we'd just end up doing them together anyway. I miss him sometimes, which is stupid because he's right here in front of me, in this kitchen. But he left—he left me. After Aunt Linda was already gone, I got home one day and he was gone too.

"Chased home early by the lightning?" He pulls a Sprite out of the fridge and sits at the kitchen table, several feet to my left; he knows I might slug him if he sits next to me.

"Something like that," I mutter.

He's going to hate me.

So what? I already hate him.

He's going to hate me.

The Stranger swishes soda in his mouth for a few moments. I can see the wheels in his brain grasping for any kind of conversation topic. If he can't talk to me now, forget it after he finds out.

"I'm going over to Lizzie's for dinner," I say.

Relief flushes over his face.

"I think I'll stay there tonight too. Bring some homework." I didn't realize this was my plan but now that the words are out of my mouth it sounds like a great idea—avoid World War Three, spend some final time with Lizzie before I'm locked in Total Isolation for the rest of my life.

"Have a good time." He pauses awkwardly. This is the part where he should say "Evelyn." But he has never called me by my name. He used to always call me "Pumpkin" or "Pumpkin face" or sometimes "Pumpking, king of the pumpkins," but right after he came back—the last time I really yelled—I exploded all over him and told him to never call me "Pumpkin" or any version of that stupid name again.

Sometimes I think that I'm too hard on him because I know that not everything was his fault. But when he left, it sucked. It really sucked. And when something sucks that badly, it's easier if you can point a finger.

I jump up from the stool. "Bye, Dad," I yell, running toward the stairs to my room. I have to get out of here immediately before Mom tries some kind of pointless grounding on me. I throw some clothes in a duffel bag, sling my backpack over my shoulder, and sprint toward the kitchen door.

"You're going now?" Dad asks. "Don't you want to shower the beach off or anything?"

I brush past him, calling "nope," and dive into my Jeep. I have no idea if Lizzie has a date or plans with her family or anything, but at this point I'll spend the night in her driveway if I have to.

Her mother puts down her glass of wine and greets me with a hug and a kiss on the forehead. She smells like vanilla all the time. She tells me Lizzie is in her room painting. She tells me I can spend the night. If my father had just stayed away like Lizzie's, would my mother be this warm?

"You're here!" Lizzie squeals when I open her door. "Great! It's time to try on outfits." She abandons her easel and jumps over the dirty clothes and dishes and books and knickknacks covering the floor to get to her monster of a closet. "Okay. I was thinking about this white halter"—she tosses it onto the floor behind her feet—"but if this lightning leads to rain, you'll be able to see, like, everything. I mean, I don't mind a little slutty but I don't want to be an exhibitionist or whatever. You know?" She leans out of the closet to look at me.

I'm standing in her doorway, deep in the mess, mouth hanging open. I forgot there was another party tonight, if I ever even knew there was another party tonight. I wrack my brain. I can't remember. I don't know whose it is or why or where.

"You forgot?" She looks hurt. "Please, E, tell me what's going on."

If I tell her everything, it will be okay. She'll stay here with me and protect me from my parents. She'll understand why I don't want to go to another loud party full of drunk jocks and giggling girls. She'll know I can't drink anyway. We'll drive to the Redbox and rent a horror movie and pop popcorn and curl up on her couch and maybe her mother will make us some herbal iced tea because herbs are good for you so they would probably be good for the bean-baby and we'll scream until it's time to go to sleep and then I'll curl up on the mattress on her floor and tell her in a whisper-song everything that I am afraid of, even the stuff that doesn't have anything to do with the baby, and she'll come down off her bed to hug me and tell me that I can just live with her and her mother and her brother and sister and that they'll take care of everything and her mother will raise the baby after it's born and it will all be okay. I just have to tell her.

"No way I forgot. I just had to come raid your closet."

She smiles. That feels good.

"I'll drive," I add as she throws me a hot-pink tube top. Hot pink does not work with my hair, but Lizzie never listens when I say that. "But can I stay here tonight? I'm expecting World War Three."

Lizzie sighs. "I want to be mad at you right now for once again not telling me whatever is going on with you, but I'm too excited for Bethany's. I'll get mad at you tomorrow." She pulls off her tank top. "I won't even ask why you're in a bikini."

With a deep breath and some serious effort, I pull my comfy gray T-shirt over my head. Of course I didn't bring my strapless—I'm still in my swimsuit—but luckily my boobs are small enough that I can just go without. For now, anyway. I yank the tube top down to meet my jeans. It's long enough, but it fits like a hot-dog casing. I imagine the little bean of a baby scrunching into the very side of my uterus, squishing smaller and smaller and smaller until it just . . .

"That looks great!" Lizzie attacks my face with a huge blush brush. She has decided to risk the white halter.

"So why the World War Three?" she asks.

"I don't know what they're fighting about now. It's just more stormy than usual there, so I am pretty sure it will explode again. Do you have a ginger ale?"

"Don't change the subject. Something's going on with you. What is it, Ev?" She abandons the blush brush and sits on the side of her bed.

"I don't know what you're talking about."

"Come on, Ev." She's almost whining now.

"I swear." I cough. "It's nothing."

"I thought you were going to tell me everything now."

"I do." Except this. "I swear." I swallow.

Lizzie stands and pushes the brush harder into my face. "Well, if you're going to keep your mouth shut, I won't tell you what I found out about my potential dad today."

When we leave I am clad in hot pink and covered in sparkles, an unwed mother masquerading as a Disney Princess.

I carry around a warm Solo cup of beer while watching my friends get drunk and avoiding Todd. He walks in the kitchen, I pull Lizzie and Bethany into the backyard. He approaches from the side of the house and he's calling Lizzie's name, so I pull Bethany and Sean to the other side. Lizzie joins us again, but a minute later, Todd starts up the driveway, so I pull her and Sean into the garage. They start making out. I abandon my full cup of beer and wander into the kitchen by myself to find a sneaky way to raid the refrigerator for a snack and a ginger ale. My stomach is confused—half nauseated, half hungry. I trace the line between the halves with the nail on my pointer finger and I walk smack into Todd. Both missions abandoned in one fell swoop.

"Where's your drink?" There's beer on his breath and his

shirt smells like weed. He's standing too close to me, like he wants something. We haven't talked since Sean's party—the Breakup of the Relationship That Never Was.

"I'm not drinking." I look him in the eye. "Were you smoking weed?"

He laughs. "No. I got this shirt out of the back of Sean's car because Bethany ripped a hole right in the chest of the one I was wearing."

This is not the image I want interrupting the shrinking baby movie that has been playing in my head.

"I'm sober, actually," he says. "Big practice on Monday."

Whatever, dumbass, it's only Saturday night. I keep looking over his shoulder like someone who I'm dying to talk to is about to show up. But the only things over there are drunk teenagers gulping and groping and running to find a place to puke.

"So," he says to my silence. "When do you need me to do that thing?"

Now I look at him. "What thing?"

"You know, the favor?" I stare blankly. "Pick you up from the . . . appointment. I have some . . . for you, too." He starts digging his hand into his back pocket.

"Oh!" I say too loudly. "I don't need you to do that anymore."

"Why?"

"Don't worry about it."

"But does this mean . . . do . . . you're going to . . . shouldn't I be worried?"

I don't know. Maybe my mom will make me sue him for child support. But I don't care. "No."

"Are you . . . are you okay?" Suddenly the jerk is gone and it's Todd in front of me—Todd who packed three sandwiches when I said I was hungry, Todd who told jokes to cover up the yelling, who asked me a thousand questions about life in the Silent House, whose naked body would feel so natural next to mine.

Sean and Lizzie burst into the kitchen in a torrent of energy and Sean runs right up to us and knocks our heads together. "Ow, jerkoff," I say, rubbing my skull.

"Will you two just bang it out already? So much sexual tension here." Sean waves his arms between Todd and me, accidentally brushing my boob with each swing and not even noticing.

Todd and I stare at him, reducing Lizzie to a fit of giggles. She won't say anything to Sean, I know that, but she also doesn't know about the Fake Breakup last week, so I hope she doesn't lean in and whisper something to Todd. I'm exhausted. I check the clock. Eleven. That has to be late enough.

"Come on, Lizzie. Let's go home."

"Home! Are you crazy?" Lizzie spits between giggles. "Don't go home, have a beer." She stares at me like it's a challenge.

"Yeah, the party's just starting!" Sean slaps me on the shoulder. "Don't be mad about the sexual tension. I didn't put it there, I just tell it like it is."

"Get over yourself, Sean. I don't care what you say. I'm just tired and I want to go home. Let's go, Lizzie."

She looks at me, confused. "No?"

"Lizzie, I'm really tired."

"So have a beer. You've barely had any."

"I don't want a beer. I want a pillow." Sean's and Todd's eyes bounce between our faces like this is a tennis match.

"So go to your own house then. I'm not ready to go."

I want to scream. I can't go to my own house. I can't stay here. "Please?"

"What the hell is wrong with you, anyway? You say there is nothing wrong with you but something clearly is. If you don't tell me, then you're not coming back to my fucking house." Lizzie's eyes look angry. I hope mine look pleading.

"I'll tell you when we get home. I promise," I say.

Todd sucks in air.

A stampede of naked boys crashes through the kitchen yelling, "Streak! Streak!"

"Sweet!" Sean says, pulling off his shirt and yanking down his shorts and boxers in one swift motion. Still in his sneakers, he chases the crowd. The sticky, sweaty smell they trail into the kitchen causes my lunch to rise dangerously high in my esophagus. Lizzie dissolves into giggles and runs after them into the pool, in all of her clothing.

I take a Solo cup, fill it with water, and hoist myself onto the kitchen counter. Todd comes over and puts his hand on my knee. I do not like it there. It feels like a spider.

"You didn't tell her?" he asks, like somehow this makes him feel worse for knocking me up, telling me he wouldn't do anything to help, and then dumping me.

"What the fuck do you care?"

"I don't. I'm just surprised."

I shrug. A symbol for if-you-want-this-conversation-to-continue-you-better-say-the-next-word.

"You really want to get out of here? You can sleep at my place. I don't think you'll get Lizzie to leave for a while."

I almost snort out my water. "Great idea. Like your mother wouldn't rip out my eyes and fry them for breakfast." Todd's mother is totally a Sitcom Mom. She knows who I am—a friend of her son—and who we all are. She honks at us when she drives by. She welcomes us at their home. But she wouldn't be happy about me if she knew I'd been screwing her son.

Todd laughs. His hand rises off my knee and even though I hated it, his laugh makes me miss it. My knee feels cold.

"I mean, in the guest bedroom. I'll tell her your parents had a fight and you didn't want to go back there after the party. She knows what they're like, anyway."

She knows about my parents? How is this possible?

"That's okay," I say. "I'll wait for Lizzie."

"Look," Todd says, "I know I'm not the person you want to accept help from right now, but you look exhausted and Lizzie is going to be here for another three hours and everyone is going to get drunk and puke more and this whole place is going to smell even worse than it already does. What I'm offering you is a double bed with clean sheets in a house that's only silent at night. Okay?"

My head feels like it weighs a thousand pounds. O-kay. Only two syllables. It foams around my voice box. Just say okay. That's it. Then you can go to sleep and this awful day will be over. You don't need to forgive him, just sleep.

Todd keeps going. "Mom and Rick will be asleep now. You can just go to bed and leave in the morning. You won't even talk to her, but we won't do anything so she wouldn't mind anyway."

The syllables finally form outside my head. "Okay."

Todd swings his keys around. "Just so you know, though. Right now we're playing Trivial Pursuit in Tom's basement." I nod, even though I don't understand how a guy with a mother like that could lie to her. But this is the guy who told me he could abandon his child, so I guess it's not that surprising.

I find Lizzie, tell her not to drive and to be safe, and leave. She barely acknowledges me but I leave anyway. I don't know what else I can do.

Just tell her.

But I can't.

26 Days Till It's Too Late to Change My Mind

I sneak out of Todd's at nine a.m., prepared to walk into a war zone. I leave the guest bed unmade so he'll have to deal with it.

But the house is silent when I get home, so I collapse into my bed, grateful.

Beneath me the coffeemaker churns and the toaster spits out a bagel. My dad's shoes squeak and my mom's heels clap; they are both in the kitchen at once. Finally, the door to the garage swings open and one Beamer hums in the driveway. They're going to Mass. Together. This is the biggest bull in our entire house. Every Sunday, they zip their mouths shut and play happily-married-couple-with-a-rebellious-teenager for the benefit of the priest and parishioners. Today they will pray for me. God will curse me further after the prayers of hypocrites.

I used to go with them. I actually kind of miss it. I don't believe in it, but I love the singing. And it felt like such a peaceful way to turn one week into the next. I didn't think about God or whatever, but I went. I didn't stop because I didn't want to go anymore or even because I got sick of those two faking it with drippy voices and somber faces. I stopped because Bad Evelyn doesn't go to church. I expected a big, satisfying fight that first Sunday that I stayed in bed, but like always they clamped their mouths shut. They never ground me, yell at me, or even question any of the Bad Evelyn decisions. They barely even look at my report cards, which is good because my GPA is the one thing I wasn't willing to risk for a Bad Girl Rep. Until now, I guess.

They're gone, so I have like ninety minutes to myself. I fall asleep.

I'm naked again, but I'm soaring on my stomach, Supergirl style, through dark-gray clouds with neon-blue edges. It's fun. I'm warm and the clouds feel like teeny-tiny raindrops tickling my skin. I clasp one hand on top of the other in front of my head and soar faster. The baby assumes the same position inside me. Even though it is encased in there, I know its little bean-body can feel all of these clouds too. And I know they are erasing us, sucking us into the blue just like the halo-vacuum. I feel happy like I haven't since before I was pregnant. Like I'm dancing with my daddy in the kitchen.

Something bangs into my door and I jolt upright, rubbing my eyes so my contact lenses scrape my retinas back and forth. "Come in."

Mom stands: her spine a ramrod, her lawyer mask securely hiding any maternal emotions. The Stranger looks like he's either going to cry or punch something. I am tiny. I'm a little ant about to drown in all of these blankets.

She told him.

"We need to talk, Evie-Teeny." She hasn't used that name for me since I was about three, but when she sits on the foot of my bed, she looks like she's perching on hot coals.

"You told him?" I guess she had to. But how did she do it? How could she string those words together when they can't even talk about the weather? How did they have that conversation and yet the house is still standing? Last week a simple question of dinner summoned a hurricane in the kitchen.

She doesn't answer. Dad stands in the doorway. "Did that kid who keeps coming over here do this to you?" he growls. He's Daddy-Dad. Angry Daddy-Dad from before. He's still Stranger-Dad, but he's also Daddy-Dad.

"What?" I ask the bare ceiling.

"Who did this to you?" he grunts, each word requiring effort and precision.

"I did this to myself, Dad." I lace my voice with the sarcasm teenagers use on television and in the movies.

"Who—" he starts again, but the Ice Queen cuts him off.

"Stop, Jim. We said we wouldn't." He storms into the hallway and the air pressure releases slowly from the room. One parent is better than two.

"What's your plan, Evelyn?"

I curl into a ball and turn away from her. She pats my knee, which twitches.

"This is scary for us, too, Evie. But we need to talk."

Sure, Mom. We don't ever talk. Silent is who we are.

"Are you keeping the baby?"

I curl my knees closer to my chin.

"Are you considering abortion?"

Would she let me get an abortion? Does she want me to get one so we can pretend everything is the same?

"Are you going to stay in school? Are you thinking about your GPA?"

She doesn't even know what my GPA is. Her presence on my bed is like a ringing in my ear—I want it to go away but I don't know how to make it stop.

She just sits there. Five minutes tick by. I start to nod off again, but she shakes my knee.

"This is serious stuff, Evelyn. Your father and I don't want to decide everything for you. What are you going to do?"

"You've got to talk to us, Pumpkin."

Somewhere in the ringing he wandered back to the doorway. I whip myself around in the bed. "You don't call me that anymore."

He throws up his arms. "I'm sorry." He retreats a step into the hallway.

Mom's eyes grow to the size of quarters. The three of us freeze for five minutes, ten minutes, half an hour, two hours, two days, two weeks. I always thought three silent people in a house was the most uncomfortable feeling imaginable: turns out that three silent people in your bedroom is worse.

After an eternity, Mom says, "If I make an appointment at a doctor tomorrow, will you go with me?"

I nod and crash back into the bed. He vaporizes. She clicks out of the room. They leave my door open and by the time I trudge across the room to close it, I'm too awake to go back to sleep, of course.

My big toe connects with something cold on the floor. I reach down: it's a can of ginger ale. Mom must have left it during all that silent lingering. It's freezing, just the way I like it. It opens with a hiss and fizzes over my fingers, but I don't care. I lick it off like it's the elixir of life.

I am the loneliest person on the planet, even though I never get to be alone. I pound my fist on my abdomen, where I imagine the beanyblob to be floating around. I can't talk to it, though.

If I call Lizzie, she'll yell at me again. If I call Todd, I'll look desperate and heartbroken. If I try to talk to my mom, we'll just stare at each other. If I go back and see Mary, I'll have to listen to her squeaking in my ears. If I call anyone else, they'll wonder why the hell I'm calling.

I settle for Lizzie.

She doesn't answer.

I wish I had asked Mary about sleeping pills. If I take a Tylenol PM I might kill the baby, but if I stay awake another minute, I might kill myself. Finally, I reach for my chemistry textbook and tell my brain to start sifting through chapter five because tomorrow is Monday and Mondays always mean quizzes.

The full weight of the textbook is resting on my abdomen, but I don't care.

25 Days Till It's Too Late to Change My Mind

Last night, I outlined the chapter, took the practice quiz, solved a hundred and fifty practice problems. I went through twenty pages of notes and turned them into flash cards. I have never been so ready for a quiz in my life, but when I wander down to the kitchen in my uniform in the morning, Mom is sitting at the table, still in her pajamas.

"Why are you wearing that?" she asks. That's my question. She should be in a suit by now, in some courtroom, looking comfortable with a ramrod back and a pinched expression.

"It's what I wear to school." Duh.

"You're not going to school. We're going to see a doctor."

"No, not now!" I feel like stomping my feet.

"Yes now. You promised yesterday, sweetie. That was the deal."

"No. Not now. After school. I have a chemistry test today."

"Evelyn, you need to get to the doctor immediately.

I couldn't make an appointment for just anytime. I had to ask Dr. Elizabeth to come in early to get you in right away. You have been preg—in this condition for a while now and still haven't seen a doctor. You need to do this." Mom stands to walk toward me.

"Dr. who?"

"Dr. Elizabeth. She's married to one of my colleagues and is the best in the field."

I just need a damn doctor, not the best in the field. "Mom, chem is first period. I spent all of yesterday studying."

I want the pressure of a pencil nudged between my fingers while they chart out the answers to equations and map atoms with the appropriate number of electrons and neutrons. I want to turn my brain off and sit down in the plastic desk answering questions that actually have answers.

"Evelyn, I'm pulling the Mom Card. I'll drop you off at school after the appointment, but you're coming with me now."

What freaking right do you have to pull the Mom Card? I just want to take a test! You won't listen to me about a chemistry test; how will you ever listen to me about this parasite?

"I'll take my own car."

Dr. Elizabeth Whatever is late. Of course. I sit on the table, sweating into my pleated skirt. The Control Freak sits on the stool next to me, shaking her sensible heel from her toes and punching buttons on her BlackBerry, until finally one of Dr. EarlyMorning's minions starts pulling things out of my body: blood, urine, whatever else she finds in my vagina with that prodder. By the time we sit down with the actual doctor, I might as well be inside out. She sits in a big burgundy armchair, and everything in the room is new and clean and white and beige. My mom and I sit on the other side of the desk, which is so big it feels like we're at a dining room table except that she has these plush and comfy armchairs that make me want to fall asleep. The doc looks at me. She can see blood running through my veins and the inside of my hair follicles and to her my eyes look like golf balls with red lines running all over them because I am inside out now. The Stiff-Ass sits on the very edge of her chair and I want to tell her to sit back and relax because the chair is so darn comfortable but she would never. She has a notebook on the edge of the desk and a pencil in her hand and she's leaning into it like she's ready to take notes even though Dr. Keep Waiting hasn't said anything yet. Finally, she looks up.

"I hear you have been drinking a lot of ginger ale, Evelyn," she says in this low, womanly voice, and I nod, thinking how she and this whole place are the opposite of Mary and her office.

"How have you been feeling?"

I shrug. My uniform feels itchy, like this blouse is made of sandpaper.

"Any morning sickness? Vomiting? Diarrhea?"

I shake my head. I did puke twice last week, but I think it was the cafeteria food.

"Well, you are in fact pregnant." I like how she says it: not like she's pitying me or expecting me to jump up with joy, and not like I'm the stupidest person on the planet for getting knocked up in high school. Just like it's a fact. Or it's not such a big deal.

"I knew that."

"So." She puts the folder she has been looking at on her desk. "What do you want to do?"

Mom repositions her pen, as if I'm the one she's going to be taking notes about.

I shrug.

"Jesus, Evelyn!" My mother's voice makes me jump in my seat. "You have to tell us something. We're all trying not to be mad at you and not to go out and murder the kid who did this to you and not to drown you with lectures on things like safe sex and contraception because we know you already know this stuff. We are not grounding you or punishing you. We're trying to be supportive. But you have to talk to us!" Her voice shakes. Is *she* mad at *me* for being silent?

My mouth opens, but nothing comes out.

After a while, Dr. Elizabeth says, "Well, let's start here. What are your goals?"

Mouth still open, I turn to look at her. Isn't that the same question?

"I mean, regardless of the pregnancy."

"Evelyn wants to go to college," Mom answers.

No duh.

"Let's give Evelyn some time to answer here. Evelyn?"

I nod.

"Any idea where you wanted to go?"

My mother says "University of Florida" at the same time that I say "One of the Ivies." I watch her face out of the corner of my eye, but I keep looking at Dr. Elizabeth, whose blond hair is loose and smooth and crinkly like tiny little waves. I wish my hair could do that. She raises one eyebrow. I wish I could do that too.

"I'm number one in my class right now: 3.9. I think I could get into one of them. Or maybe Stanford."

"You are?" my mom's voice leaks between the doctor and me, but I ignore it.

"I want to get out of Florida, as soon as possible."

"Why?" asks Dr. Elizabeth. Again, she's asking for a fact.

"Because I hate it," I answer. I expect her to push this further, but she nods. Mom scribbles in her notebook.

The doctor turns over a paper. "Your mom tells me that Mary from Planned Parenthood says that you want to deliver the baby."

I snort a laugh.

Her head jolts up. "Is that not true?"

I could still get an abortion. The idea dances into the back of my head like a sexy belly dancer swaying her hips and curling a finger right at my middle. Mom would let me. This could be over.

I lurch forward when I get punched from the inside. No, I can't. It was never about Mom anyway.

"I want to not be pregnant."

Dr. Elizabeth says, "Okay, so you're going to have an abortion?"

I glance at my mom. Her face is all lawyered, her expression unreadable. It would be so easy. She and the Stranger would pay for it. She could drive me home. She could call in to St. Mary's and tell them I have the flu and they could send my homework home with Lizzie and two years from now I would be sitting in my dorm room at Stanford or Brown or Yale and I could just completely forget it all. I'm going to do it. It will be easier now that everyone knows.

But when I look at my mom, her mouth is open. Her eyes are still but they're tan, the brown has drained out of them to somewhere deep and hurt. She'd let me do it, but I can't. The three babies she didn't get to have swim to the surface of her eyes. Damn it, I can't. I fucking can't.

I look up. "I can't."

Dr. Elizabeth pauses. "Okay, so you're going to deliver. Have you spoken with anyone at school about this?"

Only Todd. "No."

"Do you know what St. Mary's policy is on pregnant students?"

"No." The nuns can't know. They can't know.

"Well, that is something that you need to look into right away."

"No!" Four eyes swing to study my inside-out face. "I mean, I don't want anyone to know."

"What?" says Mom.

"How would that be possible?" says Dr. Forceful.

"Evelyn, you know what a pregnant person looks like eventually, right?" The Control Freak thinks I am a total bonehead. "How are you going to hide a belly like that from everyone at school?"

I shake my head. I don't know, I don't know, I don't know. I haven't cried since I found out, but there is a stinging on the inside of my eyeball, which is now the outside of my eyeball, and I imagine how ugly it will be when the tears trace their way down my inside-out face.

I wait for Dr. Elizabeth's voice, low and melodious, but instead my mom chirps in her direction. "We'll figure this out."

I snort and glance up at the Control Freak in time to see her mouthing some secret message across the white plane that separates us from the doctor.

"What about after you deliver, Evelyn?" I look at Dr. Elizabeth. "Do you want to raise this baby as a teenage parent, or place it for adoption?"

I don't know. I don't like the thing, but if I don't like it, why would anyone else?

"Evelyn," my mother's voice warns.

"I really don't know. What do you want from me?" I spit back at her. Her mouth snaps shut. "All I know is, I don't want the whole city of Jacksonville to know I'm . . . to know about this."

"We'll figure it out, Evelyn," Mom says, ignoring the way my eyebrows knit in confusion.

"Well, you really need to think about who you want to raise this baby," Dr. Elizabeth says, which must be a joke, because my mother thinks we're going to figure out a way for me to somehow keep my GPA and my class rank, and hide the fact that I'm pregnant from the entire school. Never mind that it happens to be full of nuns and prudes and horny guys who objectify all of the parts of our bodies every day and would notice if my stomach swells to the size of a grape, let alone a watermelon. But Dr. Whatever is now droning on and on about prenatal vitamins and regular checkups and the high likelihood of postpartum depression (no biggie, I've been depressed for years), and early delivery (which means my life is over even sooner than I thought—goody).

But when I finally get to school at lunchtime, I find Sister Maria and ace the chem test. Mom's fantasy plan is working so far.

21 Days Till It's
Too Late to Change
My Mind

The week goes by with no Todd, barely any Lizzie, and absolutely no fights. My parents do this weird thing they haven't done since right after Dad returned: they pretend to like each other. Dad says "good morning" when Mom walks in the room at breakfast. Mom brings Dad's mail all the way down to his office instead of sorting it and leaving it on the kitchen table. And twice we eat dinner together, all three of us. This is a huge production staged for an audience of one—me—and I hate it. They recite lines back and forth, and I'm expected to perform but I never get the script. I guess this charade is more like the old days, but somehow all the pretending feels worse than the silence.

At lunch on Friday, Lizzie jabbers to the other girls at our table—Bethany and Mandy and Cate, and I guess to me too—about how to hook up in secret at a party. She's pretending to be upset that everyone in the school knows she keeps hooking up with Sean.

"So, Evelyn, how do you do it?" She glances at me and my cheeks go pink. It's a weird thing for her to say. She usually stays as hushed about my sex life as I do.

Bethany says, "Huh?"

Mandy swerves her head. Suddenly I'm the center of attention. I much prefer life when Lizzie is in this position. I stop moving my Sharpie, stop writing "St. Mary's sucks" on the side of the cafeteria table. "Who have you done anyway, Evelyn?" Mandy asks.

"Did you hook up with someone last week at Bethany's?" Cate says.

"No. And you know me. I don't kiss and tell."

"But you also don't get an S-L-U-T reputation like yours for nothing!" Cate squeals and the four of them dissolve into laughter. I try to join it convincingly. If I weren't pregnant and if I were still screwing around with Todd, this would be a happy moment. This would make me laugh. No wonder Lizzie thinks something's wrong with me.

"So . . . have you done it with Sean?" Mandy asks. She hangs with us, though she's a prude.

"No, Mandy, I have not had *sex* with Sean." I shout the word to make her jump. They all start laughing again. I kind of hiccup alongside and enjoy the stares of the surrounding dumbasses at different tables.

Cate recovers first. "Who then?"

Bethany starts the roll call: Joe? Pete? Mark? I realize that she's going to get to Todd eventually so I stop shaking my head and start shrugging. She rattles off ten more names.

"A good girl never tells," Lizzie says, and I roll my eyes at her. She knows I hate it when she calls me that.

"What do you *know*?" Cate demands. When the bell rings, I almost feel normal again. I need to tell Lizzie. She's the soundtrack of my life. If I cut her out, my ears will starve.

I follow Lizzie home after school and she commences fashion show number three of junior year. There have never been so many parties to go to. There were always other things we did too—football games and video games and carnivals and movies at the cineplex. Ever since I got pregnant, all anyone wants to do is drink.

She's not asking me anymore. She's being too quiet, letting Jay-Z and Rihanna create noise in the room as she tosses clothes out of her closet.

I pull a black spaghetti-strap tank top over my head and shake my red mane at the mirror. My stomach is still flat, but it kind of looks pregnant to me, as if my eyes are telling the future. This must be how anorexics see their reflections— skinny and fat at the same time. I'm wearing khaki shorts, tiny ones that would show half my ass if I bent over. I look good. For now. Should I go to the party, even after I tell her, or should I just go home?

I'll decide after I tell her. I'm going to tell her. I have to tell her.

"Lizzie."

She's halfway into a red minidress, one strap pulled over her shoulder, the other hanging under her armpit.

"Yeah?"

It's the damn word. I haven't been able to say it once.

"That dress is too skimpy, even for you." She giggles.

My phone rings and I dig it out of my backpack, cursing

myself for hoping it's Todd. Maybe he's going to say, *Do you want to blow off this party?* Maybe he'll say, *Let's go to a movie and get some ice cream and my mom's out of town so you can stay in the guest room again and I'll stay with you, be a comma around your body, and stroke your inner elbow all night long but we don't have to have sex if you don't want to.* Maybe he'll say, *You can just move in with us. Your parents are crappy, but Mom and Rick are great and she'll stay home and take care of the baby so you can go to college wherever you want and get the hell out of Jacksonville and my mom will love this baby more than you ever could.*

It's the Stiff-Ass. I reject the call.

Lizzie emerges in a white sundress. "You wore that one two weeks ago, remember?"

"Damn," she says.

"Hey, Lizzie?" Maybe I can act it out for her the way I did for Todd. Maybe I can drive her down to Planned Parenthood and make Squeaky Mary tell her too.

"Yeah?" she calls from the depths of her closet while my phone rings again.

"Why the hell does the Control Freak keep calling me?"

"Who?" she asks.

"My mom," I answer.

"At least you hate her less." Lizzie laughs. She means less than my dad.

I turn my phone off. "I don't hate either of them," I say. "I just don't like them. I don't like anyone, really, you know?"

Lizzie comes out of the closet in a pale-pink dress. She

looks stunning, but it falls all the way to her knees. There's no way she will wear it.

"What about me?"

"I don't mean you. But I don't like most people."

She jumps on my lap where I'm sitting on the bed and covers my cheek in kisses. "Good. Because I looove you." After a pause she adds, "Which is why you need to tell me what's going on."

I laugh. "I know." It feels good to have her on my lap, actually, but I shove her off me. "Lizzie, I—"

Her face floods with relief because she knows I'm finally about to talk, but she cuts me off anyway. This is the game we play. She's letting me get comfortable, get laughing, then she knows I'll talk. "Uh-oh. Are you about to tell me you're a lesbian or something? Is that how you keep from falling for Todd? Did I just, like, totally turn you on?" She collapses to the floor, a giggling pile of pink. There's a knock at her door. Her mom stands there holding a phone.

"Oh honey," she says, "I do wish you would wear that." They both laugh. Then her mom crosses the room and hands the phone to me. "It's your mom. She says it's a family emergency."

Lizzie mouths, "Oh shit," so I have to force a smile as my mom tells me I have to come home for a family talk. A family talk composed of individuals who never talk.

"No." I don't need to explain.

"You can meet up with Lizzie later," she says.

That doesn't work for me. Later, Lizzie will be a drunken, stumbling mess. Later, I will be sober and outside the fun that everyone else is having. Later, I will have to share space with Todd, who makes me feel like my insides are about to explode through my belly button, bean-baby and all. Later, I won't be able to tell Lizzie anything.

"No," I say.

She puts the Stranger on the phone.

"It's time to come home now, Evelyn." Crap, he used my name. This might be the third time in sixteen years he's ever used my name.

"Later."

"It's dinnertime," he says.

I almost say, "Exactly," but I'm not that kind of Bad. I am the quiet kind of Bad. The kind that quits everything and sneaks her not-boyfriend in the house and gets knocked up but still cowers in front of her parents. "Later, please." It's not fair, them tag-teaming me like this. I've had no time to prepare for a mutual strike.

His voice loses the edge. "Why, Pumpkin? Is there something important going on right now?" Mom would never bother with this question, but it makes my blood boil. Part of me realizes I should give him points for trying, but he's not supposed to say "Pumpkin." I hang up.

"I have to go."

"Okay." Lizzie has pulled off the pink dress and is standing in the middle of her closet in a tan strapless and a white lace thong. "I would hug you but you might try to take advantage of me, so I'll just see you later."

I force a laugh. "Bye, Lizzie."

"Hey, E?" She pokes her head around the closet door.

"Yeah?"

"You'll tell me what's going on when you get back, right?"

"I promise," I say. But family dinner might at least save me from a third weekend in a row of tiptoeing around other people's puke and wishing my warm beer was ginger ale.

I'll tell her tomorrow if I can't tell her tonight.

My house is a scene from a horror movie. The lights are out in the kitchen and the upstairs hallway. A green lamp glows in the living room, shining vomit colored through the kitchen door. My parents sit in there together, the green making streaks in my mother's hair and highlighting the underside of my father's eyes. We never go in this room. They're sitting next to each other on the couch, murmuring back and forth in low voices, barely audible. They never sit next to each other. They don't murmur. If they talk, they yell. I wonder if they are planning to kill me.

Three cans of ginger ale hiss on the coffee table, straws poking out of them. The Control Freak's notebook sits in the middle. Bean-baby becomes Demon Baby, clawing at my insides when I tiptoe into the room.

Mom points to the rocking chair next to the couch. I sit. Dad hands me a ginger ale. I sip. The bubbles escape the straw and dot my tiny khaki shorts.

"We have a plan, Pumpkin," the Stranger says.

"Don't call me that," I say, without looking down. But at the edge of my vision, I can see his eyes fall to the floor. It's creepy enough in this room. I shouldn't say anything.

"We have a plan, Evelyn," Mom says.

"We think we have a plan," Dad repeats, green shadows shifting all over his face.

If they kill me, I can maintain my GPA and class rank and no one will know I'm pregnant.

"Don't you want to know what it is?" Mom asks in a hushed whisper. It's supposed to be soothing but soothing doesn't come easily to her.

I sip my ginger ale and shrug.

"You're going away for your junior year."

I wish they'd killed me.

"Starting when?" I ask.

"Well, that's why we wanted you to come home so quickly. It's up to you, really. I could drive you out there this weekend. We'll leave first thing in the morning. Or, if you want some time to say good-bye to all the kids at school"—I snort—"we can leave next weekend."

Ha. Some choice.

"Where are you driving me?" I ask.

"To your aunt Linda's. In Chicago," Dad says.

Relief floods my body in tingles. That's much better than some Unwed Mothers' Home run by nuns. But it still hurts that they'd just get rid of me, even if I did screw up.

Mom keeps talking. "I had a few meetings with Sister Maria, your guidance counselor, this week."

"Meetings? You had meetings? Like, in person?"

"Don't worry, sweetie." Mom tries to coo, sounding like a cow. "I didn't tell her that you're—about our situation. I just said that we have some family in Chicago and someone is sick and that you might be spending the school year there. She said your grades can transfer from Aunt Linda's school, especially since it's a Catholic prep school. And Aunt Linda says that there will not be any consequences to your being—to your condition at her school."

"You told Aunt Linda?" I'm horrified.

"Weren't you going to tell her? You love Aunt Linda." She says this the way she always does—like me loving Aunt Linda means that I don't love her, means that she isn't good enough. I feel guilty because she's kind of right. Aunt Linda is warm and funny and loves me so obviously. She lived here when I was a kid and we all pretended it was so my parents would help her get through college when really it was so she could take care of me when my mom shifted between health problems and depression. But Aunt Linda is ten years younger than my mother, a Chinese adoptee, and her polar opposite. They're complicated.

So why is she shoving me out the door and into Aunt Linda's arms?

And what does Aunt Linda think of this crappy situation?

"So, what do you think?" Dad says.

I can't believe you're kicking me out. You are awful excuses for parents, but I can't believe the minute I start causing the problems you send me and this thing away. That's what I think. I shrug again.

"Your father and I really think this is the right plan. Your aunt Linda will take good care of you." And we all know you wouldn't send me to her unless you were completely sick of taking care of me yourself. "We can talk about the Ivy plan depending on what you decide with the baby."

I nod.

She reaches out to grab my hand. "We'll talk every day, Teeny," she says, as if that's what I was worried about.

I move my hand away.

The Stranger finally looks at me. His eyes are red. "Are you upset, Pum—Evelyn?"

"No."

Don't pretend I have a choice when you already made it for me. When you stepped all the way out of my life, and now you want to force your way back in as the hotshot director.

"Let's leave tomorrow," I say. "But I'm going out tonight."

I walk straight out the door before they can say anything else.

Lizzie is still at her house when I pull back in the driveway, about nine o'clock. Now I really have to tell her. Right now, before she gets drunk.

She's eating a bowl of cucumbers and tomatoes at her kitchen table—no dressing. Suddenly, I am starving. Dad said it was dinnertime, but no food ever appeared.

"You're back!" she squeals, jumping up from the counter when I let myself into the kitchen door. She looks me over. "You don't have any makeup on. And you need to brush your hair. And I think I found a cuter top for you." How the hell am I going to live a year without her? "But first sit and tell me what's up. No more lesbo jokes, I promise."

She pulls out the wicker chair next to her and I crash onto it.

"Sorry. I had to leave as soon as possible after the family meeting. I'll get ready real quick here."

"You should wear that white dress," she says.

"I'm too pale for it. And you just wore it two weeks ago."

"Wear it anyway. It'll look great with your hair." My hand automatically pats the frizz on top of my head.

"Lizzie," I say. I'm going to tell her. I have to.

"Yeah?"

"My aunt Linda, remember her?" She nods. Why am I starting here? "She's sick." I hear the lie fall out of my mouth and crash to the floor. I don't need to tell her, or anyone. Ever.

Lizzie's eyes go wide. "With what?"

"I don't know. But my mother's sending me there to help take care of her. Since Aunt Linda's got the kids and all now."

Lizzie narrows her eyes, angry.

"No!" she says. "For how long?"

"Probably for the whole year."

Lizzie covers her hand with her mouth. "Then, will she be, like, dead?"

I shrug. I suck.

At the party, Lizzie is determined to get me shitfaced. It's almost like she wants to make it impossible for me to leave this party sober. She drags me to anyone who has ever been my remote acquaintance and announces that I am leaving for a year, starting tomorrow. Everyone wants to chug a beer or do a shot with me. If I hesitate their eyebrows arch with suspicion because all these drunkards are used to me being the most wild girl at the party, though not the most drunk. Lizzie always got that prize. After making up a game where we chug with our eyes closed so I can pour three entire beers in the grass, I finally find a moment when the kitchen is empty and pull a water bottle out of Sean's refrigerator and go to the bathroom. I empty the water and step on the bottle to make it look beat up, then fill it with water from the sink. The rest of the night, I take huge gulps and breathe deeply after each one. It works. No one even asks me what it is.

By the time the partiers are falling and puking and sticking dirty tongues down each other's throats, I'm almost happy I'm leaving. I sit by myself on Sean's swing set, still chugging water. Next week, I'll be in a school full of other gossipy teenagers where it's freezing and you can't party outside for eight months of the year. But in Chicago, it will be okay to bury myself in whatever bed I sleep in and not come out except to go to school. In Chicago, I won't have a stupid, wonderful best friend in my face constantly yammering on about something being wrong with me. In Chicago, Aunt Linda will— Crap, Aunt Linda. Aunt Linda will be disappointed. Aunt Linda will want to talk about it and about Todd and about what the hell I'm going to do with my life. My head is spinning. My stomach churns. I lean off the swing and puke into the grass. It's two a.m. Morning sickness has begun. My charade is complete.

Todd wanders out the side door, bare chested and carrying a wet polo shirt. His khaki shorts swing on his hip bones just under the lip of his plaid boxers. The muscles in his stomach shift back and forth while he walks. He doesn't see me, so I help myself: my final look, my good-bye to the body that caused all the damn trouble. His chest is smooth and tan, and when he spins to wring out the shirt, the flexing muscles make lines in his back and curlicues on his arms. I don't want to have sex, but I want to run my hands over his stomach. When we first did it he was wiry with muscles that ran only up and down instead of bursting through to punctuate his skin. His shoulders were probably two full inches narrower. I look the same . . . a skinny gift box of a torso with strings attached for limbs. But he never noticed that.

Soon I'll be a beach ball with a head.

He sees me kicking myself back and forth on the swing. "Hey." He wanders over in a zigzag. He's drunk. I expect him to sit on the other swing and do some dumbass confusing thing like putting his hand on my knee and inviting me to sleep in his dumb guest room, or telling me in one breath how he won't support me but that he never slept with other girls. Instead, he walks right up to me, bends over, and kisses my mouth. I just puked, but he tastes like stale beer, so I guess it doesn't matter.

He has forgotten everything. He screwed up my life and he's the one who gets to drink himself into oblivion. He's the one who gets to pretend. Soon I will feel his hands descend on my throbbing nipples in an attempt to cop a feel at nothing, and then he will be pulling me toward the hedges next to the highway. But the dumbass stands.

"Don't go. Please don't go," he says.

What the hell?

"I know this is a problem, but stay. This whole year, all these parties, all these stupid football games . . . nothing will be fun without you."

I'm not going to any parties or football games because you knocked me up, dumbass!

I say, "The Silent Parents didn't give me a choice."

He sits next to me and pulls my hand into his lap.

Rub your thumb in my elbow. Please, one more time, rub your thumb in my elbow.

He starts to swing, just a little, and so do I. It's crazy hard to swing holding hands though, so we stop.

"I'm sorry, E."

I start to tell him that it's okay, but he should be freaking sorry. For knocking me up, for convincing me so many times to have sex without a condom, for telling me I was on my own. He should be in as much trouble as I am. But I just shrug.

Then I realize something. Something desperate. I drop his hand and stop his swing. He's drunk. That sucks. I have to get this through his pea brain.

"Todd." He widens his eyes at me. I don't usually say his name.

"Yeah?"

"You have to pretend my aunt is sick. You can't say a word."

"I know."

"Have you told anyone already?" I whisper.

"No." He's looking right between my eyes, not in them. What if he's lying?

"If I hear about this from one person, even one single person, you are dead meat," I tell him.

His eyes go wide again. This time he focuses all that green right on me. I don't care, I'm too angry to look into them, so I try to burn them with my own retinas instead. "I'll tell your mom; I'll tell all your stupid friends; I'll tell the nuns and you will get kicked out of school and out of your house and I won't even care. If just one person knows where I was when I get back, that's what I'll do. I swear I will."

He looks scared, really scared. Shit, what if he told someone already? But he shakes his head. "I'm not going to tell anyone, babe"—don't call me that now!—"but Lizzie—"

"Lizzie doesn't know."

"You still didn't tell Lizzie? You told her you were going to. I heard you."

"I didn't tell anyone. You gotta keep your mouth shut, or I swear I'll ruin your life." I stand up.

"Where are you going?" He sounds like he might cry, the baby.

"Chicago," I say, and turn to walk away. It would be awesome if I could just keep walking. It would be amazing if I leave him sitting on the swing with his mouth hanging open and his arms reaching for my skinny ass. I would be like a heroine from the stupid movies if I just stroll out of the yard right now, open my car door, and drive away to Never-Never Land where I can pretend I didn't spend the past two weeks growing up on fast-forward, making the biggest decisions of my life. I can pretend I'm not scared shitless and I'm not seething mad at everyone I love, especially the stupid boy behind me.

But I'm not awesome and amazing and perfect, so I stop and turn when Todd yells my name.

He's still sitting on the swing, but he's leaning all the way forward like he might fall flat on his nose any minute and his arms are reaching for me like the dumbass thinks they could grow the five feet it would take to pull me back and his face is so puppy dog it isn't even cute, like puppy-dog-turned-cockroach. But because I am weak and stupid, I turn around and walk back over to him and let him hug me.

My arms dangle at my sides while he squeezes the crap out of my entire upper body and puts his nose in my hair.

"I'm really going to miss you," he says.

You shouldn't get to say that to me.

I don't know what to say. I'm too angry for "I'll miss you too," even though I will. I can't just shrug. I want to say "whatever," but then he'll cry again and I'll go back for more of the confusing treatment.

"I'll be back."

He finally loosens his grip. As soon as he does, I sprint for my car, running as fast as my sick, tired, pregnant, skinny body can before I go back for more of that warm, shirtless hug.

Which one is the real boy: the Todd who says he can't help me, or the Todd who begs me to stay?

7 Months, 2 Days

Somewhere in Kentucky, I roll down the window and puke all over the side of the Jeep.

"Morning sickness," Mom says pointlessly, as I text Lizzie a quick good-bye. Those are the first words of this lovely little mother-daughter road trip. My head falls back on the seat and I'm instantly asleep again. I keep my eyes closed when the car takes an exit and pulls into a gas station. I stay still as Mom sprays my puke off the side of my beloved Jeep. She climbs in, and as we sail the highway again, I am lulled back asleep.

It's good because I don't want to be awake with her. I don't want to face everything: Aunt Linda knows I'm a screwup. I have to live with three people I barely even know—Aunt Linda's wife or lover or whatever you call her, and the two little girls they just adopted. Sleep is easier. Maybe I can just sleep until April, when Dr. Elizabeth says this thing will finally be out of me. After that, I'll never sleep again.

But as we cross into Tennessee my brain starts rumbling all over the place. I squeeze my eyes shut, preferring complete boredom to Mom's company but my stomach has other ideas. I lean out the window again and leave whatever was in my stomach on the road.

"You must be hungry," she says when I pull my head back in the window.

I just shrug.

"I think we'll stay in Nashville tonight. It's about halfway. But it's going to be another two hours and you probably need to eat right now. You know, you've got to take better care of yourself, eating and sleeping."

I shrug again, even as my stomach roars.

We eat in near silence and roll back onto the road. The sky is darkening but not black. I don't know what else to do. I feel like I should do homework, but I haven't even begun my junior year yet, not really. In Chicago school doesn't start for another week. It's like the past two weeks—those days that changed my entire life—didn't even exist. I should talk to Mom but I have no idea what she wants to say to me. I should be yelling at her. I should be making her feel as crappy for kicking me out as I feel for being worthless to her.

I wish she would put on the radio or something. A real Bad Girl would just reach up and flip it on. I don't.

Finally, I pull out a pen and paper and start writing to Lizzie.

Hey Bestie,
I'm actually writing this to you, with a pen and paper and all that, because I'm in the car with my

mom and the silence is like completely suffocating. I don't know what I'm going to do without you talking and talking with me this year. I can't believe my parents are kicking me out like this in my junior year of high school.

Mom just asked me what I'm doing. She asked if I was going to mail this to you, like with a stamp. But I told her I'd type it over at the hotel tonight and e-mail it to you.

So, I hope you are feeling okay tonight after that party. It seemed like you were having fun. Also, this is the third time you hooked up with Sean in like a month . . . do you like him, Lizzie? I think it would be good if you did, you know. It's okay to have a boyfriend. I kind of wish I had made Todd my boyfriend when I had a chance, now that I have to leave him anyway.

Look, you've gotta keep an eye on Todd for me, okay? I mean, he isn't my boyfriend or anything, but if he gets some stupid new girlfriend, will you tell me about it? I don't want some bimbo surprising me when I finally get to come back. Okay?

I know you are going to want me to talk about what's going on, so I'm going to try. I'm scared. I love my aunt Linda, but she doesn't know the worst stuff about me—like drugs and sex. She just knows about Judy, the uptight big sister who squashed Aunt Linda all those years. (I have to keep inching closer to the passenger-side window while I write this. I think my mom is trying to read it over my shoulders even though she is supposed to be driving. (DRIVE, MOM. DON'T READ THIS. IT'S DANGEROUS!) Anyway, Aunt Linda has a wife or a partner or whatever, I don't know what you call it, but they had that commitment ceremony that I went to when we were freshmen, remember? That was the last time I saw her. And the woman she married or whatever, Nora. I don't know, she seems nice, I guess, but just a little, like, stiff. I don't think she'll be too happy to have another person living with them, corrupting their daughters. And I mean, they just adopted these kids like a year ago. Then here I come waltzing in to screw up the dynamic. It sucks, you know?

I want to live with you, Lizzie. Because I know you would talk to me. And because I know you would want me around.

I swallow before going on, but I know I have to lie.

And I'm scared about what will happen to Aunt Linda. I don't know any more about it because it's not like Mom is talking, but when I find out I'll let you know.

Why is it easier to open up to Lizzie with this lie than it is to tell her the truth?

I don't think I'll even bother to make friends at this new school. I'm going to take a break from being Bad and work on getting As. Plus I'm going to have to go to the school where Aunt Linda works and I think it's different from St. Mary's. I mean, I know this is bad to say or whatever, but the kids there, they don't have much money I think. Aunt Linda says that they don't teach Japanese there, so I'm going to end up taking Spanish with freshmen! Can you believe that? It sucks. No point in making friends.

Who'd want some pregnant new girl as a friend anyway?

I mean, I'm only going to be here like a year, then I'll be back with you.

"Evelyn," Mom interrupts. "It's getting too dark to write."

It's not dark at all with the highway lights on, but I'm too tired to argue. Besides, she managed to say some words. I should reward her for that. I cap my pen and lay my head back and fall asleep.

Finally, we get to Nashville. Mom made hotel reservations, but they ran out of rooms with two beds.

I walk into the cozy room and wish I were with Todd instead. The bed is huge—thank God—but Todd and I would squeeze together and only take up a little bit of it. There's a pile of board games on a table next to the bed, and a balcony off the back with a fireplace next to it. The room is gorgeous, but Mom still can barely talk to me, and now I'm supposed to sleep with her. This is awful.

The shower is huge. I imagine Todd in it with me, water sliding down all those muscley curlicues in his upper arms.

When I get back into the room, I pull my notebook out of the backpack, grab a spare key, and head toward the door.

"Where are you going, Evelyn?"

"To the computer in the lobby to type the e-mail to Lizzie."

"You need to get some sleep tonight so you can do some driving tomorrow," Mom says. But she doesn't say no, so I keep staring at her, doorknob in one hand, notebook in the other. "Hurry back," she says finally.

I find peace typing words I already wrote. I'm nervous to send her all that truth—all those fears about Aunt Linda and Nora and this different school. But I'm nauseated about sending her all the lies—between each word is the baby, crying, screaming, confused—but I just can't tell her. I can't stand another person knowing.

At the end, I add:

> Now I just typed that into this computer at a Nashville hotel. My stupid mother is making us share a bed tonight. Can you believe that?
>
> I miss you already, Lizzie. Please call me every day. I know you have other friends, but I really don't. Not like you.
>
> This is the most honest thing I've ever said to you: please don't forget about me. I need you.
>
> Ev

Even though I slept all day, I'm exhausted when I pad back into the room. I'm relieved to hear Mom's measured breathing as I slip between the sheets. I roll onto one side, away from her so I can pretend I'm alone. I put my hand on the flat part of my stomach, right beneath my belly button, and whisper so quietly that Mom wouldn't be able to hear me even if she were awake.

"I'm sorry this is so hard on you already. It's not your fault you were made by a dumbass and a dimwit. It's your bad luck to have crappy parents like Todd and me. And an even crappier mom—holy shit, she's your grandma." I turn my head and look at the back of my mom's hair, sensibly pulled away from her neck. Her ribs go up and down with even breaths. How can the Ice Queen be a grandmother? That's harder to imagine than Todd and me being parents. I curl up again and put my hand back on the bean in my belly. "I'm sorry that you're taking me away from all my friends and my maybe boyfriend. And I'm sorry that it's making me mad at you. It's not your fault." I rub my hand back and forth for a minute, as if my stomach were a baby chick or something. "I still want to get rid of you. But I'm not going to. I promise."

Then I close my eyes to fall asleep with my palm still resting there. It's only seconds until I feel her fingers in my hair, smoothing it out on the pillow behind me.

"I love you, Evelyn," she says. "I hope you know how much. I'm only this angry because I love you."

I pull my knees to my chin and lower my head toward them, trying to stop the stinging in my eyes.

"I'm so worried for you, sweetie. I don't think you know what it means to lose, to really lose something."

Of course I know what it means to lose. She's been living in the same house. She should know. There is a pause and she rolls onto her back. I almost start to fall asleep but then her voice comes back; she's talking to the ceiling.

"When I was your age, I was just so busy trying to do well in school and taking care of your aunt Linda, who was only seven then. And Nanny and Pop-Pop, you know they didn't have much money. I mean, we were fine when it was just the three of us, but they didn't have the funds to suddenly adopt another one. They were both working full time, so I was picking Linda up from school and dropping her off and sometimes even meeting with her teachers and it was a lot. I think I lost my youth then. I love Linda, but when she went from baby to kid, I went from kid to adult. It was too fast. I know you think I'm a fuddy-duddy, a stick-in-the-mud, but I'm telling you: I had to be. We would have fallen apart, my family. I was the only one who had any mind for structure—I reminded them when the mortgage was due and to make car payments and to pay for Linda's after-school care. From the time I was fifteen. It wasn't fair. I didn't want you to have to grow up so fast."

I can't help it, my knees relax, my breathing eases and my ears perk up. I didn't know any of this stuff. I don't know why she's telling me this now, and I resent the way my heart is softening toward it, but I sort of want to know. I do want to know.

"Now you're having a baby, you're probably listing all the things you will do differently than me."

Nope. I'm not thinking about that at all. Pregnancy, yes. Motherhood, no.

"And I know the list is a mile long, and it probably should be. I don't want you to be stiff like me. But I am only so stiff because I wanted to take the best possible care of you. I was the kind of mother who needed to read a book in order to figure out how to hold you. By the time I got used to supporting your head, you were able to hold it up on your own anyway. By the time I got used to you crawling, you were walking. I always knew I'd do better on the next one, but we, your dad and I . . . well, you know this part of my story. We never got that lucky. Your dad, he was so much better with you.

"And you don't really know loss until you've lost a child. You know I still talk to them? Every night when I'm going to bed, I say good night to my babies in heaven. I've been missing them so much that I haven't given your life enough attention in years. I know it's not fair. And I'm not telling you all this to make excuses for the mistakes I've made, but just to warn you—you are going to lose a lot right now. Don't let it take you over. Don't let it steal what's left."

I think she's going to stop there, but she just keeps talking. The words pile like bricks onto the bed. They keep me still, keep me awake, trap me. It's so scary to hear her talk like this after the silent car ride. All day long I just wanted her to speak, but not to lay it on like this.

I should be angry that she says good night to dead babies every night but hasn't even paid enough attention to me to know I'm in position to be valedictorian, or that I'm a total fuckup. But it's too sad. I can't be angry when the sadness in the room is so heavy.

"And then, really, I lost your father. And I know you blame him, but it was my fault too." She pauses so we can both breathe. "But he loved you so much and so well, I knew if we split up, you'd go with him." I want to tell her she's wrong, but I can't. She's probably right. "I knew he could never live without you. And neither could I. So here we are. Both of us preparing to live without you."

Now I'm crying in earnest. The first time I've cried since I got pregnant. I try to keep my shoulders still so she can't see. I keep my eyes closed so she might think I'm sleeping. It feels so good to have her fingers in my hair after all these years. I wonder if my baby feels someone stroking its head like this just because I do. I hope it does.

"I'm going to miss you so much. And I'm so worried about everything you are about to lose—your freedom, your high school, and I think you must have lost Todd."

She knows his name?

"I just don't want all that to seal you up like it sealed me up. Please talk to Linda about it. Linda is wild and flighty and we were never close, but she's happier than I am. Let Linda help you, Evelyn. Talk and talk and talk. Don't be like me. And then come home, and we'll all make it work. We'll make it all work."

It's not fair for her to finally talk to me just as soon as she's kicking me out. It isn't fair to hear her say I love you now that we're so angry at each other, now that we're going to be hundreds of miles apart. It's not fair for her to try to explain all of her mistakes away when she's still the one who made them. It's not fair for her to say that I haven't lost yet when I so clearly have—lost her, lost my dad. Lost Todd. Lost everyone but Lizzie and Aunt Linda. It isn't fair for her to pressure me to talk when she can't talk herself. Not fair.

I try to stop crying as I fake sleep breathe, deep in, deep out. Steady rhythm.

Just when my brain feels heavy enough to fall out of consciousness, she starts talking again.

"You can keep pretending if that's what's best for you, Evelyn, but I know you heard that. I love you."

Then she rolls onto her back again. My hair misses her hands. I want to keep pretending to sleep, but I remember everything she said about talking so I let the words slip out onto the pillow, so quietly, "I love you too, Mom."

But I'm not sure she hears them.

7 Months, 1 Day

Today will be better. We can't talk like we did last night and then spend silent hour after silent hour in the car like yesterday.

Mom throws the car keys at me without a word when I stumble out of the bathroom after my morning puke. As if last night didn't even happen.

Driving in silence is worse than riding in silence because I can't read or write letters or anything to distract myself from all of the words we aren't saying. But hours later, when we're pulling through the southern border of Illinois, I almost feel excited. It's been close to two years since I last saw my aunt Linda, and that was at her wedding or whatever so I didn't even get to talk to her that much. I can't wait to hear her greet me, feel her hug me.

Finally we wind our way through the city of Chicago, the buildings painting lines in the afternoon sky. They reach all the way to the clouds and are lined up all the way to the lake. The highway to the western suburbs is so jammed that there has to be at least one other pregnant girl in one of these cars, freaking out, unable to tell her best friend, ready to kill it if she only could. Someone else like me. It's a comforting thought.

A city this huge is so full of people it could never be silent. And someone else's life would always be worse than mine. The thought settles the bean-baby down to the back of my uterus.

Maybe living with Aunt Linda will be better. I should give it a chance. Aunt Linda will talk to me every day and through every meal. She's a social worker in a high school— she must have counseled pregnant teenagers before. Maybe she'll even be able to help me so I don't feel so rotten all the time.

Maybe Aunt Linda and Nora will let me babysit their daughters while they go out on their dates, and maybe those kids will start to look up to me and call me Cousin Evelyn. Maybe I'll be able to cook for them, read them bedtime stories, and help them put on pajamas and brush their teeth. Maybe I'll start to feel useful, worth something. Maybe I'll be to them what Aunt Linda was to me.

What Aunt Linda Was to Me

When my parents lost the first one, I was still tiny. Maybe only two. My mom tells me there is no way I remember, but I do. I remember her puking in the morning and I remember the way her tummy started to swell. She told me later that the doctors always told her she was too far along to lose the baby. And then, suddenly, Mommy was gone. She was just not around. She was in her room, but I never saw her face.

Aunt Linda moved in with us, supposedly because she was broke and needed a place to stay during med school. That's the reason my mom still gives for why Aunt Linda lived with us until I was eight years old, but I know that's not the real reason. Aunt Linda came to help with me because my mom was just too sad. Aunt Linda told me that every day. She would pull me out of the bath and stand me on the bathmat, a chubby, fiery two-year-old, then a quiet string bean of a six-year-old. Then she would put a corner of the towel under my arm and spin me until the towel was wrapped all the way around me. She would say, "It's my dinner: an Evie burrito!" Then she would lift me up and pretend to eat me, starting right at my middle, and I would giggle and feel her face so close to mine and smell the soap in my hair and the lilac of her hand lotion and I would feel all soft and warm. I thought Aunt Linda must be the best person God ever made.

And she would tell me, "I'm here for you, not for me, Evie-Teeny. I'm here to help take care of you because your mommy is just too sad."

And Mom says there's no way I remember that from when I was only two, but I do.

Then Aunt Linda decided to quit medicine and study social work. She moved all the way to Chicago and met Nora, who I still don't really know, but she must be cool.

And I know that now that I'm moving in with my aunt Linda, and I'm all grown up and even pregnant . . . I know that she isn't going to wrap me up like a burrito and pretend to eat me, but I think maybe she can still make me feel soft and warm, not like I'm rotting from the inside out, uterus first.

7 Months, Less Than 1 Day

Finally we pull into their driveway. The house is small and skinny, with other houses right on either side, sharing walls. I've seen houses like this on TV, but I've never been inside. You could probably fit four of Aunt Linda's house inside ours, but somehow there's supposed to be more room for me here.

I'm just starting to pull bags from the back of the Jeep when the door bursts open and Aunt Linda rushes out. Seconds later, her arms are around my waist and she spins me in the tiny driveway, saying, "Evie-Teeny, that beautiful face of yours is a relief. It has been way too long since I've seen you." I'm dizzy. Aunt Linda smells like lilacs, the same; her hug feels just as warm, but it's weird because my eyebrows are now above the top of her head. She swings my shoulders back and forth and finally stops and says, "We're going to make this work, Evie, you hear me? You are welcome here."

My eyes sting. It's such a loud greeting, such a relief that I can feel both heartbeats slowing down: the one in my chest and the one in my abdomen. I have no idea what to say.

Aunt Linda lets go and approaches my mother. "Hi, Judy."

"Hi, Linda." They share a stiff hug. My mother is in full lawyer costume despite the jeans and sweatshirt that are on her body. "Where are Nora and your girls?" Mom asks.

"They went out to dinner," Linda says, pulling some bags out of the Jeep. "I thought we'd do the same, and just get some things worked out before meeting the girls."

We step into a kitchen so small you can't fit a table in it. I wonder if this is why they're out to dinner. But we go through a little opening and end up in a living area with a TV and a couch and two tables—one normal-kitchen-sized and one that is clearly for little kids. Aunt Linda runs a hand through her black hair, strands of silver streaking through it. "So, Jude, this couch extends into a sleep sofa, full sized. I think you'll stay on it the next few days until you go back. I know it's not luxurious, but it's what we have."

She should thank Aunt Linda and tell her it's plenty, but she just nods.

"When are you going back again?" Aunt Linda asks.

"Wednesday. I've told you that, Linda," my mother says, like she is speaking to a kid. She doesn't even talk to me that way.

"Well, I hope this will do until then." Again, Mom doesn't say anything, as if Aunt Linda owes her. "You get settled for a second; I'm going to take Evie up to her room."

We climb a small staircase and enter a room right at the

top. It has bunk beds against the far wall—one comforter bright pink and one purple with a unicorn pattern.

"So this is your room," Aunt Linda says. "Appropriately decorated, as you see."

I shake my head. "Aunt Linda, I don't want to kick the girls out of their room."

She laughs and taps my throat. "Oh, good, you do have a voice in there! I was starting to get worried. Anyway, we're just putting Cecelia in Tammy's room. They both have bunk beds and they end up climbing into bed with each other anyway, so they're thrilled. You're great. You've just got to pick a bed."

Aunt Linda puts my bags in the middle of the room. She seems to be waiting for me to say something. I feel like I could curl up into either bed and sleep the two days until my mother finally leaves.

Aunt Linda says, "And here's the thing. I'm thinking you probably need some space from Mommy right now, so I'm just not going to give her the tour or mention the extra bed in here. She'll be fine on the sleep sofa, don't you think?"

My eyes well up. Exhaustion and open tear ducts, these must be pregnancy symptoms. But I'm grateful. Aunt Linda gets it. She always has. Everything is going to be okay. *You should hug her*, I tell myself. I stand, and I'm right next to her, but I just can't make my arms do it. Maybe while I'm living here she'll teach me to hug.

By the time we get back from dinner, I'm ready to kick my mother out. Aunt Linda is doing her another favor, picking up the pieces when it comes to me yet again, but my mother acts like she owes it to her. I'm so annoyed I forget to be nervous until we open the front door and Aunt Linda shushes us.

"The girls are probably sleeping by now," she says.

Nora is standing in the corner of the kitchen, sleek blond hair falling almost all the way to the waist of her black skirt, which cuts off at the knees to reveal stockinged and perfectly shaped calves on top of shiny patent-leather high heels. She turns and fuses her neon-blue eyes to my abdomen. I have to catch my breath. I thought Nora was beautiful in a wedding gown, but I had no idea she'd be breathtaking in work clothes, watching a baby monitor on her kitchen counter. She flips half of her hair over her shoulder and approaches me with a hand out.

"Hello, Evelyn," she says as if it's not easy to get the syllables out. And I'm supposed to shake her hand? She's, like, Aunt Linda's wife—that makes her my aunt or something. She should hug me or at least pat me on the arm. "Why don't you all go have a seat at the table in the family room. I'll bring in some peppermint tea and we can discuss the details of this arrangement," she says, and that's when I know: she's a lawyer. Another stiff and beautiful lawyer as the head of the house. My heart falls to my feet. The bean-baby tries to hide behind my bladder.

Aunt Linda tries to start a conversation with Mom about five times until Nora finally brings in the tea. I push mine away.

"You don't like peppermint tea, Evie-Teeny?" Aunt Linda asks, and I swear Nora starts to roll her eyes.

"I'm not supposed to drink too much caffeine because of the—" I can't finish the sentence. "You know, because of it."

"Oh boy," Nora says. Aunt Linda throws her a look.

"Peppermint tea is fine. No caffeine," my mother says. I don't know anything; I'm a total bonehead. I take a sip and it almost works like the ginger ale. I'm so tired I want to put my head on the table.

Nora is giving some speech but only the buzz words are breaking through the fog of fatigue and pepperminty relief in my brain: "Rules . . . younger girls . . . school . . . grades . . . doctor . . ." Mom echoes the same kind of thing back uselessly.

Finally, Aunt Linda tweaks my chin. "Are you getting this, Evie?"

"She's grown now. You can call her Evelyn, you know," my mother says, and I try to shoot daggers at her with my eyes.

"Getting what?"

Nora sighs like I just told her something terrible. "Well, it's good I wrote down the rules." She takes out a piece of paper. I almost ask her what kind of law she practices but I know that would sound rude.

She hands it to me. It looks like this:

```
RULE 1: E will drive herself
    to school and all doctors'
    appointments without needing
    encouragement or reminders.
RULE 2: Any possible social
    activities will be limited to
    wholesome ones that will not
    impact E's sleep and will be
    approved by L or N ahead of time.
```

RULE 3: E will be in bed with lights
out by 10:30 p.m. every night.
RULE 4: E will complete all homework
each night and maintain all As and
Bs at Santa Maria High School.
RULE 5: E will meet regularly with
L's young mothers' group.
RULE 6: E will report to all meals
and eat everything on her plate.
RULE 7: E will be responsible for the
following chores: taking out the
trash on Monday, recycling on
Thursday, and completing the after-
dinner dishes each night. E will
also maintain her own room and
laundry.
RULE 8: E will not interfere with
C or T. She will at no point be in
a room or car with them
unsupervised.

Then there is a place for me to sign, but my body has
gone numb and I can't pick up a pen. Nora drones on and on
about how this move is supposed to be positive for me and
the baby and how she and Linda want to take the very best
care of me possible. She talks about how I will need good
food and plenty of sleep to grow a healthy baby, and how
that will be provided for me as well as emotional support,
and the temptation to screw it up with substances or lack of
sleep or nutrition or care will be completely taken away
from me.

I stare at Aunt Linda, but she keeps her eyes away from me.

Nora doesn't say one word about Rule 8.

The rest of the rules are crazy overkill, but I mean, I don't really care. I don't have any friends, so where am I going to go? I need to go to the doctor anyway; they don't need a list of rules to make me do that. And the whole reason I am here is to be in school, so obviously I'm going to get As. But why won't they let me talk to my new cousins? Am I so screwed up that they think their precious daughters will be corrupted just from being in the same room as me? Am I so messed up that I can't even be a big cousin the right way?

I'm going to be a mother in seven months! And I can't even play with my cousins in their room?

"Do you get it, Evie?" Aunt Linda asks, but if I try to say anything I will start to cry and the words will get wet, salty, and garbled. I force myself to pick up a pen and sign the damn contract, noticing that it is 10:20. I have ten minutes to get the lights out, according to Rule 3.

"Can I take a shower before bed tonight? It will take me past my ten thirty bedtime."

"Of course," Nora says. Aunt Linda just sits there like she has no say. "Why don't you do that now? Let's say lights out by ten forty-five tonight, okay?" The lady I barely know imposes this rule while my mother and aunt, who have known me all my life, just watch her. I run up the stairs. Nora yells good night behind me, but Aunt Linda follows me.

"I love her, Evie," she says. I snort. "And I love you. You'll see why soon." She hugs me and my muscles let go of their resentment only slightly. I want to ask her why they think I'm too awful to even talk to her daughters. I want to ask if that means she thinks I will be a more rotten mother than my own, but I don't because she says, "I love you, little niece, and I'm glad you're here. You're very welcome."

"Thanks," I say. Which isn't much.

In the shower her words repeat through the steam: "I'm glad you're here." "I love you, little niece." "You're very welcome." "I'm glad you're here." "You're very welcome." "I love you."

I hold my hand in a little cup next to my abdomen and let the water fill it up so the bean-baby can cuddle into the warm spot. "I hope someone says those things to you one day."

I wrap myself in my own burrito and step into the hallway back toward my new room. The peppermint smell still wafts up the stairs, along with the grown-ups' words.

"I'll give you what you think you need, and also some more for renting the room," my mother is saying.

"How much does it take to feed her for a month?" Nora asks.

"I don't really know," my mother says.

"Seriously, Judy!" Nora says, sounding exasperated.

"Well, to be honest, Nora, we just don't need to worry about that, my husband and I." I wonder if this is what a courtroom sounds like. "Let's settle on four thousand a month."

Four thousand dollars a month? Just for feeding me and renting a room?

"We don't need that much," Aunt Linda's voice interjects softly.

"We're already shaking hands. It's fine, Linda," my mother says.

So Linda and Nora are getting four thousand dollars a month to pick up my mother's nasty little secret. My mother is paying four thousand dollars a month to get rid of me. No wonder I'm so welcome. A list of eight harsh rules costs four thousand a month . . . that's like thirty-two thousand dollars! I might as well be in college.

I close the bedroom door behind me and feel the tension snap back into my shoulders and legs.

I drop my towel and slap my palm into my wet abdomen so hard I can see a handprint on it. "Why do you want to be here so badly anyway?"

It's 10:40 but I'm way too wound up for sleep now, so I flip on my computer to check my e-mail after pulling on my pajamas. I have two.

The first:

> Ev—
> I know. Todd told me, like, days ago. I told him you'd tell me. I believed you'd tell me. I gave you so many chances. SO many. And you just lied and lied and lied. You're a fucking terrible best friend.
> Good luck in Chicago. Good-bye.
> —Lizzie
> P.S. You were really going to let me believe Aunt Linda was dying? Screw you.

The second:

> E—
> I'm sorry I told Lizzie. I didn't know you weren't telling her. But don't worry, if she tells anyone else,

I'll kill her. Good luck in Chicago. Drop me a line and let me know how it's going, okay? St. Mary's is going to be weird without you.

Todd

I look at my belly button. "I hate you. I hate you. I hate you." I'm still saying it when I fall asleep.

Last Day with the Stiff-Ass

My mother decides to take me shopping.

After puking my brains and the baby's brains into the toilet in the early morning, I am lying in bed, cursing my baby for the words in Lizzie's e-mail when I hear Aunt Linda and Nora wake up my cousins in the room next door. I listen to showers running and eggs being cooked and the girls backtalking Nora and climbing all over Aunt Linda like a jungle gym. The garage door opens and two cars slide out. Does Nora want to keep me from ever meeting my cousins while I live in the room next door?

I stare at the bed above me, watching as the characters in my life chase each other through my brain—bean-baby sits there like a flesh-colored blob, Lizzie bursts it out my ear as her screaming face appears then fades back into bean-baby, then Todd picks up bean-baby and throws it like a football until he fades out and Nora appears, just her lip-sticked mouth moving as she repeats Rule 8 over and over, then bean-baby sprouts from the paper again, taking center stage, then my parents stand there, neither of them looking at the blob or moving to touch it. Then there it is, all alone again, completely unaware of the hell of a life it's about to be born into when Lizzie's e-mail starts running in its eyes and the entire routine starts over again. I can't do this.

I'm still lying there watching the horror movie playing on my eyelids when there's a soft tap on the door. I roll onto my side to feign sleeping. She opens the door, and I tell myself that I want to hear her just turn around and leave me alone with the purple unicorns, but I know that I'm really pretending to sleep because I think it might make her come over and say that she'll miss me or that I can come home if I want to or that Nora and her rules are ridiculous or something, anything real. She sits on the bed and puts her hand in my hair and I feel my breath catch.

"You have two beds in here," she says. The breath rushes out of me like fire. But I don't move.

"I thought we'd go shopping today, Evelyn. You're going to need some winter clothes and some clothes for when you start . . . getting bigger. This evening you have an appointment with your new doctor. But in the meantime I thought we'd go to Michigan Avenue and shop like we are real Chicagoans. It'll be fun. Get dressed."

And she leaves. She said the whole thing like it's some great mother/daughter/bean-baby adventure but she doesn't give me a choice.

I want to tell her that at four thousand dollars a pop, Aunt Linda and Nora should be able to pay for my clothes. I want to tell her no way am I going out with her if she's stiff

Lawyer Mom. I want to tell her no. But I'm punishing her by staying silent, so I get dressed and wander downstairs, where she puts a plate of eggs in front of me and disappears to shower. I wonder how long I can go today without saying a word to her.

Turns out I make it all the way until the drive home from the doctor's office. All day she shoves clothes at me and I try them on and if she likes them she buys them and we end up with shopping bags hanging from every limb but she's too busy checking sales racks and her BlackBerry to even notice that I don't say anything. At the appointment, I answer only the doctor's questions—"When was your last period?" "When did you last have sex?" "Do you know who the father is?" "Do you know his medical history?" And I answer none of hers— "Do you understand what she's saying, Evelyn?" "How are you going to remember to take your prenatal vitamins, honey?"

On the way home, she's turning onto Aunt Linda's street and checking her BlackBerry at the same time like a complete idiot and she doesn't even see it, a bright red fox chewing on a bird carcass in the middle of the street. Our car advances at 25 mph—it's twenty feet away, fifteen feet, ten, five. Finally, I shout "Mom, watch out!" But just then the fox sees us and darts into the hedges at the side of the road, and she can say, "I wasn't going to hit that animal, Evelyn." So I used my voice for nothing.

We park in the driveway, and since I already broke my silent spell, I turn to her to ask the question that has been bugging me all day. "Do you really think I would be so bad with them that I should be banned from Tammy and Cecelia?"

My mom looks startled. "Oh, sweetie," she says.

"Because if that's true"—now that I've started I can't stop the words from coming—"then I'm going to be lousy at . . . this."

"Evelyn, I think your cousins are going to be crazy about you. I think Nora is just a bit stiff." And she takes the key out of my hand and unlocks the door.

That comment is funny for two reasons—the queen of all Sticks-in-Their-Butts has just deemed someone stiff, and she managed to answer me without saying a word about whether I would be a crappy mommy.

We're only two steps in the kitchen when I feel a startling squeeze on my thigh and look down to see a tiny body on my leg, like a koala bear wrapped around a eucalyptus tree. At first I can only see the braids that pattern the top of her head in all directions, but then she tilts her neck back and fixes her cinnamon face on mine. "I never had a cousin before."

I look at Nora chopping carrots on the counter and try to tell her with my eyes that her daughter just attacked me. I didn't say a word. I didn't break Rule 8.

"Cecelia, step back so Evelyn and Aunt Judy can get in the door."

Until I hear that—Aunt Judy—I haven't realized that these are my only cousins too. I've never had siblings or cousins or any kid around. Besides the one inside of me.

Cecelia unwraps herself from my leg, and even though I don't know how to hug, my leg immediately misses her little body, my knee longs for her chubby cheek to be pressed to it again.

"Now," says Nora, "say hello."

I'm not sure if she's talking to me or the four-year-old

who is bouncing at my feet, but either way I take that as permission and squat down to take Cecelia by the hand.

"You know, I've never had a cousin either," I say. "I'm very excited to get to know you too." I feel Nora's eyes burning a hole in my ear.

"But you're all big," says Cecelia.

"You think so?" When she nods, her little braids bouncing off her shoulders, I add, "Just you wait then." Completely forgetting every tear that's stung my eyes.

I'm shocked when I hear both Nora and Mom start to laugh.

"Do cousins play Legos?" Cecelia asks.

"I'm sure they do," I answer.

"Goody!" she squeals and she moves toward my legs as if she's trying to climb me again. "Then come and play with me and my sister in the family room. We have pink and purple and light-blue Legos. Which is your favorite?"

Her tiny hand pulls at my skinny arm. I look at Mom for guidance—I'm not supposed to be in a room alone with them. Mom looks at Nora. Nora says, "Let Evelyn go upstairs and rest before dinner, Celie. She'll eat with us when Mommy Linda gets home."

"But she said cousins play Legos!" Cecelia shouts.

"That's one for backtalk," Nora says like a robot. "If you don't get to three, we can all play Legos for fifteen minutes after dinner."

Cecelia opens her little mouth and closes it again. Then she looks at me. "I thought you were like Mommy Linda," she says, and walks out of the room. I don't know what she means: She thought I was Chinese? She thought I was talkative?

She thought I was pretty? She thought I would play Legos? Whatever she thought, I want to be that.

I turn to leave the kitchen and Nora says, "Where are you going, Evelyn?"

"To my room to rest," I answer. "Like you said."

Nora nods and I walk through the family room without even greeting Tammy because I'm not allowed to. The worst thing about Rule 8 is that these girls are going to think I don't even like them.

I drag myself and bean upstairs. I'm too sad to be angry. I'm tired, but even more than that I'm hungry, so I know there is no way I'll sleep. I open the door to the closet to start to unpack and notice the full-length mirror on the inside. It's too tempting. I strip to my bra and underwear with my back to the mirror, then turn to analyze where on my body I can see the bean.

My stomach is a little closer to round, a small mound stretching toward the mirror between my hips that you can only see if I'm naked. My feet are bigger, the fat almost pulsating at the sides of them. I have boobs. Little ones, but they actually have mass and I could squeeze them with my hands if they didn't hurt so damn badly. My butt actually arches away from my lower back. I look good, almost. Better than a sack of bones. It's temporary, though. I wish Todd could be here right now, just for a second, to cup my ass or kiss my breast when there is actually something there. Except that he's a total jerk.

"Mommy Linda!" Little girl voices erupt downstairs, and four tiny sneakers pound the kitchen floor as they are no doubt throwing themselves at my aunt the way I used to when she would come home from the library after studying. I would be so glad she was there in time for my bath that I would fling my whole body into her stomach and chest. But standing naked in my room looking for evidence of a baby, I'm not sure anyone will ever be able to hug me like that again. I want to be Cecelia's size.

When I hear Aunt Linda yell up the stairs, "Where's my niece? She must be hungry!" I allow my four-year-old smile to dance on my face before pulling my clothes back on and slumping down the stairs.

Aunt Linda brought home tacos; Nora made a salad; my mom pulled together her delicious salad dressing. We sit down and Aunt Linda says, "Now I don't know who at the table believes what, but I know all of you love me, so for me you're going to hold hands and at least pretend to join in while we pray."

Both Nora and my mom roll their eyes. I'm seated between Cecelia—who clutches my hand tight—and my mother—who lets hers hang in mine like a dead fish.

I like Aunt Linda's prayer, even if I don't believe in God. And I like that she prays for me. After she shouts amen, Cecelia turns to me and says, "You see? That's how we knew we had a cousin before we even met you. Because Mommy Linda prays for you every day at dinner. But she didn't tell God about all that orange hair on your head."

When everyone laughs I think that this could almost be normal one day.

For a minute, I think that maybe we could just stay here—me and bean. And even my mom. I can see a baby screaming at this table while Cecelia dances around it and tells it how great it is to have another cousin. I can see Mom laughing when the baby makes a sound it shouldn't or smiling when it sprouts a tooth. For a minute, everything seems like it will be okay again. But those minutes never even last a full sixty seconds.

Nora's smile straightens back into a line too quickly. "How much were the tacos, Linda?" she asks.

Aunt Linda is leaning over Tammy, wiping salsa off of her chin. "I don't remember."

In the corner of my eye, Mom shakes her head over Aunt Linda's hair. Nora sighs, exasperated, as if my aunt Linda is a little girl.

"Well, where's the receipt?"

Aunt Linda looks at her. She almost looks scared. "I don't know, Nora. I was rushing back."

"Yes, you were very late."

My eyes bounce between them.

"One of the new teachers had a total mental breakdown in the bathroom, and I was trying to help her get through it. The first day of school is Tuesday, and the teachers are not ready at all."

"Really, though, the students are your responsibility," Nora points out.

Aunt Linda shakes her head. "I don't want to get into it tonight, Nora. I'm sorry I forgot the receipt. I'll work on it."

"And call when you're on your way home so I can have the table set?"

Mom keeps her eyes on her plate, but I can see a smile playing with the ends of her lips. This is almost exactly a conversation Mom and Aunt Linda would have at our house:

money, time, responsibilities. Aunt Linda was always messing up in my mom's eyes.

Suddenly, there's a memory: Aunt Linda at my house, drying me after my Evie burrito and telling me to make sure that I listen to more than just my mom when I grow up. "Life is more than rules, Evie-Teeny. Life is actually about laughing and loving and dancing your heart out. Don't let rules steal your joy because you, my precious Evie, you are so full of joy."

And I was. I remember the screaming way I used to laugh when Aunt Linda threw me over her shoulder or Dad pulled me out of my seat in the middle of dinner for a dance. What had happened to that joy? This baby, that's what, and the Silent House.

And now I'm mad at Aunt Linda—she lectures me my whole life about Mom and her rules, about looking for a way to have more joy. She says she's searching for joy when she quits medical school to be a social worker, moves to Chicago, comes out, shocking Mom over and over. Aunt Linda told me that shocking my mother was part of the joy, that she was making Mom better by prying her mind open. The day she moved out—I was almost eight—she told me she was never going to live with someone so rule obsessed again.

What has she done?

She's married my mom—a blond, lesbian version of my mother. Screw Aunt Linda! If she hadn't married this stiff shrew I could have moved in with just her, and we'd be popping popcorn and dreaming up names for the baby and talking about what color to paint the nursery. How could she marry my mother? Now I will never be free of the Ice Queen.

After dinner, I am allowed fifteen minutes of supervised

Lego time with Cecelia and Tammy before the girls need to be put to bed. I do the dishes and listen to them get baths. When I'm sure they're getting the burrito treatment, I wrap the dish towel around my middle.

Later, I sit at my computer to deal with the e-mails I've been ignoring all day. I hear voices coming through the wall and I'm slammed with another memory. I move the desk chair over and lean against the wall, ear first, listening to Aunt Linda spinning one of her famous bedtime stories. I haven't heard this one. It must be new. Of course it's new. There are pigs—three friendly pigs who want to befriend a spider. I love Aunt Linda's description of the pigs' pink and plushy house and the spider's silvery, stringy apartment. I want to crawl in bed with Cecelia and let bean listen. Then I hear Nora say, "It's past nine, Linda." It pisses me off, but Aunt Linda just laughs and says, "To be continued, my beautiful girls." It's starting to feel like eavesdropping, so I know I should peel my ear away from the wall, but I don't move. They get good night kisses and warnings when they ask for five more minutes or a glass of water, or to snuggle.

Finally, their door clicks closed and I face my computer again. I have two new e-mails:

> My Pumpkin,
>
> I know you said not to call you that, but that is who you are to me. My Pumpkin. And I miss you. You have been gone only 48 hours and I miss you already. I know, I know. I haven't talked to you enough over the past few years to claim missing you so quickly now, but it's the truth. I've been missing you for so long, I can barely stand it anymore. I know

I messed up and I know I should have talked to you about it, but you froze as a ten-year-old in my mind and I just had no idea what I was doing. I still don't. I'm hoping that you'll e-mail or call. I'm hoping to be Daddy again and for you to be Pumpkin again. It's too much to hope for, but what is a man without his dreams?

I doubt I'll hear from you soon, but you'll hear from me tomorrow. And I promise it won't always be this cheesy.

Dad

The second:

E—

School today sucked. I got caught smoking behind the gym. I've never even done that before and I got caught today. Now I'm suspended tomorrow AND grounded forever. Can you believe it? Lizzie and Sean got caught too, but neither of them is grounded.

Todd

Since I've been in Chicago, three people have written me e-mails. I write back to the one who doesn't want to hear from me.

Lizzie—

Okay, I know this is not enough, but I'll tell you now: I'm pregnant. I'm pregnant and I'm going to have a baby and my parents kicked me out and that's why I have to move to Chicago for the year and I'm here with Aunt Linda, which would be cool except her crazy wife-lady Nora has all these rules and won't even let me really talk to my cousins and it's really just awful and I really miss you. Please don't stop talking to me just because I'm so bad at it. I know you're mad, but I need you. I don't know what I'm going to do once I have this thing and I was going to tell you, I swear, but I just didn't know how to bring it up and what to say and all that and I could barely even tell anyone. I didn't even tell my mom—I made the lady at Planned Parenthood tell her.

Please write back, Lizzie.

Ev

P.S. I know I shouldn't say this, but please don't tell anyone! The whole point of being in Chicago is so that no one needs to know!

6 Months and
30 Days Left

She barges into my room after my huge puke and endless hours of flipping around in my sheets while switching between telling the bean stories, cursing it for ruining my life, and briefly picturing it in the arms of other people—Todd, Lizzie, my dad, Todd. Even in the pictures that my brain makes it looks like an artificially enhanced chickpea, not an actual human. And I still might hate it. If I didn't hate it, I wouldn't think about it so damn much.

She opens the door without even knocking and shoves her behind onto my bed.

She strokes my hair like she's going to be Mom, but it's the Lawyer who speaks. "We have a lot to talk about, Evelyn. The car is coming to take me to the airport in an hour, and we still have a lot to work out. I guess I thought between the drive and two days in Chicago, there would be more time to talk. And now we have to talk it all out in this last hour." She pauses. "I wish I could stay longer." *No, no. Please don't stay any longer.* "But I just can't take any more days off." I wonder why I feel disappointed.

I roll over but I don't look at her. "Good morning," I say.

"Oh, don't give me that attitude," she answers and I know that she will never understand me and I will probably never understand bean.

"What else is there to talk about?"

"Evelyn, everything! We haven't even scratched the surface."

I've decided not to have an abortion, I've gone through hours of counseling, I've lied to and probably lost my best friend, I've broken up with the boyfriend I never had, and now I've moved across the country into some stranger's house—and she says I've barely scratched the surface? Please.

I do my best to keep any edge out of my voice when I say, "Everything like what?"

She's dressed in a suit, ready to go straight to work when she gets back to Jacksonville. It makes me feel embarrassed to be under the unicorns and in a pink tank top with no bra.

She sighs like I'm stupid. "My biggest question is if you're going to keep the baby. I have opinions on this, but Dr. Elizabeth and Dr. Moran both told me to keep them to myself. The rest of the decisions really stem from there. But you can't have this baby until these decisions have been made."

Obviously I'm keeping the baby. I just went through all that decision making. Besides, it's too late, isn't it? The possibility of abortion slinks back into my brain—a scantily clad belly dancer. It wiggles up to me and says, "You could still opt out of this. You can go back to being a kid. You can go back home." But I know I can't. I have nothing to go home to anymore anyway.

"I'm having the baby. I told you that. Besides, I think it's too late not to," I say.

"No," my mother explains. "I know that you plan to carry to term. I respect that, Evelyn. That was a difficult decision, and, as much as all of our lives would have been easier if you decided otherwise, I am proud that that is the decision you made." God, she even talks like a lawyer when she's trying to sound mushy. "I am asking about after you give birth: do you plan to parent this child or do you plan to place it in a home for adoption?"

Adoption. I've mostly decided against it, but I'm not ready to say that out loud.

"You haven't even thought about this, have you?" my mom says, not giving me any credit.

What are her opinions anyway? Aunt Linda was adopted but that was from China and she would have been killed or something if she wasn't, so that's a different story, right? And Mom lost all of those babies and it was awful, so does she think I should keep this one and "parent" it, as she says? Or does she think I should give it away because she couldn't tell me that I wouldn't be a lousy mother and she doesn't want to have to deal with it anyway?

I don't want to give away my cluelessness, so I don't say anything.

"Jesus, Evelyn, how could you not think of this? Do you even realize you are pregnant?"

I wish she were Mary, even sitting on my bed and encroaching on my space like this. Mary annoyed me, but she never made me feel like I was the size of bean.

I put an edge in my stare.

"And pray tell, my dear, how do you plan to go off and study at some Ivy League school if you have a child?" Ah, so there's the opinion she wasn't going to state. But then she keeps talking. "And how will you ever pick up your life and move on once you have to leave this baby? Have you thought about that? You might choose adoption, but you're a mom either way."

"Both ideas sound terrible."

My mom sucks in her breath.

"Besides," I continue, "do I really need to decide so soon? I have until April."

"You're making big decisions here, Evelyn. You need to be responsible. Either choice is going to be compounded by a whole new list of decisions."

"Like what?"

"Like how will you choose a family? Will you have an open or a closed adoption? Or where will you live with the baby? What will you do for money? Who will care for the baby while you're at school? How much will you expect from Todd?"

"Nothing," I answer, flinching at the sound of his name. The sting of him telling me "I just can't" buzzes like a wasp in my ear.

"Well, that hardly makes sense. He's around; he has as much time and money as you. If you end up parenting you should insist that he help financially and/or otherwise."

I don't say anything.

"See, you need to think about these things, Evelyn."

I give up. "You said you had opinions. What are they?"

Mom shakes her head, her bun plastered, unmoving, on

the back of her neck. "I'm told that if I share them, I risk isolating myself from you even further. I risk you following my advice blindly and then resenting me for it. Or else I risk you assuming that I am upset with you for your choices forever."

If the Stiff-Ass is going to tell me she has opinions, she needs to tell me what they are. If she isn't going to tell me about them, she shouldn't tell me she has them.

She gives me a death stare. I pull up my blankets, still feeling awkward for wearing pajamas during this conversation.

"Evelyn."

"I'm keeping it." The truth is that adoption appeals to me the same way abortion does: I get to be a kid again, smoke weed, have (protected) sex, go to college far away. But I've screwed up. I don't deserve those things anymore.

Mom breaths a stiff sniff up her nostrils. I gave the wrong answer. "And you'll live with me? With the baby?"

Do I have another choice? "Are we welcome?" I don't bother to hide the edge from my voice this time.

She chokes as my words go in her ears. "Of course you are. I'll help however I can." The doorbell rings. She looks at her watch. "We have so much more to discuss, but . . . I have to go." I nod but I'm thinking: *Take me with you, please. Please take me with you.*

She stands, and I can tell from the way her eyes rest on the car outside my window that she isn't even thinking about taking me with her. "We'll talk every day," she says. We will? Oh, goody.

She starts to go, then quickly turns back on her heel. She

bends hastily and pecks my forehead. It tingles like Tinker Bell has just alighted above my eyes. "I'll miss you. I love you, Evie."

I'm still considering whether I want to respond to either of these statements when she shuts herself out of the room. If she'll miss me, why'd she drop me here?

Pregnant and Parentless

The five days until school starts swim by in a slow-motion blur. Aunt Linda's little house is a lot louder than the one I grew up in, but I don't do any talking. I sit still and watch nightmarish visions of myself—holding a baby, nursing, changing a diaper—on repeat while real life goes on outside my head. My body spends the day sitting in front of the TV, switching channels every five minutes or picking up books and magazines and putting them down. In an early evening flurry of activity Nora and Cecelia and Tammy burst in the front door and all at once there are toys on the floor and screaming and laughing and dinner preparation and I'm banished to my room the second that Cecelia asks me to play and then called down for dinner where I sit at the table while Nora cuts Cecelia's hamburger into bites and tries to get Tammy to answer a question about her day with more than one syllable. At some point, Aunt Linda will call and Nora will roll her eyes and explain over the girls' braids that Aunt Linda is working late. The food goes in my mouth but I can't taste it; the prenatal vitamins get swallowed without any sort of lump registering in my throat. I do dishes without feeling the suds on my fingers. Cecelia asks to play with me and either I'm allowed or Nora is too busy to supervise and I'm not. Aunt Linda rushes in the door for bedtime, swinging by to kiss me on the jaw, and it strikes me that I could try to talk to her about all this but she's been working all day and probably doesn't want to hear any more problems. It should make me angry that I'm barely living with Aunt Linda; I'm living with three people I didn't know a few days ago, but I don't have enough brain left to be angry. Aunt Linda and Nora get busy with bathtime and storytime and I'm so exhausted that I put myself to bed earlier and earlier—9:30, 9:15, 9:00, 8:15. The sounds of Nora and Aunt Linda arguing creep under my door while I close my eyes and beg sleep to come over me and quiet my brain. But it never quiets.

All day—if I'm asleep or awake—it's the same thing inside my mind: the baby taking over, my world shrinking to just my Silent House, which grows noisy with the baby's screams, and I'm always feeling bad because I have no idea what I'm doing.

What kind of mom should I be? I wouldn't be like my mom—never talking, stiff and formal. I wouldn't be like Aunt Linda either—always working, then showing up like a magical fairy. I wouldn't be like Lizzie's—hugging and kissing my daughter even when she outgrows me, bestowing the same kind of boundless affection onto all of her friends. I don't even know how to hug. I wouldn't be like Nora—she's just like Mom. Even if I wanted to be a mom, I would have no idea how. I have to decide everything for this thing: its name, its last name, where it lives, what it eats, where it goes to school. If it's a boy I have to decide whether to circumcise it. How do you even decide that?

I can't be a mother. It's like asking me to be a man. Impossible.

But I already am one. As much as I don't like him/her, bean is here. Already here. How can I say that I will make space for it in my body but not my life? What does this thing deserve?

And really, it's ruined everything already, so I might as well just keep it.

I note the days, minutes until the start of school—if I can't even concentrate on a fashion magazine, how the hell am I going to read a chemistry book?

My dreams are the same stressful succession of words; I'd prefer nightmares of demon babies or being thrown into hell to the string of words continuing into my subconscious.

The night before the first day of school a question flies into my brain that causes me to sit upright: Why does this feel even harder now? I already have one decision down—I didn't kill the thing. Shouldn't that be a check on the to-do list? Shouldn't each check make it a little easier?

It's because I got so used to talking. Mary made all of these crazy sentences leave my brain during those hot afternoons in her office. That witch. I feel a pang for her stronger than I have for anyone yet. I don't want to miss the little lady. Who knows what the hell she would say to me, but she would let these damn nightmares escape my skull. I need to talk to Aunt Linda.

My eyelids are heavier than lead blocks. Maybe I don't need some conclusion in order to be able to move on with my life; maybe I just need to know how to make a step forward.

6 Months, 26 Days Left

I stand outside my Jeep about twenty feet from the entrance to Santa Maria High School, gaping as swarms of students rush by me, hugging and squealing. They are all girls—chatty, squeaky girls in maroon-plaid skirts that reach their knees. They flock around each other, hugging and kissing and playing with one another's hair. And even though I can see hundreds of students from where I'm standing, I'm fairly sure not one of them is white. You'd think someone would mention these things to me.

I scan the parking lot for anyone who looks male or white or Bad or just slightly out of place. My eyes land on a swollen abdomen—just a tiny throw-pillow shape underneath the blue cotton shirt of her summer uniform. She leans against a car in the junior parking lot, batting her hands at another girl who is giggling loudly. Her hair is a black glossy curtain swinging back and forth over the car's hood. She must not be pregnant. She's too happy.

But when I dodge my way through the crowd and settle in

a seat in the back of the dingy auditorium for what they call morning assembly, I see them everywhere—girls with just throw-pillow-sized bellies to undeniable watermelon ones. I notice maybe five of them among the three hundred and fifty girls who wander into the auditorium, chatting English peppered with Spanish. Maybe when I start to sprout a belly I will just blend in. Maybe no one at this place will even notice.

Of course, I'll never blend in here. I'm the wrong freaking color.

But I'm not going to make friends this year anyway, so it doesn't matter.

As soon as they can tell I'm pregnant these girls will know this is the reason I got pawned onto my Aunt Linda—just another girl whose parents kicked her out and gave up on her.

I'm looking at the spot where my shirt is tucked into my pleated uniform skirt, wondering if they can possibly see the little preggo-pouch I see. I stare at that spot as they start the day with some nun saying some prayer and some teacher explaining the theme for the year. My eyes move up to inspect my boobs, which make actual mounds beneath my collar, and I don't know if you can tell they're pregnancy boobs or if they just look like natural B-cups. How long until these strangers know my secrets?

And why are there more pregnant girls here? It has to be because Santa Maria doesn't punish you if you're pregnant. This means there were probably more pregnant girls at St. Mary's than I ever realized and they all either got an abortion or just disappeared. Like me. I wonder if I will be able to find them when I get back.

A girl plops heavily into the seat next to mine and leans over the arm. "Can I sit here?" she asks, which is weird because she's already sitting there.

At that moment, Aunt Linda steps onto the stage. The girl leans toward me again. "That's your aunt, right?"

How can she possibly know that? We're only ten minutes into the first day of school and I haven't said a word to anyone. And I might be the only white girl here, but Aunt Linda is Chinese. That doesn't seem like it could be a hint. Is it bad to have an aunt who I live with be the social worker at my school? Can I deny it?

"I wish Ms. Clark was my aunt. She gives better advice than anyone I'm related to," she says, and I finally look at her. My eyes automatically spring to her belly.

"Five months," she says. "How about you?"

Shit. She can tell. How can she tell?

I shrug noncommittally.

"Ms. Clark told us that you're going to be joining our group."

"What group?" What does a social worker even do, anyway?

"Our group. Expectant Young Mothers. We meet with Ms. Clark during sixth period on Wednesdays."

I blink. This is impossible. "She told you that?"

"Didn't you know that already?"

I shake my head. There was something about some group on the list of rules, but I didn't bother figuring out what it meant.

"Well, it's good actually. It's good to talk to other people who are kind of going through the same thing." She's talking fast, like she's trying to cover her ass, or maybe Aunt Linda's.

She's talking crap, but I love the way her voice lingers whenever she makes an *l* sound.

"So she basically told you that I'm pregnant?" All I remember Aunt Linda saying about school is that I'm not supposed to mention Nora or that she is gay. But she gets to spill my secrets.

"She . . . ," the girl stammers. "She did." She looks at me dead on. "I'm sorry. I love Ms. Clark, but if people blabbed that about me on my first day at a new school, I'd go ballistic."

"Evelyn," I say. It's a gift. I didn't plan on saying even that much to anyone today.

"Huh?"

"Evelyn. My name."

She holds out her hand, "I'm Maryellie. I'm in all the APs possible, so I think we're going to have some classes together."

This girl is the loser. She has no friends. She's jumping at the first opportunity to scoop up a weird-looking, pregnant new kid. But the second Aunt Linda says, "And God bless, students," seven or eight girls reach over chairs to hug Maryellie. They pat her belly and ask how she's feeling and when was the last time that she puked.

I turn to leave, but she starts to introduce me. I'm forced to spend the day with a plastered smile so phony my cheeks ache within seconds. I keep raising my eyebrows to prevent bean from forcing my eyes closed in the middle of the day.

Then it's over. I trudge to the front door of the school, my back weighed down with textbooks and lists of homework already, my front weighed down with bean and the fact that I can't talk to Aunt Linda about it anymore. On my way out, Aunt Linda leans out of her office and calls down the hall for me to stop. Her voice is nails on chalkboard. All this time she's been a fake too. I really thought she was perfect, and then she goes and tells everyone what I want to hide the most. I traipse over to her.

"How was day one?"

I shrug.

"Okay, you're being quiet again. I won't push it." She lowers her voice. "Can you tell Nora I'll be home late and to go ahead and start dinner without me?" So I get to go home and deliver her bad news when she can't even keep mine to herself.

"And don't go to bed until I get home. We need to start having those heart-to-hearts, you and me."

I make it a point to be entirely asleep by the time she gets home. I don't want her catching me pretending, so I force myself into a kind of wordy coma—What kind of mom will I be? How will I name this thing? Do I really have to push it out of my vagina?

My brain spins when I lie down and when I fall asleep and when I wake up to pee every three minutes and when I fall back asleep. It rolls in endless circles.

Finally I give up. I need to talk to someone, and it can't be Aunt Linda. But I need to talk to someone.

I go to my computer and e-mail her. I ignore the list in my in-box alternating between Dad's and Todd's e-mail addresses. I know she doesn't want to hear from me, but maybe if I apologize . . .

Lizzie—

It's me again. The worst friend ever.

I'm sorry again, Lizzie. And I really need you. Can you call me tomorrow?

—E

And even though she's mad at me, I'm sure she will. She always does.

She Doesn't

During group with Aunt Linda the next day, I keep my teeth glued together, saying only my name. There are seven other girls in the room, fawning over Aunt Linda and talking and talking but I let my brain get caught up in the nightmare that my life will become in seven months and tell myself not to hear anything. And I don't.

A week and a half without Lizzie's voice has driven me to desperation. When Lizzie still hasn't called or texted or e-mailed or anything, several hours after I get home I call my mom before she has a chance to call me.

"Evelyn!" I picture her in her office. She probably just put down some brief she is working on to talk to me. I better talk.

"Aunt Linda told all these girls at school that I'm pregnant."

"She shouldn't have done that," Mom answers, letting my heart go light before slamming it down again. "Have you thought any more about a plan?"

When I don't reply, she keeps talking.

"Like how do you plan to ensure this baby is cared for while you finish your senior year? How will you apply to colleges? How will you work out a plan with Todd?"

She stops and the silence on the phone is a screaming banshee in my ear. Finally I say, "I don't know."

She sighs. "Evelyn."

"I don't understand why you get to ask me all these questions after you kicked me out of your house." I didn't mean to say that out loud.

My mom emits a one-note sob like the one when she first found out I was pregnant, and I immediately wish I could take it back: sweep the words off the floor and cram them into my lungs again.

"We didn't kick you out, Evie-Teeny! Is that what you think?"

Stupidly, I shrug. She keeps talking anyway.

"We thought you wanted to make sure no one at St. Mary's knew, so we let you hide out at Aunt Linda's. And we know you've been missing your aunt Linda for years now." She's using the voice she used to when Aunt Linda first moved away: one made of such thin glass that if I speak back it will break. So I stay quiet. But then she says, "Do you want to come home? I'll book an airline ticket right now and drive back with you."

"No," I say, and wow, I don't. This phone call has been hard enough. Living there would stress me out in that way that Mary said is dangerous. "I guess you were right. Thank you."

"Okay." She should tell me that she won't make any more

plans for me without talking to me first. She should tell me that I can come home whenever I want. She should tell me she's sorry.

"Honey, I'm in the middle of a brief here. I'll call you back after dinner and we can try to iron out a plan, okay?"

"Okay," I lie. But I can't make a plan. I'm being dumb, but I just can't. I don't know what else to do but avoid my mom now.

Pregnancy Brain

By the time my first marking-period progress report is mailed to Aunt Linda's house, my stomach is the size of a mixing bowl and my life is nothing but panic. Loneliness, indecisiveness, and anxiety pile in my gut every day, like layers of dirt under the earth's crust. I get home from school afraid my heart will stop. By the time I go to bed, it's hard to breathe.

I've stopped checking my e-mail altogether. What's the point? I don't want to hear another word from Todd. Seeing the Stranger's name on the screen brings back my morning sickness. And my mother calls me. She strings endless lists of questions together, terrifying questions that I have never even thought of before. They scratch into my voice mail and I call her back during study hall or lunch, when I know she's in court.

Outside my head, life in Aunt Linda and Nora's house moves slowly. The girls zoom in and out of rooms but take forever to actually accomplish the smallest tasks—changing clothes after school, brushing teeth, even spitting out a sentence.

Today, I'm sitting at the little desk in the purple unicorn room, letting the letters in my chemistry book shuffle around and rearrange themselves into words I don't want to see: pregnant, baby, crib, labor, name, parent, abortion even. I'm trying to take notes on acids and bases, but the layers in my chest won't dissipate. At least if they suffocate me or stop my heart I won't need to figure out my life: if I die, so does the baby. That will be the end.

Someone knocks on the door, which is already open, and without looking up I call, "Come in." My head is still bent over my pencil, which is converting pH levels completely separately from the actual workings of my brain. When no one surfaces after a few moments, I look up. In the door frame, Tammy switches from her left foot to her right foot and back, the beads on the end of her braids swinging with the momentum.

We stare at each other.

If this were Cecelia, I would know what to do. I'd send her down to Nora, who would be in the kitchen or doing some work in the family room, to ask if she can visit with me. Nora always says she should let me rest or let me finish my homework.

But Tammy doesn't seek me out. I've been living here for over a month now and the only times Tammy has actually spoken to me are when she's directly told to.

She freezes in the doorway, leaning onto her left foot, her little peanut-butter hand clutching a sheet of paper and a pencil.

"I need help with my math."

I still don't know what to say for a few seconds, the kind of seconds that feel like minutes. Her feet stay solidly outside the threshold of my door, but my heart starts beating wildly, aware of how close we are to breaking Rule 8 right now. But I think about what's on that page in her hand—I could show her how to count on her fingers. I could draw her a number line. I know how to help her, and maybe if I do, the bean bean bean on my brain will stop for a minute.

"I'll help you, but go ask Mommy Nora if it's all right," I say.

"She's on the phone," Tammy says, barely audible. Her eyes look into mine like she wishes she could just transmit whatever is in her brain and never need to say anything out loud. "And she doesn't help me that much. I don't get what she explains."

I stand up and scoot past her. Her little body stays planted in my doorway. I tiptoe down the stairs and peer over the banister to see that, in fact, Nora is involved in a heated conversation on the phone. I recognize the lawyer in her voice and body language. As a state's attorney, she trades the astronomical salary she could get at a firm for a five p.m. sharp stop time, but it doesn't always work out that way. Her back is toward me, and I see that it's straighter than it would be at, say, dinner; her chin pointed slightly up, one hip thrust out. It strikes me that when she comes home she is actually Mom-Nora, not Lawyer-Nora. Her mom self is that stiff. I lose a second just looking at her before scurrying back up the stairs, which I feel in my knees.

Tammy has swiveled her head but not moved her feet. She's watching me, her expression impossible to read.

"Okay," I say. "Let's get this math done."

I expect her to look happy, but her demeanor barely changes.

"Here's how we'll do this. You sit right where you are, and I'll sit on this side of the doorway."

"On the floor?" she asks.

"Yes." I plop myself down to show her it is not a big deal.

She sits. Both of us are still in Catholic uniform skirts and, sitting Indian style, our legs make a nest for her homework. I know that even though we're not technically in the same room, I'm breaking Rule 8. And I don't even care. The list of rules I used to break is so long it would take an entire notebook for Nora to write them all down, so why have I been sweating her stupid list? This is just one rule. I used to rebel by drinking beer and smoking pot and having sex. Now I'm helping my tiny cousin with her homework. Sue me. Seriously, try to kick me out for this one, Auntie Nora.

The homework is harder than I thought. It's fractions. It's asking which fraction is bigger: one-half or one-third? One-fifth or two-fifths? Was homework really this hard in the first grade?

It takes about thirty seconds before I start to doubt myself, start to wonder if I can teach this little girl first-grade math, but she's trying so sincerely. I feel some of the nausea in my system drain out of my fingers.

I'm saying, "Bigger number on the bottom means small. Bigger number on the top means big," and showing her a pie on the back of the homework sheet that I keep shading and erasing with her pencil. She's on the verge of getting it, so I'm leaning almost out of my room, my butt barely on the carpet. She grabs the pencil from me, saying, "I can shade in one-third of the pie," and she starts to make a scratchy back-and-forth motion with the pencil. I'm stretching toward her, thinking that she might actually have it this time—it might have actually sunk in—when I hear Nora say, "Evelyn."

That's when I see her feet, right behind Tammy's bottom.

Tammy and I both freeze, as if she also knows that meeting with me is not allowed.

When I first look at Nora, I haven't quite finished wiping the fear off my face, but by the time she starts talking to me, I've met her eyes in a "bring it on" expression. If you want to kick me out, just do it. What the hell do I care? You think I'm not used to this shit by now?

"Tammy," she says, and Tammy jumps. Nora's face softens. She squats behind her daughter, leaning her blond hair into Tammy's dark braids. "It's okay, sweetie. Just go work in your room for a few minutes because I have to talk to Evelyn. I'll send her in there to help you when we're done if you want, okay?"

She'll what?

Tammy nods, but her chin is wobbling like she's close to tears.

Nora closes her in a hug before Tammy disappears into what the girls call the Pink Room.

I feel grateful to Tammy at this minute and not just for distracting me from my puke-layers with fractions, but also because when Nora speaks, the edge in her voice is gone. "You were doing really well with her," she says.

How long had she been there? "I . . . I'm sorry."

Nora sighs and drops onto my bed. "Don't be. She came to you, that's good. She's so skittish and afraid; I just don't know what to do with her." She's talking to me like I'm an adult, like I might have something useful to say, like I'm also a mother, which—I jolt—I am. Maybe. Well, definitely. Right? Well, maybe.

What makes you a mother anyway?

Nora is clearly a mother, and she was never even pregnant. My mom is barely a mother, and she was pregnant four times. And when I have this baby I'm going to be a worse mother than either of them.

I say, "I know you don't want me talking to her without you around."

Nora shrugs. She has made such a big deal of this anytime one of the girls wants to do anything with me, so how can she just be shrugging it off now?

"So how are things going, Evelyn?"

I look at her, startled, then quickly look away. Things are sucky. But that's not her fault. It's mine for getting pregnant. And things were always sucky anyway.

My gaze drifts to the window where the colors in the backyard tree compete with the blazing blue sky. Everyone warned me about freezing weather and massive snow piles in Chicago; no one mentioned the leaves. When it is time for all the nature to die, it suddenly bursts into more life than you can see in a single glance. No one mentioned the way that driving down the highway, orange and red and yellow and brown would streak by my window, painting the world happy. The way a tree could take weeks to adopt a sort of noncommittal peach and then suddenly burst into the brightest red you've ever seen for an unsatisfying twenty-four hours before settling into a cardboard brown.

I'm still contemplating the leaves when Nora says, "Evelyn?"

Maybe my baby is like that too. Maybe if it bursts into a frenzy of activity right at the end of my third trimester, it will mean that it's time for it to disappear, to live again, but somewhere far, far away. Maybe I can give it away. But how can I wait that long to know?

"Evelyn?" she says a third time.

"Fine," I say. "It's fine."

"Evelyn," she says, and hands me a coaster-sized piece of cardboard with my name at the top: my grades. A row of little half-moon Cs laugh at me for thinking that disappearing to Chicago would mean that I could be valedictorian after all.

"I'm sorry," I say. Is she going to kick me out for this?

"Let's not just say that. Let's talk. Is this just pregnancy brain?"

What the hell is pregnancy brain? "Maybe."

"How do you like Santa Maria?"

The truth is, I have no idea. I go through the day like a very visible ghost—everyone staring at me but no one speaking. Except Maryellie. I eat lunch at her table, and the other girls seem to put up with me out of pity or grace or something but I don't have any friends. I stupidly froze them out with my silence the first few days. Lectures and labs and tests *whoosh* by my ears and regular high school life swirls around my head, but my brain is located in my uterus at every second of the day.

Still, I've never gotten a B before, let alone a C. I'm a failure as a mother and a student.

"It's okay," I say.

"Is it harder than your old school?" she asks.

"No. It's easier." Then, thinking about how being a visible ghost is better than being the slut of the school while I dodge Todd in hallways and pine for Lizzie's voice, I say, "Please don't send me back. I'll work harder."

I expect an argument but she just says, "Okay, whatever you want." Then she stands to go.

I realize that I don't know if I'm supposed to finish helping Tammy, so I say, "Nora?" This might be the first time I'm calling her by name.

She crosses the room in two steps and collapses back on the bottom bunk. She doesn't hug me or take my hand, but she looks at me like we're in the middle of a genuine moment. "Yes? Evelyn, tell me what I can do for you."

"What?"

"Aunt Linda and I, we don't know what we're doing."

They don't?

"We don't know how to help you. We've never been pregnant. We've never had ex-boyfriends to move away from or little bodies inside of ours. We—neither of us—had stakes as high as valedictorianship or"—she breaks to swallow—"an unloving house either."

How does she know about my house?

"I thought what you would need coming here was structure, and, except for this"—she gestures to the progress report, lying facedown on the carpet at my feet—"you've maintained the structure perfectly and still managed to secede from the family. You get smaller every day even as you get bigger. I have no idea what you're feeling or thinking about but I know whatever it is, it's deeply sad. And even Linda has no idea how to pull you back into the world, but you need to be in the world for that baby. And for you. For yourself too. Please, what can I do?"

She's like Lizzie at this minute, asking for even just a pinky's worth of who I am. She's open and vulnerable and pleading. And I almost consider telling her that I think I might want to give it up, but I don't know her. I don't trust her. She doesn't trust me. And I can't do that, anyway.

So I give her less than a pinky.

"Could you buy some ginger ale the next time you're at the store? It calms my stomach."

She laughs. Before now, I've only heard her tiny laugh aimed at SpongeBob or some silly song. Now her laugh matches her looks—beautiful and sharp, high enough to hit the ceiling. I can't help laughing back. The sound escaping my lips is as unfamiliar as Nora's and I wonder how long it's been since I laughed—even just a two-syllable chuckle like this.

"I'm going to take Celie out for a minute before dinner," she says. "Will you keep helping Tammy?"

There's a warm feeling in my chest, like a washcloth on a sore muscle, when I nod. I think about wringing it out and spilling some warm drops on the bean, because it could use them too.

When Tammy and I walk down to dinner, she's playing with her index finger, examining how it's divided into thirds, and her homework is done. At my place there's a can of ginger ale and it hits me like a baseball bat that that is where Nora took Cecelia. And maybe I could be a mom if I was like Nora. Maybe she's the best mom I know.

The warm feeling dulls but lingers through dinner, and washing dishes, and a shower, and a chapter of my history textbook that I actually pay attention to. It lasts until bean makes my eyes close on the book and I climb my expanding body into bed, listening to the mattress squeak.

But then I'm back on my chemistry book, the blue ring humming in my ears and casting an eerie glow on my pale flesh. I look to the book, for some reason checking to see if it's my Santa Maria chem book or my St. Mary's chem book. Just then it tips and knocks me forward and I fall into nothingness. I fall faster and faster, air and black swirling around me, and when I wake up I'm sweating and freezing and my heart is beating so fast it shakes my newly grown boobs.

I don't have anyone else to talk to, so I jump across the room, flip on my computer, and dig in my still half-packed suitcase for the little business card of the only person I know will always listen to me:

MARY MULDOON
PLANNED PARENTHOOD
Jacksonville, Florida

I ignore my brimming inbox, open a new mail window, and type as fast as I can.

Mary,

I still need to talk. I'm sorry, but I don't know what to do. I know you thought you were done dealing with me, but I don't know who else to talk to.

Evelyn

P.S. I've been taking my vitamins and stuff, just so you know.

When I climb back into my bed, I'm actually expecting to fall asleep the way I did a month ago when I wrote to Lizzie and truly believed she'd write back. I know Mary will write back. She's the wrong person, but she'll write back.

She's tiny and she never just tells me what to do. She'll probably try to mail me pamphlets or she might even just show up at SMHS and hand me a ginger ale and expect me to understand what she means when she tells me some other cryptic story. But I also know she'll tell me something. She'll give me some other piece of information that I don't already have. First, she'll tell me to write down everything I do know. I'm not sleeping, so I lug my laptop into my bed, thinking maybe putting it on paper will allow me to fall asleep, and maybe it will impress Mary if I have a list already.

I type:

1. Raising a baby is hard work.
2. I don't know how to do it and I will probably be very bad at it.
3. I will have to move back into the Silent House.
4. My parents will help me but they won't be any better at it than me.

5. I need to find something to do with it while I'm at school and stuff.
6. I need to figure out how to go to college with a baby.
7. I don't even like bean, and I'm supposed to love it if I'm its mother.
8. That's not its fault.
9. If I work hard enough, I think I can learn how to be a mom and love it.
10. I don't know how to name it.
11. Once I have the baby, Todd will have to stay in touch with me.

But I delete that one immediately.

I'm still pressing backspace when I hear murmured voices in the hallway. My first impulse is panic—technically my lights are out but I'm pretty sure sitting in my bed with an open laptop at 3:04 a.m. breaks the "lights out" rule. And I don't want Nora to kick me out. I want to be here while I decide what to do with this thing—away from Todd and Lizzie and my Silent House. I can focus on bean here.

I snap my laptop shut so they won't see a glow underneath my door and hold my breath, waiting for Nora to catch me. Instead, they keep talking. And then I start to hear my name passing back and forth between them. At first it's just my name I notice—a football tossed in a snowstorm—but then I start to hear the context.

"Her mother said she hasn't talked to her in weeks?" I hear Nora ask. "Who's she talking to, then?"

Aunt Linda's voice is more muffled: ". . . friends . . . Evelyn is . . . father . . ."

"Does Evelyn speak during your group at school?" I don't need to hear Aunt Linda's answer because I already know it: no.

"She doesn't seem to have any friends there, really." That's not my fault. They ignore me. But even as I think that, I know it's mostly my own fault.

Nora's pointing a lot of fingers at Aunt Linda, which isn't fair. I mean, they're just supposed to give me room and board. They didn't sign on for anything else. They aren't my parents.

I'm expecting Aunt Linda to raise her voice, because she always does. Not the kind of screaming explosions that used to startle me awake in the Silent House, but some loud, earnest communication that for some reason always makes me picture them both naked.

But Aunt Linda's voice is laced with more concern than I've heard since my days as a burrito and she says, "You're really worried about her, aren't you?" I know she has taken strong and stiff Nora into her arms, right there in the hallway. She says, "I think you're right. She's not really talking. She needs to be."

"I tried to talk to her tonight," Nora says. "Do you know she even got Tammy talking? Evelyn helped her with her math homework. She has your gift."

Gift? With math? That's definitely not true.

Nora goes on. "She wouldn't talk to me, Linda. You have to take care of it. I'm not as good as you are."

There's several seconds of silence and I think that they went to bed, but when they start talking again I'm pretty sure that they just paused to kiss for a while.

Then Aunt Linda says, "But you are good at letting me

know where my services are needed. I'm not too good at that. Let's let Evie take the girls costume shopping and trick-or-treating. What do you think?"

My heart races. I'm not sure why. It's not like I've been pining away for the old days of trick-or-treating. But I find my brain saying, *Say yes, Nora, please say yes.* I don't hear her say anything, though. I hear their bedroom door open. I hear it click closed. I'm glad they decided to have that conversation in the hallway, even though it makes no sense.

"If I get to go trick-or-treating," I tell the bean, "I'll think of it as practice. And I'll know how to take you trick-or-treating next year."

5 Months, 22 Days Left

Mary writes back and tells me to call her. She doesn't have my phone number, so when I don't call, she writes and writes and writes and sends me links to websites that are supposed to tell me about adoption and how to do it and I don't want to know anything about that so she didn't understand my question at all.

She says that I can choose adoption right up to the end and that I need to be very careful about having a plan for this baby after it's born—a solid plan that I don't change once I give birth—and all that, blah-blah. All she does is put that damn belly dancer back in my brain again. The abortion/adoption ship has sailed. I'm having this baby. She has no idea what she's doing. She's about as much help as Lizzie.

I know I should start listening to somebody but whenever I try, it just seems too hard.

I leave all the e-mails that piled up during that panic spat glowing unread in my inbox. But I read the new ones.

Todd sends one about once a week. Dad writes every day and it's usually completely boring and all about anthropology or archaeology or some crap. He's trying. He's finally really trying to be the old Daddy-Dad from before, so sometimes I think about writing him back. But with everything that's going on in my life, it's so much easier to stay mad at him.

Today, I'm sitting at my desk drawing molecules for my chemistry homework and trying to keep my head from wandering into my uterus. Aunt Linda yells my name the second she walks in the door, the way people at a party yell "surprise!" She's like this at school—she greets every girl like a long-lost friend. She hugs them. She gives every student a birthday card every year. She smiles and frowns through their stories. She looks them in the eyes like they are the only thing existing in the world anytime they try to talk to her. I used to think all of this affection was just for me. Moving here, I was prepared to share it with Cecelia and Tammy, but not the whole city.

"Evie, get your butt down here," she says. "I'm taking my favorite niece out to dinner."

I almost call back "I'm your only niece," but that sounds too lovey-dovey sitcomy and that's just not me. I pull on a coat, the one my mom bought me during that crazy Michigan Avenue shopping trip, and pound my swollen body down the stairs.

"Olive Garden?" she says, and I think about how I've never been there because it's not the kind of place my parents would ever go.

Over our salad, Aunt Linda says, "I talked to your mom yesterday. She misses you."

I feel my mouth open with shock when my eyes well up. The way I'm reacting to my own body makes me laugh and then I'm crying and laughing and gaping in shock all at once. I feel Aunt Linda's eyes on me as I start hiccupping with excess emotion. She hands me a tissue and says, "Well, I'll be damned," which makes us both laugh harder. It takes a good five minutes before I'm breathing normally and my face is wiped off.

"Is crying a symptom?"

Aunt Linda chuckles. "It can be, I think, but maybe it's not. When we first got Celie and Tammy, I cried every day for weeks."

"You?" I try to picture it. It's impossible. My imagination can't even iron her smile into a straight line.

"I had no idea what I was doing," Aunt Linda says, helping herself to another breadstick.

"You didn't?"

Nora was the one who read all the books and she was ready for the day-to-day stuff—bedtime routines and balanced diets and educational options. I was supposed to be ready for them emotionally—talk to them about the adjustment, about having parents that would always be there for them, about learning to trust again. And on top of that, I knew that one day I'd need to prepare them for how unusual their family looks. Cecelia was still so little and so full of affection. She trusted us immediately. Of course, that trusting nature comes with its own concerns. But Tammy is a different barrel of monkeys. Every time I tried to talk to her, she just went stiff as a board. I was a total failure."

"How did you figure it out?"

Aunt Linda laughs. "I'm glad I give off that impression. I still have no idea what I'm doing."

But that's exactly how I feel.

"If you have no idea what you're doing . . ." I pause, a breadstick halfway to my mouth. I don't know how to ask the question. "Then what do you do?"

Aunt Linda hears the question I was really asking, the question with words that are too scary and binding.

"I just love them so much. There's no choice but to do what I think is best. They are the little loves of my life."

For some reason, my eyes start stinging again. Our food arrives and I watch the waiter until they dry out. He puts a steaming plate of chicken alfredo in front of me.

"Evie," Aunt Linda says, looking at her plate while I pause to look at her. "Your mom says you haven't talked to her in a while. Why is that?"

Excuses fly to my tongue—I'm busy, I don't want to, I'm mad at her, I'm hiding my progress report results. But I think about Nora in the hallway last night, saying that I need to start talking to someone. Nora doesn't need to care about me. She's not my family. I guess I owe it to her to try.

My voice, same as whenever I'm trying to tell the truth, gets small and high.

"She's rushing me into figuring everything out. And Mary keeps telling me not to rush."

Aunt Linda's eyebrows knot in the center of her head. "What do you mean, rushing you?"

"She wants me to have everything figured out." It gets easier with each word. This is Aunt Linda. And she can still love me even if I'm not Cecelia or Tammy—the little loves of her life.

Aunt Linda raises her eyebrows so high I think they might bounce right off her forehead. "You mean you are considering adoption?"

I expect to see disappointment fall on her face, the way I imagine it did when she first found out that I got pregnant or the way it would if she found out I'd done drugs. But it almost seems like a light goes on behind her eyes.

"Sweetie, you need to talk to people about that."

"But I'm not really considering it. And I don't have anyone to talk to anyway." The words fall on the table faster than I can catch them. They feel huge and incriminating, but Aunt Linda dismisses them with a wave of her hand.

"Please. You're falling down with people to talk to. Starting with yours truly."

I nod.

"So let's start here. Why aren't you considering adoption?"

I shrug.

"Would it be too hard to give up your baby after all this time? Do you feel like no one can love it the way you will?" Aunt Linda spears a piece of chicken and blows at the steam.

I shake my head. "Nothing like that."

"Then what is it?"

My life is over anyway. It's my fault the bean is here, so I'm the one who should have to deal with it. But I don't say anything.

"Okay," she says. "I don't want to push you so far that you stop talking to me. We'll enjoy our meal. Tomorrow you're going to call your mother, but not until after I talk to her and tell her to stop pressuring you, because Mary—whoever she is—is right. You need to make all of these plans seriously and carefully."

I'm relieved.

"But what we do need to do immediately is start to fill in the ifs about those decisions. Like: If adoption, what agency? What kind of family? Or, if parenting: Where are you going to live, get money, what will you do about school?"

I feel my pulse quicken. "I'm not thinking about adoption."

"But for now, we'll just enjoy ourselves. Serious talking starts tomorrow. Am I a good person for this talking to happen with, or do you want to use someone else?"

Lizzie's face appears in my head, and, strangely, so does Nora's. "No. You. You're good."

"And you'll talk to your parents, if I get them off your back?" she asks. She hasn't said anything about the Stranger before this and I know I should tell her that I haven't been talking to him at all, but I nod because she said that was the end of the tough conversation for tonight.

"And will you talk at group on Wednesday?"

Geez. I thought we were going to just enjoy ourselves. I shrug.

"Will you at least talk to Maryellie before group? That girl's tongue is going numb trying to talk to you while you just smile and nod in her face as if she can't tell she's part of a two-month-long, one-sided conversation."

"I'll try," I say.

She nods. "So who is Mary anyway?" she asks.

And I start to describe how little she was and her crazy curlicue handwriting and how I never knew what she was writing. Aunt Linda laughs. I know she's kind of just laughing to be nice, but she's laughing a lot.

"The best thing she did for me was turn me on to this," I say, tapping my glass of ginger ale.

Aunt Linda laughs again. "I know. Nora says we're going to spend all four thousand dollars this month on ginger ale alone."

I stop laughing immediately. The money. I can't believe she brought it up. It makes me want to ask the question I've been itching to ask since I first got to Chicago. But I can't. Or can I? Maybe I can decide to be Talkative Evelyn the way I decided to be Bad Evelyn. "Why did you and Nora take me, anyway?"

Aunt Linda pulls my hand across the table into both of hers, even though I'm still holding a fork. "We wanted to, Evie-Teeny," she says.

I could let it go there, but she didn't answer my question, so I push the rest of the words out of me. "But you just said it has been hard with the girls already and I know things aren't perfect with you and Nora, so why? I mean, why take on one more thing?" Aunt Linda squeezes my hand. I keep talking. "If it was really for the money, just tell me, because it's okay, but I need to know."

She shakes her head and now her smile disappears and tears gather in her eyes. "Evelyn, don't you know you're the love of my life? How could I not help you? We would have done it for free. We could use the money, so we're taking it. But you better believe we would do it for free. We would pay to help you if we had to."

My cheeks feel wet again, and I yank my hand to get it out of her grasp because I hate these stupid tears and I hate seeming like such a sissy and I'm just not used to it. But she won't let me.

"And you're wrong, you know?"

I look at her. Now I have no idea what she's talking about.

"About Nora and me. You're wrong. We're different as different can be, and sometimes it takes talking—a lot of talking—to figure out where the happy medium is, but I love that woman and she loves me. We're in good shape."

I think of my mom and dad and how they will never, ever find a happy medium. And I wonder if Todd came back to me if we could ever find a happy medium. But I know we couldn't because he's a dumbass and now he's a jerk and there is no way to know if I will even have anyone to talk to about bean back in Jacksonville, or if I'll ever get to talk to someone so honestly that it sounds like an argument even when we're in good shape. So the tears just keep flying and I hate them and we're in public and it's so embarrassing the way they pile up on the table in front of me until Aunt Linda finally says, "Do you want to take Cecelia and Tammy costume shopping tomorrow? And take them trick-or-treating next week?"

I smile in spite of myself and imagine Cecelia's little hand in mine as she yaps in my ear and Tammy walks next to us with big eyes looking at everything there is to see in the mall.

"So she said yes?" I don't realize how this incriminates me of eavesdropping until the words are already out of my mouth.

"Both Nora and I would be thrilled if you would do that." She doesn't seem to notice.

When we get home, I have an e-mail from Todd.

> E—
>
> Bethany brought you up at lunch today. She was talking about how you used to do those impressions when you were drunk. Remember how you used to imitate Sister Face? Your voice would be all high and your back would be all hunched and you would even use the words she would use, like "negligible" and "youngsters." It made me laugh thinking of you.
>
> Do you have anyone to imitate at your new school?
>
> I hope things are good and you feel all right and all that,
>
> Todd

It's the first one I'm tempted to answer. Somewhere in my mind I know my life would be easier if I started answering some of these e-mails. But I don't.

Talking

Next Wednesday, before group, Maryellie asks me what my Halloween plans are and I shrug. I don't know why this girl is so interested in me, pushing her big belly into my thoughts almost every day, preventing me from just daydreaming about bean or Todd throughout group, always curious as to what I'm doing after school or for the weekend. I have no idea what Maryellie wants from me.

But I remind myself, Talkative Evelyn. Talkative Evelyn.

So I end up saying, "I'm taking my cousins trick-or-treating. Do you want to come?"

I can't believe the invitation leaves my mouth. I'm nervous enough to take out those two. Costume shopping was hectic with Tammy refusing to talk and Cecelia's legs getting tired and both of them getting hungry and pulling me in all sorts of directions and getting pouty about one costume and angry about another. Eventually we got them both princess dresses and I went home feeling certain that I could never, ever, do this every year for ten or twelve years, but also profoundly proud of getting the job done. Even if it took four hours.

But adding the potential of a friend? It's been forever since I had to make friends. Lizzie and I had been friends for so long and since then, she just kind of made the friends for me. But I miss her. And Maryellie is right in front of me. I feel guilty—as if hanging out with Maryellie will be cheating on Lizzie. Or not exactly. More like by hanging out with Maryellie I will be doing something I don't deserve; every laugh will be one I'm not supposed to feel.

But Maryellie doesn't even answer. She says, "Ms. Clark has kids?" And I remember that at school we have to pretend like Aunt Linda is single because of the whole dumbass Catholics-aren't-supposed-to-be-gay thing.

"No." I have no idea what else to say. "Other cousins."

"I don't know," Maryellie says, laughing. "Do you really think I could go trick-or-treating in the suburbs with a bunch of white girls?" It still surprises me, that term: white girl. There were always some nonwhite people around me, but in my white world we pretended that not talking about it would make the difference in races just disappear.

I smile. "They're black. My cousins."

Maryellie says, "You better believe I'm coming. This I gotta see. You all have one colorful family!" Then she pats bean and says, "Besides, we need the practice." I wonder if she knows all that stuff I'm supposed to know.

Now I just have to tell Aunt Linda. I look across the room and see her and realize that she's heard the whole thing. I try to tell her that I'm sorry with my eyes, but hers are smiling.

Practice

By the time Halloween arrives, Aunt Linda has told Mary-ellie everything. She and Nora even had one of those loud, passionate nonarguments about it right in front of me one night while I washed dishes and the girls played Legos in the next room. It ended when Aunt Linda said, "Nora, my love, you have to trust me."

Nora came up behind her and put her arms around Aunt Linda's waist. "You know I do," she said, and they kissed, right in front of me.

Whenever they get affectionate like that, it makes me feel like I'm standing on a boat during a storm, but I don't think it's because they're both women. I've just never seen that kind of affection.

Then Nora put her hand on my head and said, "And I'm proud of you, you know." And I felt like I just got an A.

🕐🕑🕒

On Halloween, Tammy insists that I be the one to zip up her princess dress. And Nora steps away from the costume, laughing. The girls have on pink sparkling dresses and tiaras; in their hands they clutch wands and plastic pumpkin buckets. I disappear up the stairs when the camera comes out. I retrieve my silver sparkling eye shadow and I use it to paint their cheeks. Cecelia is giggling nonstop, and Tammy is even smiling intermittently.

I pull on a sweatshirt with a pumpkin picture on the stomach and my bean-bump makes it stick out like a real pumpkin. This sends Celie into a fit of gleeful giggles.

Maryellie and I walk with the girls between the houses, but we let them climb the front steps themselves. Cecelia yells "Trick-or-treat," while Tammy just looks at her plastic high heels.

It's so easy that we have time to talk.

Maryellie tells me about her brother who's in college and how he's the first one from their family to go. The concept is so foreign to me that I find myself asking questions.

Then she's asking questions.

"So did your parents, like, kick you out when you got pregnant?"

"It wasn't really like that," I say as Cecelia catapults into my leg screaming, "Laffy-Taffy! They gave me Laffy-Taffy!"

"Is that your favorite?" Maryellie asks, swooping down over her big belly and guiding Cecelia's hand so she remembers to put the Laffy-Taffy in her pumpkin. I would never know to do that. I'm going to suck at this.

"No, it's Tammy's!" she shouts and pulls it out of her

bucket, throwing it in Tammy's when she comes lumbering up the walk. Cecelia sticks her tongue out at Maryellie, and I don't know what to do.

"You are very nice to give your sister your candy, you know," Maryellie says. "But it's not so nice to stick your tongue out at people who are just trying to help you."

Oh, I think, as if I'm learning along with Cecelia. Cecelia just stares for a few seconds before Tammy pulls on her arm and they walk toward the next stoop.

"So," Maryellie turns back to me. "Are you glad they sent you here?"

"Yes." I'm still surprised that this is true.

"Don't you miss your parents?" We're both watching the girls ring the doorbell, not looking at each other, so it's easier to talk.

"Not really." I remind myself every second to be Talkative E. "They yell a lot. Or else they just don't say anything. But I miss my friend." And the next thing I know I'm telling Maryellie all about Lizzie and her monster closet and her dad search and the way we used to laugh and every minute that I'm not watching Maryellie perform mom-magic on my little cousins I'm spilling my guts all over the shelf her pregnant stomach has formed.

Finally she says, "So when was the last time you tried with her?"

"Maybe a month ago?"

"You should try again." We turn to walk back down the other side of the street. Cecelia is hanging onto my hand. There are several undecorated houses in a row on this side of the street, which, as I have learned tonight from

Maryellie, means we aren't supposed to trick-or-treat at them. Cecelia puts her face on my thigh. "You should pick her up," Maryellie says, and I do. "And you should try again."

I know she's talking about Lizzie. "She doesn't want to talk to me."

"No, she doesn't want to be a sounding board for your problems now that you're ready to talk. Ask about her life. And if she doesn't reply, try again. And if she doesn't reply, try again."

"It's not going to work." I set Cecelia down to scurry to another doorway.

But, once the girls are in bed, I try.

> Lizzie—
> I miss you.
> How are you? How is Sean? Any news on your dad? I know you don't want to just worry about me. I'll take anything at this point.
> Still sorry,
> Ev

The Dumbass

A little fantasy has been flirting with my imagination when I'm awake and asleep. In it, I've got bean in my arms, and even though I can't see it, it's warm and snuggly. And Todd has changed his mind. He figures out that he better work hard his senior year and he gets a football scholarship to Stanford, and I get into the same school. And we move to California together and he gets some really good summer job. I take care of bean in the nice apartment he gets for us, and when he comes home from work every day, I've cooked him dinner and we put bean to bed and have sex and then he strokes my elbow pit. And we get to talk about our families and to go out in public, the two of us holding hands or letting our bodies touch familiarly. And when we disagree we talk like Nora and Aunt Linda and then we kiss and we share a bed all the time and he's always feeding me when I'm hungry just like he did that one night. And he comes to Chicago with me every Christmas to spend it with Aunt

Linda and Nora and Cecelia and Tammy, and they start to call him Uncle Todd and eventually we graduate and we both get good jobs and he gives me a ring and we get married and we are just happy.

And when this is the ribbon winding through my brain—at night before I fall asleep, or when I wake up, or in class, or during group, or when I'm looking at one of Mary's websites, or when I'm on the phone with my mom trying to find something to talk about that's not the baby, or when I'm getting Tammy dressed for bed, or when I'm playing Legos with Cecelia, or when I'm doing my chemistry homework—I feel even better about keeping bean. Because if I don't how will I ever know?

But I remember when he said, "I just can't." "I just can't." And bean is what broke us up in the first place. And I hate it.

4 Months, 29 Days Left

Before going downstairs for another terrifying Aunt Linda meeting, I check my e-mail.

> E—
> Sean had a wild party for Halloween. I remembered you walking around last year there dressed in that crazy Tin Man outfit. I know that Lizzie was supposed to be a sexy Dorothy but I couldn't keep my eyes off of you that night, that tinfoil wrapped around your legs like that. I wanted to be the one who put it there.
> Did you dress up this year? I guess you didn't party.
> Don't worry. Sean's kind of sucked.
> Todd

Then . . .

Pumpkin,

Your mother tells me you took your cousins trick-or-treating. Linda tells me you have quite a way with them. It doesn't surprise me—you have always been so gentle and so fun. Linda tells me you dressed them as princesses, which is far from what Linda and Nora would have chosen for their daughters, I surmise! But nonetheless, I am sure they loved it. Nora sent me a picture and they look adorable. You all do.

I still wish you were here, but I am glad you are being helpful to your aunts and getting to know your cousins out there. We never did have enough family around for you, ever since Linda moved out, that is.

I miss you.

Love, Dad

And then, with a racing heart . . .

Ev,

I went to Sean's party last night as a sexy nurse. Boring, I know.

Sean's an asshole now, by the way.

Lizzie

P.S. I'm still mad, but I'll read it if you write back.

P.P.S. I do have some more info on my dad, but I'm going to make you sweat it out. See how you like it.

By the time I get down the stairs for my meeting with Aunt Linda I feel almost happy. She's sitting on the couch, a stack of paper in front of her on the coffee table.

I plop down next to her.

"Okay," she says, and immediately morphs into Mary. "So, you have some decisions to make." She pulls a pen out of her pocket and uncaps it.

I shrug. I don't like the pen and paper. I don't want her to take mysterious notes on me like Mary did.

"Have you made up your mind, Evie? Are you keeping it?"

"I keep telling you I am."

Aunt Linda's eyes look perfectly normal. She isn't even bothering to lace them with fake sincerity the way Mary does.

"Do you not want to do this with me, Evelyn?"

"I don't get why I have to do it at all. You told me I have plenty of time."

"Not exactly," Aunt Linda says. "You have time but not forever. No one's going to rush you into figuring this all out because if we do, you're too likely to make a decision you'll regret. And the stakes are too high here, babe. But that doesn't mean you shouldn't be thinking about it."

Ha. What else have I even been thinking about?

"It doesn't mean you shouldn't be putting plans into motion."

But how can I plan anything before I decide anything?

"And if you're living in my house, making a decision this big means talking about it. I know your parents sent you here so you could still graduate from St. Mary's next year and so that you wouldn't lose your spot as valedictorian, but I think your mother also recognizes that I might be better at this part of life than she is."

"What part?" I ask, reminding myself to be Talkative Evelyn even though it would be easier to be Silent Evelyn.

"The part where you need to talk about and figure out the icky-sticky emotional hard stuff."

I laugh.

"What?"

"Mom doesn't talk about anything at all ever."

Aunt Linda nods. "She's had a rough go of it, you know. But she loves you, Evie. Probably more than anything in the world."

She loves me. I think of the other people who love me. Dad. Lizzie. Mary. Todd, maybe, a little. My eyes well up, and I curse bean for taking away the crying immunity I enjoyed for so many years.

"Oh, Evie-Teeny," Aunt Linda says, putting her hand on my knee then scooting over so she's right next to me. She fits her arm all the way around my shoulders, and I feel them tighten into ropes. "She does."

I shake my head.

"What is it, Evie?"

"Just . . . why are all the people who love me so bad at it?" I laugh when I say this, making it into a joke. I'm not even sure if I should include Aunt Linda on this list. She used to be the best at loving me, but living here I realize I don't have nearly as much of her heart as I always thought I did.

Aunt Linda doesn't laugh. She squeezes my shoulders tighter and says, "You really think Cecelia is bad at it?"

I think of her round face sticking out of the layers of sweatshirts and winter coats that Nora wraps her in before sending her off to preschool for the day. That face that now insists on one more Evie-kiss after breakfast, one before they walk out the door, one more when they get in the car. Is this what it's like to have a kid? A huge responsibility that loves you fiercely?

"Not Cecelia." To be fair, I add, "Or Tammy."

Aunt Linda smiles. "Okay. Now, as I was saying, you need to be working toward a decision here. You need to start putting plans in motion. You need to start loving that baby."

Fat chance of that.

"But you don't need to do it with me. We'll hire someone else to talk this out with you if that's what you need. But you do need to be talking. Talking and taking action."

Before I moved here, I never thought Aunt Linda and my mom had anything in common, but now I'm watching Aunt Linda slip in and out of her aunt role as suddenly as my mom puts on and takes off her lawyer mask.

"I'll talk to you." I hope we aren't at the point where we have to hire someone to care about me.

"Good." Aunt Linda leans over the coffee table with her pen. "I want you to do one more thing for me, though, Evie-Teeny. I'm not going to pressure you into it, but I don't want you to dismiss anything before really considering it. I want you to really think about adoption."

On one sheet of paper she writes: PARENT and on the other: ADOPTION. So she isn't going to take all sorts of hidden, cryptic notes: she's going to show me everything she writes down.

"Tell me why exactly parenting appeals to you over adoption?" Aunt Linda asks.

"They both seem like pretty bad ideas." I expect Aunt

Linda to laugh the way Mary did when I said something like this.

But Aunt Linda just says, "Actually, either of these ideas will work. Neither of them is a bad idea. That's why this is a hard decision."

I wait for what I know Mary's next question would be: Why? Why don't you want to parent? Why don't you want to give the baby up? Just the thought makes me itchy again and makes my stomach start bouncing around bean.

Aunt Linda says, "Let's say you do keep the baby. Where will you live?"

My heart quickens. Can we live here? Is that what she's saying? Do I even want that?

"Evie, you really need to start making a plan here."

I shift so my feet are pulled up on the couch, my thighs pushing directly into my big belly and probably squishing bean into my ribs or something.

Aunt Linda leans over, resting her cheek on my knee. "How uncomfortable are you on a scale of one to ten?"

"Ten," I squeak.

"Okay. Let's try this. Get through five questions today and we'll do five more tomorrow."

I nod. Aunt Linda holds one of the papers in each of her hands then puts her hands behind her back. "Pick one." I reach out and touch her left arm.

She pulls it in front of her. PARENT is written across the top.

"Okay," she says. "I'm going to keep asking you questions until we hit five we can answer, all right? We'll make this a game. We could even do it like we did Celie's potty training last year: should we give you an M&M every time you successfully answer a question?" Aunt Linda chuckles a little, but my face remains stony.

"No."

"Okay, here goes: if you keep this baby you're going to need help. Will your parents help?"

"Maybe."

"That doesn't count as an answer." I like that she's being my aunt and not some social worker, but this game is pretty stupid. "I'll try an easier question: will you ask your parents for help?"

"My mom, I guess. I'd ask my mom if I had to." If I can't ask Todd. Or you.

"Okay, that's one. You wouldn't ask your dad?" Aunt Linda looks genuinely surprised, as if my dad and I have been talking on the phone daily since I got here. She has no idea I've been ignoring him, which means, I realize, neither does my mom.

My dad left me. He left and then he came back as if everything could just be okay. As if we should have been waiting for him while he had some affair with our dentist. If he had stayed away, it would be forgivable—it would make sense. Or if he had given me a choice, offered to take me with him. Instead he was just gone. He fell out of love with my mom and then chained us all to that Silent House when he showed up again. No, Aunt Linda, I don't want bean anywhere near him. But my throat closes against all these words and instead I just say "no" again.

Aunt Linda writes: 1. ASK MOM FOR HELP.

"What about Todd?"

"You know about Todd?" Those words rush out of me like a pipe bursting open. His name feels too intimate in my mouth. I can't control anything. I am simultaneously holding myself back and spitting words all over everyone. I can't even control my mouth, and I'm supposed to grow up and control this baby in just a few months? It's impossible.

But Todd. I could do it with Todd. If we both got away from Jacksonville and we could create a little family . . .

"Your mom told me about him. He's your boyfriend, right?"

"No," I answer. "And that's two." Now is where Bad Evelyn finally climbs out of her shell and shows herself to Aunt Linda—stoned and drunk and naked. This is the part where my aunt who used to turn me into a burrito, who came to my rescue this year, who trusts me with her children—this is where she realizes that she never liked me to begin with. This is where I get kicked out again. This is where I really have nowhere else to go. This is where I lose the last person I have to talk to.

"Your mom said you were quite fond of him."

I nod.

"So what do you expect from him?"

"I don't know."

"Think, Evie. Would you ask him for help?"

I shut my eyes and picture him—running out of the locker room in his football uniform, passing me a beer in Sean's backyard, tearing into a sandwich with his teeth after bringing me an army's worth of food. Him naked underneath me, pulling at my legs and ass to get as close to me as possible. I try to remember what we used to say to each other. Can I ask him to think about helping me again? I try to imagine sitting down with him and his mom and Rick, working out a plan, because they would be darn good grandparents.

I can't see any of it.

But he shouldn't be off the hook. It's his mistake too.

I imagine telling him I'm taking him to court and the picture is really clear. I see his mom finding out after he gets served. She's crying rivers down her face, then forcing him to do the right thing. This makes sense.

But I can also see us living somewhere far away, just us two—three, I mean. I can see myself cooking for him and see us sitting next to each other at a dining room table with textbooks open between us, learning, loving, being in college.

"I would ask him for help," I say. And what will he say? What will he say?

Aunt Linda writes 3. ASK TODD FOR HELP. And I'm touched because she didn't even write number 2 on the list. So, even though I'm not sure about this, I add, "And if he says no, I'll get my mom to help me take him to court."

Aunt Linda widens her eyes. "Okay, I guess that answers the question as to where you'll live then."

What's she talking about? "I don't think I have much of a choice about that, actually."

"Evelyn, they both love you. You could live at either place."

Todd? Love me? She thinks I could live with Todd? I want this so much, I almost believe her, even though she's never met him.

"I don't know what's going on with you and your father,

but I do know he loves you no matter how he messed up. He would take you in, I'm sure."

"I'm going to have to live with him," I say.

"No . . . Evie . . . you . . ." Shock crosses Aunt Linda's face like a slow-motion slap. And then I get it too.

"He . . . he moved out again?" I ask.

"They didn't tell you?" she says.

Fuck. Fuck these tears.

"Hold on," Aunt Linda says. "We're calling your mom right now."

Fuck these fucking tears. "No!"

"Evie!" Aunt Linda calls, but I'm already running up the stairs.

I run to my desk and hit Reply.

So you finally got a clue and moved out, huh, Daddy? Finally set Mom free from the stupid Silent House? Congratulations. I hope you and your dentist live happily ever after.

Strangely, as soon as I hit Send, my tears are gone. All the anger seeps out my fingers and into my computer. I'm nothing but exhausted. I crash onto my bed and listen as Aunt Linda berates my mom on the phone downstairs. I know she is talking loudly so I can hear.

"Judy, she's seventeen almost. You really can't think you don't need to tell her this stuff . . . When . . . act like a family. . . . It is despicable to let her find out this way. . . . Yes, you should. . . . Yes, you do need to listen to this from your little sister, and another thing . . ."

But Aunt Linda doesn't get it. It's not my mom's fault. Mom doesn't talk. She doesn't know how. We never really talked. We just don't. It's not how we work. Of course Aunt Linda doesn't get it, her family is so filled with noise and talking and planning and cooking together and eating together and dishes together and homework together and playing together. That's not how we work, though. Besides, what was Mom supposed to do? Yesterday when we were on the phone was she just supposed to say, "And by the way, your father left again"? In the middle of asking me how I feel and how my grades are and how cold it is here, she's just supposed to throw that into a conversation? That's ridiculous.

No, it's all the Stranger's fault. Again.

But. I can picture my senior year now—living with my mom in that big house, which will be just as silent but not as creepy. And not as silent at all because the bean will be there, probably screaming because I have no idea what I'm doing. Maybe I won't get to move away to some romantic tiny apartment with Todd, but he'll come over and play with the baby and maybe sometimes I'll cook everyone dinner. And my mom will pay for someone to take care of bean while I'm in school. Life will go on, but with a baby in it. We'll just put up caution tape and avoid the Stranger's half of the hallway: that house is huge for just two—three—people anyway. We'll make the house smaller and just forget about him.

The weirder thing is that I can almost imagine the Stranger too: taking bean on a Sunday and showing up at his apartment downtown or wherever and letting him play grandpa while I drink tea or some stupid thing they do in real families. Maybe life will just move forward.

But he should have told me. He knows how to talk. It's not something you just forget.

"Do you want to live with me and Mom, beanie?" I ask my belly button. "How does that sound?"

I step down the stairs to the kitchen, where Aunt Linda is still having what she calls an "assertive" conversation with the phone. I know my mom is on the other end, rolling her eyes and trying to use as few words as possible to get Aunt Linda to hang up.

I put my hand out to show her I want the phone.

Aunt Linda stops in midsentence and puts it in my palm. "Linda?" Mom is saying. "I'm trying to consider your points, but I am still extremely disappointed in your decision to inform my daughter about the dissolving of her parents' marriage at a moment when she is extremely vulnerable and truly needs to focus elsewhere."

"It's me, Mom." I almost just call her Lawyer outright.

"Oh, Evelyn! I'm so sorry, Evelyn."

"I don't want to talk about it," I say, turning so I can't see Aunt Linda's reaction to that statement.

"Okay."

"I just want to know, can the baby and I come live with you for my senior year? Will you help me with the baby and, like, bills or whatever? Like, finding someone to take care of it while I'm in school?"

"Of course, my Evie! I'm so pleased to hear you've made a decision."

A decision. I didn't even realize that's what I was doing,

but it is. Three decisions down, who knows how many to go. The phone starts shaking in my hand so I push it back toward Aunt Linda and walk on unsteady knees up the stairs. I puke for the first time since the morning sickness ended, then lie down on my bed. "Well, bean, I hope you like us," I say.

Dads

Every morning I sit at my desk and reread the e-mail I know I need to send soon.

> Todd,
> I'm bringing your baby home. The baby and I are moving in with my mom, I guess. You're going to need to help. You are a dad. We need to talk. I think maybe you should call me.
> E

He keeps writing me stupid things about school and our classmates (whose lives seem so easy now) and basketball and Sean's parties and sometimes how he misses me, which is probably complete bull, but I hope not. I don't respond. I keep e-mailing Lizzie dumb questions about school and parties and her family and her dad. She doesn't usually respond. When she does she always reminds me how mad she is at me.

I imagine Todd reading the e-mail and immediately jumping for his phone, calling me and saying he'll help however he can until we can get away together. He'll say that he can get an after-school job, and I'll say he probably doesn't have to do that (because, let's face it, he probably doesn't). He just needs to come over and spend time with us every day. And he'll say he can't wait until he gets to see me every day again.

I know he told me I'd have to take him to court. But there's no way. Once he sees bean, once he realizes it's a real person, there's no way.

Still, it takes me weeks to actually send the e-mail. I send it the Friday morning that's two weeks before winter break, two and a half weeks before Christmas.

At lunch that day, I sit across from Maryellie and ask, "What do you think he'll say?" I make my face look nervous, but actually, I'm excited.

"What can he say?" Maryellie asks. "You're right. He needs to help."

I sigh.

"This is why I'm glad I only had sex with Mario." Mario, Maryellie's boyfriend and soon-to-be baby daddy, is a year out of high school and works in a gas station. Maryellie says they're going to move in together before she has the baby, but she's due in a month so that seems unlikely.

Although Maryellie is still my only friend at school, and she's no Lizzie, school is okay now. My brain wanders, so even though the curriculum—except for AP chem—is much easier than it was at St. Mary's, I still have trouble pulling Bs. But somehow I don't care. The rest of the girls mostly ignore me, but when they talk to me there's a softness in their voices that I've never heard before going to school here. The teachers, too, seem to really want me to be happy. Everyone is gentle with each other here. I don't walk around on eggshells. I don't refer to these classmates as jerks and boneheads, even in the privacy of my own brain.

"I only had sex with Todd," I reply to Maryellie.

Her eyebrows shoot toward her forehead and she shifts her butt around on the Plexiglas bench. "Really?" It's hard to fit the table between her gargantuan belly and my slightly swollen one.

"Don't sound so surprised!" I say and she laughs, and I love how easy it is to make her laugh like that.

"I just figured, because he's not your boyfriend, right?"

"No . . . it was complicated." I remember how few people know about this. I want to talk about him, but the words stick to my tongue. I don't know why: it's not like Maryellie is going to spread rumors about Todd and me at Saint Mary's.

"So why'd you do it with him?" she asks.

I remember Aunt Linda telling me that when you talk to people, you're giving a little bit of yourself to them. If I don't start talking, I'll stay alone forever.

"I was punishing my parents," I answer and laugh.

Maryellie nods like this makes perfect sense. "You did that well." We laugh again. "Hey, will you come to my baby shower on Sunday?" she says, and it surprises me. Maryellie has come over a bunch of times now to help me watch my cousins, but she's never invited me to her house.

"Yeah," I say. "Of course. Do I get to meet Mario?"

"At a baby shower?" she asks, laughing again. "No. It will just be me and my mom and my aunts and cousins and a few of the other girls." With each word the laughing leaves her voice more definitively. Finally she says, "You know, we don't have a big house or anything. It'll just be in my apartment."

I nod, although I have no idea where she lives. "I'll come. Thanks."

When I get home, Todd has not replied. He was always forgetting his phone at home, though. And he probably left for school before I sent the e-mail because it's an hour later in Florida. And he wouldn't be home yet because of basketball practice.

A question floats in the back of my brain—how is Todd going to come over to help with the baby after school if he's at practice all the time? Will he have to stop all those sports? Will he—? But I leave it there.

I'll take a nap before dinner and by the time I wake up, he'll have replied.

His face looms when I close my eyes and I think about him the way I do most often: naked and cuddled next to me. I imagine his football-player arms hoisting himself up, one hand planted on either side of my shoulders as he whispers how hot I look. In my fantasy, I flatten Bean out of my stomach, but I keep my boobs and legs just the way they are: curvy, full of texture so his hands can grab at my ass and actually take hold. He would always whisper "Is this okay?" right before he started. After, he settles his body behind me, our skin touching in every place possible and whispers questions about my life through my hair and into my ear.

Yeah, I know: sex was the problem.

I always make him put condoms on in these fantasies, even though, really, it's a fantasy. It can't make me more or less pregnant than I already am.

When I wake up it's dark and Nora is yelling up the stairs for me to come down and join them for dinner. I blink and rub my eyes, briefly looking at the pile of books on my desk that I will have to tackle later in the weekend. My door bursts open and Cecelia jumps onto my bed, covering my forehead in kisses.

"Dinnertime, Evie-Teeny!" she sings. "Dinnnnnertime! Dinnnnnertime!"

I hoist her onto my hip and swing my feet to the ground. I'm still in my skirt.

"How do you have so much energy, Little Cousin?" I ask her.

She squeezes her arms around my neck, and I wonder if bean will be this full of affection in four years.

"Evie, I don't think you should call me that anymore," she says. "I'm getting pretty big, you know."

I laugh and tilt my head back to look at her. "So what do you want me to call you?" I ask.

"I think I'm your Medium Cousin now." And when I burst into laughter I realize it's offending her so I suck it back in. It's nice to be sucking in laughter instead of tears.

"You got it," I tell her, slipping my feet into slippers and nuzzling my nose into her neck.

"And if he asks, will you tell Santa I've been good?"

"Good? You're the best medium girl I know!" I put her down and she scurries to the kitchen.

It's hard to imagine that I won't live here next year. If I could guarantee that bean would be just like Cecelia—affectionate, full of energy, always making noise—or even Tammy—contemplative, intelligent, and gentle—it would be easier to picture loving it.

I check my e-mail again after dinner and I talk my heart out of speeding up when he still hasn't replied.

To distract myself, I click on the Daily Dad Mail. I've replied to a few now—curt and nasty things that I need to shake out of my fingers so I can manage to fall asleep.

> Pumpkin—
> I need to see you. I'm not sure if they will have told you already, but I arranged with Linda to spend the Christmas holidays with you in Chicago.

Oh, hell no.

> Your mother and I both agree that I really need to come. Of course, she'll come too if you'd like to see her, but we'll leave that up to you. My coming is non-negotiable. We need to talk. I'm afraid you are very misinformed. I miss you terribly. I love you more than anything. I cannot let you disappear from me no matter what mistakes I've made or how hard you try.
> I arrive the morning of Christmas Eve. I know this might be a difficult holiday, but I am truly excited to see you regardless.
> Love, Dad

At the words Christmas Eve, I remember being Christmas Evie—my dad would spend the entire Christmas season every year until I was maybe ten coming up with a Christmas Evie outfit. On the morning of the twenty-fourth he'd put me in a white sweat suit and wrap me in red tape to make me a candy cane, or he'd cover an entire leotard in holly and dress me as a wreath, or he'd plaster me in pine needles and turn me into a tree. I was a Christmas cookie, a Christmas star, a Christmas present, a Christmas snowflake. But no matter the costume, he called me the Great Christmas Evie. Then we'd go out caroling, just the two of us, while Mom made soup for dinner. We'd go around our Jacksonville neighborhood and usually it wasn't even cold enough to need a coat yet and we'd ring the doorbells of all the neighbors and we'd scream Christmas carols into the night with absolutely no talent at all. The neighbors started expecting us; they'd show up on the porch saying, "It's the Christmas Evie!" and the best houses would give us hot chocolate or cookies. The Christmas Evie.

It's weird when you realize how easy it would be to make someone smile and you still don't want to. If I showed up at the airport on Christmas Eve in antlers or a Santa hat—even something that simple—I know he would see me and call out "The Christmas Evie!" and his eyes would light up even before they wander to my swollen middle.

It's almost tempting.

Except that I don't want the jerk to come here to begin with. The wimp. The fool. He can't torture Mom anymore, so he decides to show up in Chicago and ruin my Christmas—maybe the only one I'll ever have with Cecelia and

Tammy—and bean—all of us together? He has to come and interrupt Santa? He has to negate the fact that Nora and Aunt Linda have even asked for my input as to what Santa should bring the girls? He gets to watch their faces light up when I give them the princess dolls I bought at the mall—a pink dress for Celie and a purple one for Tammy, complete with glitter and a matching tiara for each little girl?

He gets to hear me call Cecelia "Medium" and he gets to see how Tammy follows me around and how I became Good Evelyn again as soon as I got away from him? I don't want him anywhere near here. How could none of them ask me about this? What's he going to do anyway? Where's he going to stay?

I run down the stairs and watch Nora for a minute, her eyes buried in a pile of legal papers in the family room. Aunt Linda is still at work.

"How come you didn't tell me?" I try not to sound completely pissed. Her eyes snap up.

"Tell you what?"

"That my dad is coming for Christmas."

Nora's eyebrows knit together. "You didn't know?"

"My dad just e-mailed me."

Nora sighs and puts her highlighter down. "I'm sorry, Evelyn. When he asked us today, I figured he had run it by you already."

"I don't want him anywhere near me." I hear the edge in my voice. Anger rattles my words the way it used to.

"We're going to have to talk to Linda about this, then," Nora says. "I'm sorry this is such a surprise, Evie. Did you take your vitamins tonight?"

How can she just change the subject like that?

I nod. "Where's he going to stay?"

"I don't know, sweetie. Is Tammy done with her math?"

"Yes," I say. *This is not Nora's fault. Don't get mad at Nora.* "Is he staying here?"

"Well, he's your father. It's hard to imagine that we wouldn't offer to put him up over Christmas."

Because he will ruin Christmas. I spin on my heel. Before I've reached the stairs, I turn back to Nora.

"Well, he can't stay down here," I say. "Because then the girls won't know how Santa got to the tree without waking him up."

I'm trying to sound as pissy as possible but Nora smiles. "Evelyn, I've come to truly love you over the past few months. I hope you know that."

I have no idea what to say to that, so I just disappear back up the stairs to check my e-mail. No reply.

3 Months, 23 Days Left

Todd still hasn't replied when I pull out a dress to wear to Maryellie's baby shower. It's burgundy and velvet and ugly but it's the only winter dress I have, and the only maternity dress I have, so I'm glad my mother bought it during that crazy shopping spree.

I climb into the car, telling myself that he will have replied when I get back.

When I trudge up two flights of stairs to step into the living room, crowded with about twenty women and girls sitting and standing and shifting in the door frames, I attempt to steel my face so no one can tell that I've never been in an apartment this small before. It makes Aunt Linda's house look like a castle. It makes my Silent House look like an entire country. How the hell is Maryellie going to raise a baby here? Where will she even fit a crib?

Even though my face is blank, an army of brown eyes rests on my pale nose. I've gotten so used to being the only white face in a room of females, I forgot it would be surprising to these aunts and cousins. Maryellie shouts my name from the shoe-box kitchen to the right, trilling the "l" as usual, and rushes in to plant a kiss on my cheek. Her mother wraps her arms around me, and it should make me miss Mrs. Gates but instead it opens up a cave deep in my heart that I know is the space my own dad used to fill.

We women sit in a circle and play games: we measure Maryellie's belly with toilet paper, we pass baby gifts, we bet on the birthday, we make up a poem for the baby's name: Emanuella. The whole time, Maryellie's mother keeps kissing her and hugging her and putting her hand on her stomach to feel Emanuella kick. The aunts pile compliments high onto Maryellie's belly. Her cousins shower her with gifts and offers to babysit. By the end of the party, I almost ask if bean can live in this crazy crowded apartment too. There's a lot more room for a baby here than in my giant house.

If you combined Maryellie's family with my family's resources, maybe raising a baby wouldn't seem so daunting.

When everyone starts leaving, I suck my breath in and give Maryellie's aunts and mother a kiss. My friend walks me out to my Jeep.

"Did he reply?" she asks.

I shake my head.

"Well, I've been thinking and it's probably going to take him a while, you know? He'll need to tell his parents and everything before he can figure out how to help."

She's right. I'll hear from him, but not for a while.

"I like your family," I say. "You're lucky."

She laughs. "We'd be luckier if I knew I could graduate, you know?"

My eyes go wide. "What do you mean? You might not graduate?"

"I don't know who's going to take Emanuella next year so I can go back to school. My mom has a job and Mario, who knows about him?"

"But you're an honors student. What's the point of all those APs?"

She says, "No, don't worry. I'll figure it out and graduate eventually." But I'm afraid she's just trying to quiet my concern.

She kisses me again, and I hoist my belly into the car. I'm really not sure which one of us has it easier.

Christmas Ev(i)e

I'm helping Cecelia and Tammy stir cookie dough, each of them taking ten turns to whip it together before they switch. It's sticky and thick and we aren't getting anywhere, but who cares. Cecelia was stirring it at first when the brattiest voice came from Tammy's little mouth: "That's not fair she stirs! I'm bigger!"

Bratty has never sounded so beautiful. Aunt Linda and Nora, who were two feet away dicing vegetables for the soup, both let their jaws drop along with mine while Cecelia just handed her sister the bowl of dough, saying, "Here, Tammy. We'll take turns."

Stirring this cookie dough is going to take more bicep than either of their little bodies have grown so far, but it doesn't matter. I pull the bowl from Cecelia and hand it to Tammy, who starts chopping the wood against the steel.

"Long, smooth strokes," I remind her, and the doorbell rings.

I'm almost surprised. I've lost myself in this little domestic moment. *This is my family*, I keep telling myself. Cecelia and Tammy and Aunt Linda and Nora. No Dad. No Mom. No bean. This is it. It's a fantasy, but it's what I have.

But Aunt Linda rinses her hands in the sink and walks to the door. He flew into O'Hare and rented a car. He got a hotel room, too, because Nora told him what I said about Santa Claus. I told Mom not to come. Two parents are always harder than one.

He walks in the door—my dad. His shoulders stoop so he seems a foot shorter than he should be. His dark hair is flecked with gray. The wrinkles around his eyes and mouth—which have been there as long as I can remember—have changed direction, each of them pointing directly to the floor. He looks older, even though it's only been a few months.

He reaches to shake Aunt Linda's hand as she opens her arms to hug him.

"For Pete's sake, Jim," she says, wrapping her arms around the outside of his biceps. "We lived together for years. I would think you could hug me." Even though he's hugging her, I feel his eyes on my inflated stomach, my boobs that actually need the bra I'm wearing, my thick legs in my jeans.

Nora approaches him and shakes his hand.

I don't even remember picking it up, but the steel bowl is in my grasp and my arm is whipping around the cookie dough, the spoon clanging back and forth in the bowl, making a satisfying racket.

"Girls," Nora says, "this is your uncle Jim."

That's all it takes for Cecelia to wrap herself around his

leg, pressing her ruddy cheek into his knee. The Stranger stiffens like she has a runny nose. He pats her braids.

"Well, hello. You must be Tammy."

"I'm Celie!" she shouts. Tammy, in fact, is peering at the scene from behind the door frame. She hides behind objects while I hide behind noise. *Clang, clang, clang* goes the spoon and the bowl. "What makes you my uncle?"

My dad looks speechless, so Nora leans over to pry Cecelia's hands from his leg, saying, "Well, you know that Evelyn is your cousin, and this is her daddy. Your cousin's daddy is your uncle."

Cecelia jumps onto Nora's leg and peers up at her. "So what's your cousin's mommy?"

"Your aunt," she says. "Evelyn's mother, Judy, is your aunt. And your Mommy Linda is Evelyn's aunt." *Clang, clang, clang.* I'm glad to have something to look at besides his old face.

"Well . . ." We all watch as the wheels in Cecelia's head turn and it does not escape me that he is still standing in the doorway. Not looking at me. Not even hearing the racket I'm making with the cookie dough. "Why doesn't she call you Aunt Nora then?"

Nora looks at me. "I don't know, sweetie. But if she wants to call me that, Evelyn should call me Aunt Nora."

I'm so surprised I stop slamming the spoon around and inspect the dough. It's ready. I feel my dad's eyes on me as I pull the spoon out and hand it to Cecelia. I take a second one from the drawer, dip it in the dough and hand it to Tammy around the door frame. He's still in the front door.

The girls lick their spoons. I start to put balls of dough on the cookie sheet.

"I know y'all have arrangements for dinner, but I'd like to take my daughter for lunch."

I feel all eyes swing to me. "No!" I want to say it. I want to scream it. I want to get in his face and tell him to leave. I want to just keep stirring dough and ignore him completely, not even dignifying his coming with a single word. But two of the eyes on me are Cecelia's, and I don't want to be Bad Evelyn in front of her. So I don't say anything while I hand Aunt Linda the bowl and cross the kitchen to the coat closet.

Is this what it means to have a kid? To have to do the right thing even when you'd rather throw a temper tantrum?

"Be back in time for dinner, okay?" Nora, or Aunt Nora, or whoever, says to me as if I'm off to some exciting social engagement, and I follow the Stranger outside and climb into the car.

He reaches and pats my back and smiles so huge I almost wish I had some reindeer antlers to pull out of my pocket and make him laugh, but I wish more that I was back in Aunt Linda's house helping Cecelia and Tammy form the dough into cookie shapes and teaching them to use a rolling pin and convincing myself that that is my real family and being right about it.

I know I need to talk to my dad eventually. Maybe I even want to. Maybe I even hope I'll forgive him one day. But I hate that he's making my one Christmas with my cousins so hard.

At lunch we are silent. This is pointless but at least I'm used to it.

He starts with the sitcom questions again: How are my grades? Am I being a good big cousin? Am I staying out of trouble? Have I made any friends? But away from the girls, I'm free to snub him. I could snub him for two straight days. It won't be that bad. I just wish that those two days weren't Christmas.

I'm halfway through my hamburger when he says, "Pumpkin, your mother left me."

I stop chewing.

"I'm not saying she lied to you. It seems to me that no one tells you enough of anything, or maybe that no one knows how much to tell you and how much to leave you alone because you have so much"—his eyes involuntarily jump to my stomach, then back to his plate—"going on yourself right now."

I stare at him.

"And I'm not saying it's not my fault. I'm not even saying it's not what I want. But you, Pumpkin, you are the most important person in my life. I can't stand the idea that you would think I'm leaving you or tearing your family—crappy as it may be—apart."

For some reason, the question my mouth forms is this: "So you're the one who still lives in the house?"

"No. I guess she kicked me out more than left me."

I don't know what to feel. "Did you cheat on her again?"

"No," he says. Then, "God, I'm so sorry."

Then you shouldn't have done it, jerkface.

"Look, Evelyn, this is not really your concern. Your parents' marriage, I mean. It's your business, but it's not your concern." He's stuttering. He's as nervous as I am right now. We're both not used to honesty anymore. "I mean, there is nothing you can do to control your parents' marriage. But we both love you. We both love you so much. That's why we lived like that for so long."

"But that was no good for me," I hear Talkative Evelyn say. The words feel like fresh water; they are coming from somewhere really pure in me, maybe from right where I keep bean, and I'm not saying them on purpose but not by accident either.

"I know," he says. "We messed up. We fucked everything up, Pumpkin. I'm so sorry. I loved your mother, but she got so sad and it just . . . it just was so sad for so long. I guess there's only so much sadness a person can take before she breaks. Or he breaks, I guess. But I don't want that to happen to you, Pumpkin. I'm so sorry."

I've never heard my father curse before. He seems like he might cry. I've never heard that before either.

I don't know what to do. I don't even know if I'm still mad at him or what.

So I pull two paper napkins into straight lines and tie them together, fanning out each side so it looks like a big bow. Then I stick it on my head and say, "Hey—look, Dad. I'm a Christmas Present for Christmas Evie."

But when he smiles so big I can see the fillings in his molars I put it back on the table and say, "I still don't want you to call me Pumpkin, though. Not yet."

He nods.

Making Plans

When I call Mom on Christmas, I can't help wishing she's here too. Not with Dad. I stand by that decision, especially now that they're getting divorced. But if she could be here separately . . . I wish she could also see how Tammy and Celie pull out the tiaras that come with the dolls and shove them right on their heads. I wish she could see me being good at something. Practicing.

I call her to give her a gift. The only one that will really matter.

I say, "Which room will we use for the nursery?"

She pauses a minute as if she can't believe I actually brought up part of the plan. She says, "I was thinking we would use the one between your room and my office. How does that sound?"

"Sounds good." I'm ready to keep planning, but I don't know what else to ask. I wonder what she's doing today. Probably sitting by herself with a bunch of legal briefs. It's so depressing. Which is my fault, I realize suddenly. When I told her not to come, I was only thinking about how hard Christmas would be for me. Maybe I should have thought about her too.

"Do you want to paint it?" she asks.

"Yeah, sure."

"What color?"

"I don't know." How do you decide that?

"Okay, Evelyn, don't get mad at me for asking this one, okay? Is it a boy or a girl?"

"I don't know. I keep telling them that I don't want to know."

She hesitates. "Okay, we'll paint it yellow. How's that?"

By the time we hang up, we've gone online and ordered a bassinet and a changing table and made plans for her to come to Chicago two weeks before I'm due to wait for the baby, which means she'll get to see how good I am with the girls after all.

3 Months, 1 Day Left

Chicago is so cold. The air bites my face if I just step outside to my car or the mailbox. I spend every second outside simultaneously apologizing to bean for the cold and wondering how, even as I am shivering, I can still be sweating pig-sized drops of perspiration from my armpits.

But we go out on New Year's Day anyway because the suburban zoo is having some sort of holiday party and Cecelia has been begging to go. The whole family goes. Aunt Linda, Nora, and I sip hot chocolate and herbal tea while the girls do different crafts at different habitats. And when we are all so frozen it feels like our limbs will never untangle themselves from our coats and one another's coats as we nuzzle up and snuggle together, we climb back into Aunt Linda's car and wait for it to warm up so we can go home. As the car purrs in the parking space, Cecilia climbs onto my lap to keep warm, her car seat empty for now. She curls up, resting her head right on my bump.

"Hi, baby," she says. "It's your big, big cousin, Cecelia."

And then, I feel it. It's not at all the same as when I thought the blob was bashing around in my insides trying to save its life. No. This doesn't feel haphazard or random or crashing. This feels like a foot kicking me from the inside out; it feels so exactly like what I would have thought it would feel. It makes tears come to my eyes.

And I know I'm not crazy either because Celie says, "It kicked me!"

"It did?" Aunt Linda and Nora whip their heads around to see me in the backseat. Tammy reaches her stubby arm across Cecelia and starts groping my stomach.

"Oh, Evie-Teeny!" Aunt Linda says, letting her own eyes fill up. "How exciting!" She reaches behind the driver's seat and grabs my hand.

I nod. I go with it. But that's not why I'm crying. I'm terrified. Terrified. The bean has a foot. There's a person in there, in me.

Aunt Linda whips out her cell phone and dials my mom. "Judy, your grandbaby just kicked! She just kicked!" Aunt Linda keeps forgetting that bean might be a boy. Sometimes I think she forgets there are penises in the world.

"Yeah, yeah, here you go," she says, and passes back the phone to me. I steel myself for my mother's stony reaction, but when she starts talking she's a blubbery mess too.

"Oh baby, my baby," she says. "Isn't it incredible?"

"Incredible," I repeat, leaving off the question mark. I don't know why I was such a disappointment when all that was in me was a pack of cells, but now that it's cells in the shape of a foot, it makes all these women cry with joy.

"Evelyn," my mom calls into the phone once she has pulled the weepiness out of her words. "I sent you a few links to some cribs I think you should consider. I want you to get back to me today, okay?"

I try to keep my rising heart rate out of my voice. "Sure, Mom."

Mary says stress can hurt the fetus, and so I'm sorry, bean, but I mean, you have a foot. I have to take care of your foot, and I have no idea what I'm doing.

As Nora straps Cecelia in her seat and Aunt Linda pulls out of the parking lot, I squeeze my eyes shut and imagine Todd standing behind me while I hold a purring, sleeping little baby in my arms. I take a deep breath. It's going to be okay.

I don't even see the e-mail right away when I get to my computer. Instead, I spend an hour looking at the cribs. I open up a picture of each and I imagine myself putting a baby in it. In my imagination, I look old. My arms are still swollen with baby pounds and my butt, when I bend to put down the baby, is still round. The baby is tiny. Then I watch myself lean over the side of a white crib, lowering what looks like a bundle of blankets onto a tiny mattress and *boom*, I drop it. I do it again with the next crib and it repeats and repeats. I've never heard of a parent who drops her kid but that's me. I'm going to be a terrible mother. Maybe it's because I *want* to drop it. It. This little person who is destroying my life from the inside out.

I switch to Todd. I imagine his football arms holding a baby over each crib. I see his back go taut with the effort to keep the baby balanced while putting it down. He manages to make contact with all six cribs.

What am I actually supposed to be looking for in these cribs anyway? I'm pretty sure I'm not just supposed to be imagining my baby daddy not dropping my future baby. What makes one crib better than the other? Who cares?

I close the link and see the e-mail. The subject line is just my name: EVELYN. It's sitting there bold and obvious in my inbox, this e-mail I've been waiting for forever, for days and weeks, and it was just sitting there all day. It says SENT: 3:33 A.M. It was there when I woke up and I just hadn't checked.

It says: TODD ARNOLD.

All of his letters spelled out like that sends shivers up my spine and stretches my lips into a smile.

I put my cursor on his name to open the e-mail, but I pause, remembering the way he smells like salt and Axe body spray, the way he always says "E" like he's happy to be saying it, the way he could chew and smile at the same time without even opening his mouth.

I felt like this baby was going to make me lose him, but it's actually going to tie him to me forever. My baby will always be half him, and half me. Our DNA is together forever, so we might as well be.

> E—
> I told you, I can't. I just can't. I hope you know I did think about it, but I just can't.
> Todd

I am such an idiot. What the hell am I doing? I curl under my blankets and allow myself to sleep through most of New Year's Day, my pillow wet from my stupid leaking eyes.

Aunt Linda sits on the side of my bed and rubs cold hands over my shoulders.

I roll over and look at her. Her face is painted with pity, and I don't know if I want it, even if it does mean she loves me.

"There's just too much going on for you, isn't there?" she says, and she gets it so completely it feels relaxing, like a foot rub or a hot bath. I sag into her arms.

"Your parents . . . you know, they should've let each other go a long time ago, if you ask me. I know you're blaming your dad, but maybe just don't blame either of them. Maybe think about how to make your relationships work in the future." So she has no idea what I'm upset about. Her palm is tracing big circles into my shoulder blades and I hate it because it's such a lie, her just rubbing my back like that, like she understands me, and then getting it so wrong. It makes my blood boil.

"Do you want to come down to dinner?"

I shake my head.

"If you aren't feeling up to it, I'll bring some up."

I nod, pretending I'm not the angriest person on the planet.

"Do you want to talk about it?"

I shake my head.

"Evelyn, please talk to someone. You don't need to talk to me, but talk to someone, baby. Don't just let this fester."

I do. I love Aunt Linda, so when she leaves my room, I force myself to pick up my cell and call Maryellie. She's not coming back to school after break because she's due on Friday. I don't know how it's possible, but that building of friendly, distant girls is going to be even lonelier without her.

I read Maryellie the e-mail three times. Finally, she says, "Yes, he can."

"What?"

"Yes, he can. He can do this. He needs to do this just as much as you do."

"What do I do?"

"I don't know. You make him. I mean, take him to court. Or just tell his mom."

Next thing I know, I'm using Aunt Linda's house phone to dial Mrs. Arnold three times. She answers each ring, but I hang up. She doesn't call back, thank God.

Then I make a pretend call. I actually pretend to hit the numbers to dial, and then, when she pretend answers, I say out loud, "Mrs. Arnold, I'm not sure if you will remember me, but I am acquainted with your son, Todd. In fact, Todd and I have been sexually involved for quite some time and he recently impregnated me. I am extending you the courtesy of a phone call so you can try to influence him to do the right thing before I need to go to the courts." Except this sounds too much like Lawyer Mom.

I say to the empty phone: "Your dumbass son screwed me and then he screwed me over and his bastard child will be here in three months and you better make that jerkoff son of yours pull it together and do the right thing or I'll have the courts skin his ass."

That sounds like Bad Evelyn, but I'm sure she won't get me what I want.

I hardly pay attention as my fingers start hitting the buttons again, and then a voice rings into the phone.

"Hello?"

"Hello? Mrs. Gates? Can I please speak to Lizzie?" I hope she doesn't ask me to call on her cell phone because I know Lizzie won't answer.

"Evelyn!" she says. "It is so nice to hear from you, honey. How is your aunt doing now anyway? Any better?" And I remember that this is all a secret. If I could just find some way for it to go away, no one would know. I could go back to normal Bad Girl/Honor Student. I don't need to torture myself.

But I deserve this torture. Except the part that's Todd's fault, it's all my fault.

If there's going to be some baby torturing me, it's going to torture Todd too.

"She's doing better, but I'm going to be here the rest of the year," I am saying. "Can I speak to Lizzie, please?" I hear all the kids yelling in the background. With a jolt to my heart, I recognize Lizzie's voice and I realize that if Mrs. Gates comes back and says Lizzie isn't there, I'll know it's a lie and that will hurt terribly.

"Of course, she'll be so glad you got your phone privileges back. Lizzie?"

She gets on the phone yelling, "Hang up, Mom!"

When we hear the click she says, "What? What do you want, Evelyn?"

I shrug even though she can't see that through the phone.

"I hope you know the only reason I even came to the phone is that I'm telling everyone as little as I possibly can about our fight so they don't end up suspecting the truth."

"What truth?" I ask.

"That you're pregnant, duh," she says, and it strikes me

funny. She's too mad at me to reply to e-mails or call, but she still goes out of her way to keep my secrets.

"So . . ." I can hear the impatience in her voice but I also know it's the kind that she's putting there on purpose, her pride blocking out what's underneath: the part of her that's happy to hear from me. My words almost lock up in my throat, but if that happens, I'll lose her for sure.

"Should I call Mrs. Arnold and tell her about the baby? Todd is saying he won't help me at all."

Lizzie hesitates. "Guys suck," she says finally.

I have no idea what to say, but what comes out is "But I'm going to need some help." I won't tell her everything. I won't tell her about the daydream where Todd and I live in an apartment in California and cook homemade pizza for each other, even though it's so close I can almost smell the dough rising. If I can just get Todd's mother to talk some sense into him, maybe. Maybe.

There's a catch in Lizzie's voice. "Evelyn, don't you realize that if you bring home a baby, everyone's going to know you were pregnant before and that's why you left?"

"I guess."

"And if you make Todd help you—not that you shouldn't— but if you do, everyone will know that you were having sex with him."

"I guess I just don't really care anymore."

"Then there was no point in you going away?"

Lizzie misses me. Maybe that's even part of why she's mad.

"Well, I don't know. I'm glad no one has to see me so fat."

"Oh my God!" she squeals, forgetting herself. "What do you look like?"

"There's an entire watermelon under my shirt. But on the bright side, I actually have some boobs!"

When she laughs, it sounds like music.

"Okay," she says, "I'm finally going to tell you. You'll never believe it. I found my birth certificate." I pull the phone back and look at it. The nonsequitur throws me off balance.

"And?" I ask.

"It had his name on it: Joseph Appleton-Smith." Her father. My eyes go wide. I wish she could see them.

"So what's next?"

"I already looked it up . . . he has a LinkedIn page. Bethany is making up a fake one so we can try to see where he lives and works."

"Wow. Then what?"

"I don't know. I'll keep you posted."

Yes! "So are we friends again?"

"I'm still mad," Lizzie says, without even hesitating. "But I'll think of something big you can do to make it up to me and then we'll be all good."

"I'll do anything," I say. "So, before that, can you tell me what you think I should do about Todd?"

"Evelyn," she says, and I hear the way her heart is breaking for me in each syllable. "I don't know if I should tell you this."

"Tell me what?"

"He's—Todd—he's going out with Amber Sallisbury."

Crash. Boom. Bang.

My heart falls past bean all the way to my knees.

"How do you know?"

"He . . . he was kissing her. Like, at school. And, I don't know, she told me."

"You *talked* to her?"

"I almost *slapped* her, Ev. Really. Only I couldn't because no one knows about you two. No one even knows you're pregnant. Everyone thinks you're taking care of your tragically ill aunt."

"No one knows I'm pregnant."

"When I couldn't slap her, I went to slap Todd. He said you were giving him the silent treatment, anyway," Lizzie says and I don't know how to explain it. Why did I even do that? "You know," she continues, "he should still have to help you. He doesn't get off scot-free just because he's dating someone or because he doesn't have a vagina. It's trashy anyway, to date someone while you got someone else pregnant."

I'm finally having a real conversation with Lizzie again, and I end up feeling like a piece of crap anyway.

That night, once I go unconscious, I'm back in the blue circle. It doesn't *whoosh*. It just gets smaller and smaller until it is only a ring around my pregnant belly. When it turns on, my skin pops off like a shell and a million electric-blue kidney beans spill out. Then my skin fits itself back on and I'm standing in my old room, exactly like I was before—no belly, no boobs, all bones.

My eyes pop open.

Just like before. That's all I want now. And the baby kicks and kicks at my insides until I finally fall back asleep.

Faking It

For three weeks I pretend my way through life. I go shopping with Maryellie right before her due date and we pick out a pink, frilly outfit for her to take her baby home from the hospital. I pick out a crib with my mom and let her pay hundreds of dollars for it. I make a lists of names with Aunt Linda. Now that I know it's really over, now that I'm really alone, I can do all this stuff. Beatrice for a girl, I say. Benjamin for a boy. I like names that start with B because right now it's bean.

Maybe I can do it. Maybe I won't be awful at this.

Maybe I can take Todd to court to make him be a dad.

Maybe I can be happy living with my mom if my dad's not there. Or with my dad without my mom.

Maybe I can go to school and put bean in day care and get home every day to the bottles and the diapers and whatever else there is.

Maybe I can just forget about college and be happy being a mom.

Maybe I can love bean.

So I don't say anything. If I tell Aunt Linda or my mom that behind every thought and every conversation I want to give this thing away, then I will have to give it away. I keep tying up my lips and wandering around in a daze filled with babies and my mother's mask and Amber Sallisbury's cheerful laughing.

At my six-month ultrasound, I shiver when the tech smears the goop all over the mound that used to be my stomach and squeeze my eyes shut. Aunt Linda is supposed to be here with me, but there was some emergency with some other girl at school, so I wind up driving myself here alone. It's good, I tell myself. Aunt Linda would want to talk all about why I keep shutting my eyes when bean appears on the little screen, and I'm done talking. No more Talkative Evelyn. I'm sick of her. I talked and talked. Since I got to Chicago, I've said more words than I have in my whole life, and it got me nothing: no Todd, no valedictorian, no family. I feel homeless now. It's good I'm here alone. I told Aunt Linda I didn't care; it's not like an ultrasound would hurt. And it doesn't hurt. It doesn't.

A few times I forget, open my eyes and glance at the screen. Bean floats there, a translucent outline, in almost the same blue from my dreams. Through my eyelashes, I catch the outline of a nose; a mouth opening and closing, a hand curled by its chin. I squeeze my eyes shut.

"Do you want to know the gender?"

"You can see its gender?" At my last ultrasound, they said the picture was too blurry, bean's position too twisted.

"Yup!" Her voice bubbles with excitement. "You want to know the gender?"

What is she so chipper for anyway? She doesn't even

know me. Why would she be excited to know the gender of something that's living inside me?

And I'm thinking about how even though sometimes I call this thing "bean," I still call it "it." Bean is a thing. Once it has a gender, it will be a person. No one calls anything with a gender "it."

"Do you want to know the gender of your baby?" she asks one more time, her voice about to spill rainbows and butter-flies all over the ultrasound machine.

"It's not my baby."

She doesn't say anything else as she shuts the machines down and hands me a tissue to wipe off.

The fog in my head is thick as I wander to my car through the chilly day, hear the phone ring, reach for it through the nothingness.

It's Maryellie.

"Emanuella is here! She's here! Come and meet her."

I shake some clouds out of my brain and do a U-turn on the road, following my Jeep's GPS back into the city. I call Nora from the parking lot and walk into the hospital, still in a daze.

First, I walk past a bed where a woman holds a baby to her breast, cooing to it so gently you almost can't tell the woman is crying. There's a white curtain hanging from the ceiling separating this woman's side of the room from Mary-ellie's, and the outline of all the people surrounding her with chatter and whoops for joy shines through the sheet.

This is the side of the room where I belong. The lonely side.

"Evelyn!" Maryellie exclaims when I push my way through the curtain and into the crowd.

Maryellie is propped up in her bed, her long dark hair

loose and crinkly over her shoulders. I've never seen it down before. Her mother sits on her bed, holding her hand, and talking a mile a minute in Spanish to two aunts who are in a corner by the window. Rosie and Lelani from school are on the other side, still in their uniforms.

I scan the room so full of women looking for the baby.

"She's right behind you," Maryellie says, and I turn.

Mario sits in a chair tucked into the corner, curled over the bundle in his arms like a cocoon. He mumbles such soft Spanish it could put me to sleep. His thumb strokes her cheek.

"*Mi amor, mi amor, mi amor*," he says, over and over again, even though it's clear she's sleeping.

"Wash your hands and sit down on the bottom of the bed, Evie. And you can hold her." Maryellie is smiling, but she still looks all pregnant.

Mario gives me a look—it's not exactly nasty, but it's clear he doesn't want to let her go.

And then she's in my arms. She's surprisingly warm and surprisingly alive. My forearms feel it when her little body takes in and lets out air. And her mouth opens in little sighs. She smells like powdery flowers and her head is covered in a fluff of dark hair. Her little fist keeps coming free of her blanket and running the length of her face. Every time that happens, Maryellie's mother stands and tucks it back into the blanket, and I think about how I don't even know how to do that.

I think about seeing Mario bent over her like that and how Todd will never bend over bean and tell it he loves it in any language.

Can I even tell bean I love it?

The next time I'm sitting in a hospital holding something this small and this alive, I'll be alone.

Why did I need anything to change, anyway? What was wrong with the way things were—a house where I knew I lived, even if it was always silent; a boy to sleep with and talk to, even if he wasn't my boyfriend; a best friend to listen to, even if she got mad at me for keeping secrets. And the other stuff I had too—doing well in school, even if I had to quit track; getting invited to all the parties, even if it meant drinking too much. Why did anything need to change to begin with?

I won't be happy like Maryellie is when bean is born. All I want is to get this thing out of me and run away from it so everything can go back to normal, back to the way it was before.

Mario stands and takes Emanuella back, and when Maryellie is saying "Don't you just love her?" I'm already mumbling congratulations and wandering out the door, past the lonely woman, ignoring the fact that my body already misses Emanuella's little weight and warmth in my arms.

On the way home, I call Todd.

"E!" he answers, surprised. But I don't let him talk.

"This is your last chance."

"Last chance for what?"

"This is your last chance to do anything right. You know it's your fault that my life is over now and there's not a single thing you will do about it. Not a fucking thing. All you do is screw Amber Sallisbury and pretend like you're a hotshot. I've had enough of your shit."

"Evelyn."

"No. You're not talking. You're listening. You better be fucking glad I'm not keeping this baby because if I was, I'd be calling your mom or Amber or both and telling them exactly who you are, you stupid, fake bastard. You know I loved you. And you just screwed me over."

"Evelyn," he says, and my name just hangs there like a dirty sheet abandoned on a clothesline.

"What? Do you have anything to say?"

"You aren't keeping the baby? What are you going to do with it?"

I hang up.

When I get home, I slam the front door harder than I mean to, and Aunt Linda comes rushing into the kitchen. "Evie-Teeny? You okay?"

"I don't want to do this, Aunt Linda. I'm done." Those stupid tears paint my face pathetic.

"Oh, sweetie." She puts her arms around me. "You've barely begun."

"No, I'm done. I'm going to get this thing out of me, give it away, go to Jacksonville, and let everything go back to normal."

Aunt Linda starts to make those circles on my shoulder blades again. "It's not going to work like that, Evie-Teeny. It's just not."

I pull away so I can face her. "Listen, Aunt Linda. I don't want it anymore. I'm done."

She puts me back into her arms and sways me from side to side. "Okay. If you're sure, Evie, okay. But nothing's ever going to be the same anyway."

But she's wrong about that. She has to be.

Done Means Done

Aunt Linda starts bombarding me with adoption information. I refuse to look at it.

My mom calls to try to get me to think about it. I hang up.

Aunt Linda resorts to shoving bits of any idea into every conversation imaginable: different agencies, different kinds of families, different visitation rights. I keep walking away. She pulls a Mary and starts leaving pamphlets everywhere I'm sure to see them—at the sink when it's time for me to do dishes, on the kitchen table at breakfast, even in my bed. I could call an agency that specializes in Catholic families, or one for gay couples who want to be parents, or one for open-minded families. I could choose a family that already has some kids or a family that doesn't have any. I could choose a family that lives in Chicago, or a family from Florida that would have to come all the way up here when I go into labor. Or I could choose a family from somewhere else completely.

I open a pamphlet with glossy pictures of smiling babies and young, beautiful, upper-class parents of all races and sexual orientations, and I just look at them until I feel my heart start to race and then I put them down. I pick up a school book and take deep breaths until everything evens out.

How is anyone supposed to decide this anyway? I'm supposed to interview people and meet with them and let them reimburse all my medical bills. And Mom says to go with a Catholic family and Aunt Linda wants me to choose a gay couple, I'm sure, and Dad says I need to make sure they love each other when I go meet them and I keep hanging up or walking away from conversations because I just can't do it. I just want to be done with it and have everything go back to normal.

I call Lizzie.

"Just let your aunt Linda decide," she says.

"Can I really do that? Is it, like, legal?"

"How would anyone know?" Lizzie asks.

I think about it. I don't know if Aunt Linda would do that, but if I just refuse to do anything about it, she'd have to.

"So when's your spring break?" Lizzie asks.

"The third week in March," I say.

"Good! I'm coming."

"What?" She shoves me so fast into another conversation topic it feels like rolling down a hill.

"Yeah, I'm coming, and you're going to drive me around. This is how you're going to make it up to me that you were such a bad friend."

That's it? Drive her around Chicago during spring break? Let her visit me?

"Um, okay. When are you coming?"

"I'm booking my ticket right now. You're not going to believe this, but my dad, he lives in Chicago. We're going to find him."

"Oh." Can I tell Lizzie that I barely know my way around Chicago or that I'm not sure if my aunts will be okay with her coming or that I'll be so huge by March I won't want to go anywhere or that I don't want her to see me this pregnant or that I don't want to make any plans at all until I'm done with this thing and I can go back to my normal life in Jacksonville?

But she hears all the hesitancy in my voice. "You have to do this for me, Ev. You have to."

And I know I do.

All These Parents

"I want you to do it," I tell Aunt Linda while we do the dishes.

Her eyes go wide. "Oh, Evelyn. I don't think we can. We have our hands full with these two and that would just be . . . I mean . . ."

"No!" I interrupt. Although if Aunt Linda and Nora just took bean, I'd always know it was okay. I know they would love it and I know it would grow up safe and educated and healthy. Unless it wasn't healthy. Unless it gets leukemia or something and then I wouldn't want to know that. Or if that day I got drunk right after I found out means it's born with fetal alcohol whatever like I read about in Mary's dumb pamphlets, I wouldn't want to know that either. And then when it finds out that its cousin is actually its mom. That would just not be fair. We wouldn't go back to normal that way.

"I mean, I want you to decide on the family."

Aunt Linda looks even more surprised. "But, Evelyn,

these people are going to be in your life forever. Don't you want to decide who they are?"

"What do you mean they're going to be in my life forever? Your parents aren't in your life," I spit back.

Aunt Linda nods. "My biological parents were in a different situation. They live somewhere in impoverished China. Since the resources are available to you, I thought you'd want an open adoption."

I know I should know what an open adoption is by now. I know Aunt Linda is trying to do everything for me and I'm just closing myself off. I know I suck. "What does that even mean?"

I can hear all the research Aunt Linda did for me and all the ways she tried to make my life easier the past few months in her sigh. "It can mean a lot of things. It can mean you get pictures and yearly updates on how your baby is doing. It can mean you visit or you're legally allowed to visit a certain amount." Even as she's talking, I'm shaking my head.

"I just want everything to go back to normal."

"Evie-Teeny, that's not going to happen."

Yes, it is. "I want a closed adoption."

"I'm not sure you do. I'm not sure you're really thinking anymore."

"I want a closed adoption, and I want you to handle it."

"I don't think I can find a family for you, sweetie."

"Then I'll ask my mom. Or my dad." I didn't even realize this plan was wedged into the back of my head. "But I trust you more. And I'm not doing it." I'm exactly like Todd. If he gets off scot-free, then so do I. Even if that means I have to hate myself as much as I hate him.

Aunt Linda just stares at me, her hands frozen in the soapy sink. I'm like a little kid holding my breath until I get my way. I'm crazy; my brain is swimming with questions about open adoptions and the right way to do this, but I'm not inside my brain right now.

"They'd do it for me. Either one. The second I ask."

She nods. "I know they would. I'll call them. The four of us will do it together."

2 Months, 10 Days
Till Normal

I go back to ignoring the bean in my belly. I mean, I'm still eating right and going to the doctor and swallowing those crazy-huge vitamins, but I think about school. I come home after my last class and log hours of homework. I open books at lunch because Maryellie isn't there anyway.

When Aunt Nora shows me my third-quarter report card, my Bs have all pulled themselves into pointy As.

"This is impressive, Evelyn."

I shrug, but I let myself smile. I'll go to college, and no one will know this happened to me.

Cecelia catapults herself into my room and slams her little body onto my lap.

"Congratulations on your reporter card." She nuzzles into my neck.

Then she starts bouncing, her knees in my lap, her little palms right on bean.

"Medium, you have to be careful," I say, taking her hands in mine. "Remember, there's a baby in there."

"When's the baby coming?" Tammy asks, and I jump. I hadn't even seen her hovering in the doorway. Nora watches from a few feet away, her eyes on the top of our heads.

"April."

"Is she going to live here?" Tammy asks.

"No." I have no idea how to explain this to a four-year-old and a six-year-old who are themselves adopted. "It's going to live with its own family, just like you live with your mommies and they are your family."

Cecelia starts bouncing again, her braids flying across her face, ignoring Tammy's questions.

"Will the baby look like you and Mommy Nora or like Mommy Linda or like Cecelia and me?"

"Well." I stall, motioning for Tammy to come closer so I can put my hands on her shoulders over Cecelia's little body. "I think the baby will look like me, but I don't know."

"Will me and Cecelia get to meet the baby?"

I shake my head. "I'm not sure, but I don't think so."

"And once you have the baby, are you leaving?"

So there's the real question. "No, I'm here until the summer. Right, Nora?" I look at her for backup.

"If that's what you want, Evelyn, you got it."

"After you leave, when will you come back?" Tammy asks. "I need you for my math homework."

I look at Nora. "I'll visit."

Tammy runs away and Nora runs after her. But it's not my fault I'm leaving, Tammy.

After the girls and Nora have cleared out of my room, after we've eaten family dinner and I've done the dishes, after Tammy's math is complete and packed away for tomorrow, after my own homework is done and sitting in a folder on my desk, my mom calls.

"We think we found them," she says, and I know she means the family for bean but I don't care. Or at least, I'm trying not to care.

"Okay," I say.

"Your aunts met them last week but they wanted me to tell you. We're hoping this is it, but the final decision is yours. We're all going to meet them during your spring break. Your father and I will fly out."

"Not me."

"I think you have to, Evelyn."

"Lizzie's going to be here for break."

She answers like that's no big deal. "Lizzie will understand if you have to go somewhere for one afternoon. You need to do this, Evelyn. I'm not sure you'll forgive yourself if you don't."

"I'm not going." A tiny part of my heart detaches and flies around my rib cage, reminding the rest of me that I haven't even thought about it. It's a mistake, but I ignore that little part and say, "I don't think you and Dad need to come all the way out here anyway. Aunt Linda and Nora already met them. They have to be fine. I trust Aunt Linda."

"I'm going to give you some time to think about this," Mom says, even though I already decided. "You also need to start thinking about with whom you would like to live when you return to Jacksonville." Full lawyer mode.

"I just want everything to go back to normal, Mom."

She laughs the lawyer laugh that makes even my huge pregnant body feel puny. "What is normal, Evelyn?"

1 Month, 17 Days
Till Normal

A few days later, I call Lizzie.

"Do you think I need to meet this family?"

She laughs. "I mean, combining your mother, your father who is now heartbroken by her, and your crazy aunt . . . they must have come up with the best possibility, right?" She says it like a joke, but I actually believe it.

"I don't want to go meet them."

"Why not?"

"I just . . . I don't want to know who they are. I want to be far away. I want everything to go back to normal."

"Not me," Lizzie says. "I'm hoping everything changes when I meet my dad. Maybe he'll be rich and give me lots of big presents. There are rich people in Chicago, right?"

"Yeah, rich people and poor people." Lizzie is crazy to think her dad wants her stalking him and finding him this way after all this time, but I can't say that. I have to do this for her.

"What do you think he'll say when he sees me?"

I pause, still thinking of bean and the strangers, real strangers, raising it and all that. Maybe I should just keep bean myself. Whenever I think about bean just out there in the world, I get so worried. But if I don't think about it, it seems okay to just go through labor and send it on its way. With strangers. I could meet them, but if I do, then won't I be worried forever?

"I think he'll be surprised."

"Good surprised or bad surprised?" she presses, not bothering to squelch the excitement lacing her voice.

Bad, I think. But I give her what she wants. "You're the amazing Lizzie. Good surprised, of course."

1 Month, 10 Days
Till Normal

Maryellie finally comes back to school in March, having found day care she can afford. I start driving her home after school—now that I know where she lives—because the bus takes too long and she wants to get back to Emanuella as quickly as possible.

"I can't believe you're going to go through all this and let someone else watch it grow up," she says, but I see the dark circles lining her eyes, I hear her complaining about gross diapers, and even though Mario is still working at the gas station, it doesn't look like Maryellie is moving out of that crowded apartment anytime soon.

I know I have things that she doesn't—money, parents who will buy cribs and pay for day care. But if I had to decide between our resources, I'd choose hers—a baby daddy who loves the baby, a mom who can't stop hugging. She'd probably choose mine.

"I'm serious!" she says, seeing the doubt in my eyes. "I'd

give up everything for Emanuella now. She's the happiest thing to happen to me."

I shake my head.

"Well, it would be even happier if she happened a decade from now," Maryellie admits with a bashful shrug. "But now that she's here, I couldn't stand to have her be somewhere else. I just wish Mario would help take care of her more."

"You're going to go to college, right?" I ask. I'm still not completely used to the way this is not an obvious outcome at SMHS.

"Community college, maybe." Maryellie shrugs. "For a while."

"Maryellie, you're in AP chem."

She nods. "I just can't imagine spending four years focused on studying more than Emanuella. I'm going to graduate, though, don't worry." I lower my eyebrows. "Oh, I don't know," she says. "Maybe Loyola or DePaul will let me go part time or something."

She's playing with her fingers, and I feel bad for pushing, like Lizzie, so I say, "Aunt Linda and my parents want me to go with the three of them to meet the baby's family next week."

"Oh, good," Maryellie says, still looking out the window.

I laugh. "No, Maryellie. I'm not going."

"Evelyn." She puts her hands on my right bicep, even though I'm driving. "You have to go. You have to meet them."

"Why?" I ask, eyebrows still lowered.

"What if you hate them? They're going to be your baby's parents," she says.

"No, I don't think so. I'm not like you. I don't need to know anything about them."

"Evelyn, you have to go," she says again.

I feel the tears coming back, those stupid tears. I pull over, shoulders shaking. My entire eyeballs turn into liquid and spill into my lap in big, goopy globs. I'm trying to tell Maryellie that I'm sorry for the delay because I know she wants to get home to Emanuella, but I can't even get words out between all the goop running out of my eyes and nostrils and all over my face.

I feel a tissue dabbing at my nose. I can't believe she actually just wiped my snot.

The tears slow down enough that I can look at her. "I just need everything to go back to the way it was before I got pregnant."

She reaches out and takes another swipe under my nose. She's so motherly right now, as if going through labor actually turns you into a mother.

"But wouldn't that mean your parents would have to be together?"

"Well, besides that." Because I can't control that.

"And would that mean you're sleeping with Todd?"

"Well, not that either. Screw him," I say, and I win a little laugh out of her.

"But you see, not everything is going to go back. I don't think you're actually going to be able to forget this baby."

"I can't do it, Maryellie. I'm not like you."

"I'm not saying you should raise it, but I really think you should meet them." The words hang like a curtain between us until I pull back into the driving lane and drive her home. She's right. That's why I'm crying. But I just can't.

1 Month Till Normal

Chicago is still cold, but the air loses its teeth. You can walk out the door without immediately hugging yourself and holding your breath so you don't get cold from the inside as well as the outside.

Lizzie starts calling me every day before she comes. Her bouncing words fill the space between my ears with plans to explore Chicago and stalk her absentee dad. Adrenaline races through my veins every time I see her name on my phone and I imagine it makes bean smile as well.

"You'd like her if you met her, bean," I tell it in the moments I forget I'm ignoring it.

A week before she's due to arrive, she says "Okay, let's go through the plan day by day."

"Okay," I say. I've started looking forward to her visit. Without school for the week, it would be much harder to ignore bean without her around.

"So I arrive Friday night. I don't think we should go

looking for him right away, do you? Maybe I'll just meet your little cousins that night? We can all watch a Disney movie or something."

"Or something. Remember that I'm not telling any of these parents that we're really spending our break stalking a middle-aged man neither of us has ever met, for obvious reasons. We're going to have to come up with two plans— our real plan and our cover plan."

"Yeah, okay, good idea," Lizzie says. "So Friday we'll just hang out at your place. And Saturday, I guess we can't really do anything because you have your thing, right?"

"What thing?"

"I ran into your mom in Publix yesterday. She said y'all have to meet the baby's new parents on Saturday. Oh my God, do you want me to go with you to that? That would make so much sense: you help me find my dad, I help you find your baby's new dad and mom."

"No! I'm not going to that."

"What do you mean you're not going to that?"

"I'm not going. I told them and you and everyone I'm done making all these decisions. Aunt Linda picked the people. I'm sure they're fine. I don't want to meet them."

After a long time, Lizzie says, "I really think you should meet them, Ev."

My God, not Lizzie. "Why would I want to meet them? All that will do is turn this thing into a real person."

"It's a person anyway. Don't you want to make sure they're not crazy?"

"They're not. Let's start the hunt on Saturday while all those parents are away at that meeting."

Lizzie laughs. "How do you suddenly have parents coming out your ass?"

"I don't know!" I join in, and we're both laughing. "Apparently all it takes to find your parents is to get pregnant."

"If that's how it is, I better have a lot of sex before next Saturday."

We let the fact that she told me to go to the meeting disappear. We talk about shopping on Michigan Avenue and whether or not Lizzie will get to see snow. We talk about sneaking into a club, even though I won't drink and I look like a hippo and it sounds terrible, but I'll do it if she wants to. It's a relief to have her in my life again.

Twenty minutes go by before she says, "You know it's okay with me if you go to that meeting, right? Like, don't skip it just 'cause I'm there and I said this is how you make it up to me."

"Lizzie, I'm not going."

"I really think you should, though."

Lizzie's not saying that I should meet bean's parents so bean isn't like her one day—searching for any clue of who Todd and I were and are, wondering all the time why we disappeared. But I know that's what she's thinking.

When we hang up all of their voices swim in my mind: Lizzie's, Mom's, Dad's, Aunt Linda's, Aunt Nora's, Maryellie's. *It won't go back to normal ever. It is a real person. Think about open adoption. Meet these people. You need to meet these people. You won't be able to forget about this baby.*

But the thing inside me is just as much a stranger as the people who will raise it.

I can't stand it, so I'm ending it.

As I'm shuffling through Aunt Linda's papers in her night-table drawer, my heart hammers Morse code in my brain: this is a mistake. As I'm pulling out the driveway heading toward the address on the envelope, the mistakeness of it grows, ready to stop my pulse. My elbows go stiff as I make the turns and sit through the traffic into downtown. Even though the freeze is out of the air, my hands shake when I accept the stub at the parking garage. My stomach is trying to climb past bean and into my mouth when I finally step out of the elevator and push the door open to the agency.

This is a mistake.

I enter the office for Marcia Cooper. "My name is Evelyn Jones," I say. "My aunt Linda and my mom and my dad have been working with you to place my baby for adoption."

She nods. Behind her eyes I see that she's afraid I'm about to take the baby back.

"I'm ready to sign these papers."

It's that easy. Bean isn't mine anymore.

I cry the whole way home, but it's just relief rushing out of my eyes.

Right?

I don't tell anyone but Lizzie by text: *I signed the papers. Baby is adopted. I'm all yours next week.*

Waiting

It will be the worst explosion ever. There will be four adults yelling. And they will be yelling about me. At me. And I guess I know that in some way, they'll all be right.

24 Days Till Normal

Wednesday, when I'm refilling Cecelia's milk at dinner, Aunt Linda slams open the front door, making Tammy hide behind her hands.

"What is this, Evelyn?" She waves around an envelope. "You tell me, what is this?" She isn't yelling, but she's using a scary voice, like the voice of a very calm murderer on a movie.

"Baby, calm down," Nora says.

"Tell her, Evelyn. You tell her and then you can call your parents and you can tell them. Tell her what you did."

Nora's eyes go wide and she turns to me. My eyes are on my plate.

"What did you do?" Nora asks

I shake my head.

"Tell her!" Now Aunt Linda yells.

"Linda, let's . . . come on, girls, I'll let you watch *The Little Mermaid*," Nora says, but Tammy is already in the other room. Cecelia follows Nora, and I hear the volume go up.

Aunt Linda is standing above me, daggers in her eyes, flames shooting out her nose. Nora comes back.

"Linda, this isn't like you. What's going on?"

"Tell her what you did!" Aunt Linda yells and I feel my body betraying me yet again with tears. One fat, salty drop rolling down my cheek.

"I signed the papers," I whisper.

Nora sits and holds my hand. She must have no idea what's going on.

"What papers? Linda, please just tell me."

"You're going to have to tell your parents, Evelyn," Aunt Linda says, back to her calm-murderer voice. "She went to the agency and signed away her baby. It's done."

Nora throws herself back in her chair in disbelief. "Why would you do that, honey? Why would you do that?"

"I didn't want to meet them."

"You're still going to have to meet them, my dear." Aunt Linda's breath comes down hot on the top of my head. "I just talked to them and, thank God, they agreed to meet with us all on Saturday anyway. But really, Evelyn. What if you don't like them? Now you have no choice. What were you thinking? Huh? What were you thinking?"

I meet her gaze as Nora quietly says some lawyer-talk about it not really being over because I'm a minor, quiet words I don't have to hear if I don't want to.

I say, "Maybe I was thinking that I just trust my aunt. Ever think of that?"

"No," Aunt Linda says. "Don't you throw this back on me, little girl. I didn't sign up for this. Taking care of you is one thing but watching you completely ruin your life, finding a place for you to just throw your child away, that's not what I was planning on."

The tears on my face go hot. "Well, I'm sorry I'm such a burden."

"Just because your little friend is coming, after Nora and I graciously agreed to squeeze her in here, you're going to turn this into the biggest mistake of your life. What's wrong with you, Evelyn?" Aunt Linda's voice gets louder and louder and Nora's hand gets tighter and tighter, and I guess she's trying to be sympathetic but it starts to feel like a trap, like a handcuff anchoring me to the table. "Why do you go through life turned off? As if talking to the people who love you will threaten your very existence? As if the only thing that matters is your grades and not people? Wake up, little girl. You better wake up before it's too late."

I yank my hand away from Nora and slam up the stairs, flying from the door to my bed and burying my hot face in my pillow. I am a four-year-old who's about to have a baby.

But when I still hear voices over *The Little Mermaid*, I sneak to the top of the stairs to eavesdrop.

"You're forgetting there are two children involved here," Nora is saying. "She's a kid. A pregnant kid, but she's still a kid. How is she supposed to make a decision like this?"

"What kind of kid is she?" They aren't arguing. They're having one of those loud work-it-out conversations. "She doesn't laugh. She doesn't play. She doesn't have friends. She just seals herself in a cocoon and she's going to rot in there if she doesn't come out." Aunt Linda might be crying. I picture them sitting at the table, Nora's arm draped across her shoulders.

"She will. And when she does, she's going to miss that baby and it's going to hurt more than even her favorite aunt biting her head off."

They're quiet for a while, then Aunt Linda says, "Thank you, Nora."

"Thank you?" Nora laughs. "I was too horrified to even say anything."

"No, thank you for loving her. I know you didn't want her here, but thank you."

I feel the tears coming on again, but their meaning changes quickly when Nora says, "I was crazy. I'm wild about that niece of yours. And you see how great she is with Celie and Tammy, especially Tammy. It took someone with a shell as thick as Evie's to get Tammy to take even the smallest chisel to her own."

"They are two peas in a pod," Aunt Linda says. "I'm so scared of the day when she regrets this. And what is Judy going to say?"

"Let me tell her," Nora says. "Judy and me . . . we're two peas also, aren't we?"

Yes, Aunt Linda. Let Nora tell her.

She says, "Okay. You might be right."

"And as for when she regrets this, you and me, we'll be here. Okay? When you take a kid in during the worst year of her life, you commit to her forever. I see that now."

I'll take them up on that, even though I'm not going to regret it.

The Next Day

It's my dad who calls me. I've been responding to most of his daily e-mails but I haven't actually spoken to him since Christmas.

"Is Mom going to call me too?" I ask when I answer the phone, before even saying hello.

"Only if you hang up on me. We decided to let me handle this one."

"Oh, so what, now that you're divorced, you guys are a team?" I snap, but I'm actually relieved.

Then he knocks my guard down completely by laughing. "It's amazing how much easier it is to get along without all the pretending. And neither of us are ever pretending when we love you."

I stay silent.

"Listen, everyone is done trying to force you. You are both too old and too young for that much pressure. But we really think you should go this Saturday, meet these people, and find out if they will negotiate something so that if, one day, you really want to know what's up with that person inside you, you can find out."

"I'm not going to want to know, Dad," I say, with a certainty I don't feel.

"It's not like it'll be too late on Saturday. But if you walk out of that hospital without a plan, it might be too late."

Why doesn't anyone ever listen to what I say? "I want to walk out of that hospital and never think about this again."

He sighs. I'm getting used to people sighing into my cell phone. "Think about it, Pumpkin. That's not going to happen. You really aren't thinking."

21 Days Till Normal

Friday after school, it's finally spring break. Maryellie and I walk through the school parking lot talking about Lizzie, who's arriving in a few hours.

"Hey," I say. "Do you and Mario and Emanuella want to come over tonight? Aunt Nora is cooking a big lasagna for everyone because my parents are going to be there too. And you could meet Lizzie." And everyone will be less likely to keep talking about what a mistake I'm making by refusing to go with them tomorrow if they're meeting Maryellie for the first time.

"Oh my God! Yes! It's like now that I have a baby I can never hang out anymore, you know? But Mario got his car back last week, so yes. Yes! What time?"

"Seven thirty?"

"Yes. So fun!"

I look at her, picking up her enthusiasm. "And the girls haven't met Emanuella yet. They'll be so thrilled."

And so we're all crammed into Aunt Linda's little living room. Cecelia, Tammy, Maryellie, Mario, and Emanuella at the kid table. Aunt Linda, Aunt Nora, Mom, Dad, Lizzie, and me around the big table. My dad is telling a story about one of his students making up an entire ancient community for a class presentation on native peoples. He gets out of his seat to demonstrate the "rain dance" the kid fabricated, and everyone doubles over with laughter when my dad hops up and down, waving his hands over his face. Even Cecelia, who has no idea what he's doing. Even Tammy, who's still afraid of her uncle Jim. Even Emanuella, who just learned how to laugh. Even Mom.

There are six parents in the room—Mom, Dad, Aunt Linda, Aunt Nora, Maryellie, and Mario—and they're all here because of me. Everyone in this room is here because of me.

It's enough to make me think about going to their stupid meeting tomorrow.

I get up to go to the bathroom and it rushes down my legs, soaking my socks before I can even get to the toilet. I'm mortified, thinking I peed myself, until I realize what this really is—my water broke.

"Mom," I say, waddling back into the room. "I need to go to the hospital."

Waiting for Normal

They finally have to tear him right out of my middle.

Then there he is: a bloody, slimy, screaming, miraculous creature writhing around on my chest.

Oh, I think, *there you are, Bean. That's you.*

He's beautiful.

There is night and day and he is here and not here and here and not here and they keep shoving words in our room—healthy, eight pounds, male, healthy—but I don't talk or think. I just take in his weight in my arms, his feet cracked and red and kicking, his hairless eyebrow muscles bouncing like kittens, his red hair in my nose and so many lips on his head—female lips, male lips, Chinese lips, Latina lips, white lips, black lips. He goes around and around like a hot potato and it rips the scar on my gut deeper every time the eight pounds leaves my elbow pit and everyone, everyone—Mom and Dad, Aunt Nora and Aunt Linda, Lizzie and Maryellie, Celie and Tammy—crying and apologizing and showering tears on me like a baptism.

Him

When my eyes open, all the kissing, crying people are gone, and it's just the two of us—Bean fastened tight in the crook of my arm. His nose is a tiny white-chocolate Hershey's kiss. His mouth is a pink oval, opening and closing with each breath. He has a shock of red hair on top of his white head. He's beautiful.

"I love him," says a voice from the chair next to my bed.

My head whips to the side. Todd. His eyes are big and round and pleading. I can't hate him because his eyes are just like Bean's. I'm too tired to be angry right now. And I can't be in love with him because I'm too in love with my baby.

"Lizzie and your friend Maryellie called while you were in labor last night. Told me to get my butt over here," he says, though I haven't had enough active brain cells to wonder.

He puts his arms out and, instinctively, I hand the warm bundle of baby to his father. To say hello. And good-bye.

I look at Todd. His eyes are glued to Bean's sleeping ones. "I even had to tell my mom," he says over the red hair. I hadn't thought to wonder about this either. Todd leans over the bed, holding Bean right next to his face. "E," he says. "He's perfect."

Todd puts Bean on my shoulder but keeps holding him. We stare at our baby. A family. A pathetic little family, but a family. For a day or two.

The nurse comes to give me more meds and I fall asleep with Bean on my shoulder.

When I wake up again my arms are empty, like my uterus.

The room is full, so full it looks like a party. I remember visiting Maryellie and Emanuella, thinking that my hospital room would be as empty and lonely as the other side of her curtain. What was I thinking?

Mom and Aunt Linda are in the corner with their arms around each other; Aunt Nora and Lizzie and Dad play cards in front of the window; Bean yawns in Todd's arms in the chair, his mom looking over his shoulder.

Todd's hand is on Bean's forehead. "I'm your daddy. You're my little man," he says.

My body has been strained and torn and stretched to its limit, but the pain doesn't register through the fog and the love in the room.

The room goes fuzzy and blue. Todd sees my eyes open and puts my baby back in my arms. I sniff in his powdery scent and take him with me back to dreamland where we can be a family.

Them

And then they come. And they cry different tears.

And they say "thank you" instead of "I'm sorry."

And she smells like sugar and lavender and when she kisses my cheek, I can feel how plump her face is, and he has a voice deep and smooth as chocolate milk and he keeps telling me how wonderful I am. But he is wrong and she is wrong and I can't look at them.

I haven't been able to say a word to them. To anyone.

Then my arms are tight around his little body and there are tears all over his hair and his ears and it's not that I think I should keep him, but I don't know how to make my arms any less tight around this squirming, red-haired, pink, and wrinkly little miracle.

And then he's gone.

My insides are empty. And everything can go back to normal.

Normal

I wake up and go home from the hospital. He is not with me. It was a mistake.

Empty

I try to study. The words in my textbooks still swim. My breasts swell and ache pointlessly. I think about Bean and I think about Lizzie and I don't think about Todd and I talk to Maryellie and Aunt Linda and everyone in group and I tell them all that it was a mistake.

I play with Celie and Tammy.

I go back to school at Santa Maria.

I tell Aunt Nora in the kitchen and Mom on the phone and Dad by e-mail: it was a mistake.

Everyone talks but the words are nonsense, bugs flying around my ears. Pointless. I keep talking anyway.

1 Month Empty

It was a mistake. I talk and talk and talk. I think and think and think. I am the biggest dumbass ever. It was all a mistake.

Maryellie

We're at lunch, the table fitting easily between our stomachs—mine a plump, empty mush, hers back to skinny.

"It's Mario's and my third anniversary Friday," Maryellie tells me.

I look up from my turkey sandwich. "Congrats."

"Do you think you could come over and watch Emanuella so we can go out to dinner?" she asks.

My jaw drops. *You'd trust me with her? A baby?*

Yes. I want to say yes. I want to help her.

An evening with a baby. She thinks I can do it. I could sit and coo and smell her flowery skin.

Open your mouth and say yes, I tell my brain.

Before I can, a big, fat, salty drop falls from my eye to my sandwich. Maryellie reaches out and puts her hand on mine.

"It's okay. My mom will do it. I just thought it might be good for you. Let me know when you're ready."

I nod. "Thank you. Thank you for asking," I say, trying to convey how much it means that she would trust me.

But I don't think I will ever be able to watch her. Because Emanuella will never be Bean.

2 Months Empty

Mistake, mistake, mistake, mistake.

An Empty Senior

Aunt Linda pulls me into her office to look at my final report card for my junior year: a row of As with only a tiny minus or two to signify that Bean was ever inside of me.

I shrug. "It's easier here than at St. Mary's."

She says, "Does this show you at all that maybe part of your decision wasn't a mistake? That you met at least one of your goals. You're probably still going to be valedictorian."

I shrug.

Her face falls. "No?"

"Aunt Linda . . . I don't deserve to be valedictorian." It's true. I'm a worthless, ugly fool who closed her ears to her own child. I did the same thing my parents did to me. I'm awful.

"Look, Evelyn, I'm glad you're talking, but you have to listen now." And she is speaking with an edge in her voice that makes all the bugs settle down and stop flying. For good measure, she takes my cheeks in both of her palms and forces my eyes to focus on her face. "He's going to have a good life. He has parents who are ready—more ready than you and Todd, or Aunt Nora and me, or your own parents." I wonder if that could be true. "He has parents who want him more than they want anything. Who aren't going to see faded dreams of Ivy League schools and football scholarships every time they look in his eyes. He's going to be happy. I'm not saying you wouldn't have made him happy too, but I'm not sure you could have been happy the way he's going to be in this new family." Something makes me nod, even though she doesn't get it, like usual. The adoption wasn't the part that was a mistake.

"What is it, Evie? What is this mistake you think you made?"

The words are sticky in my throat, a Laffy-Taffy gumming up my molars, but I get them out into her office. "That I don't even know his name."

Aunt Linda's face cracks open and she wraps her arms around me, and I cry on her shoulder and I don't even hate the crying or the hugging.

Summer

I stay in Chicago to take care of Cecelia and Tammy while my aunts work. Things get better some days, but on others the world comes crashing back onto my scar and I'm the emptiest person alive.

I miss him. I don't even know who I'm missing.

My body thins and stretches back into the me I used to be. I tell myself that's the first step back to normal, but each pound I shed reminds me that he's gone.

And the me I used to be is Bad Evelyn. Or Good Evelyn. Or Sullen, Silent, Unhappy, Slutty, Perfect, Smart, Stony Evelyn. Why do I want normal anyway?

Good-bye

Tammy and Celie sit side by side and spooky silent on the couch, watching Aunt Linda, Mom, and me carry boxes and bags down the stairs and out to my Jeep. I'm avoiding looking at them, but I see Tammy crying big, silent tears, Cecelia kicking her feet against the bottom of the coffee table.

Aunt Nora hangs up the phone in the kitchen and finds me in the driveway, hoisting a final bag into the trunk. "You have to give them a real good-bye," she says.

I slam the hatchback. "Of course," I say.

And she throws her arms around me. This is Aunt Nora, not Aunt Linda, so the hug takes me by surprise, wakes me up. "No, Evelyn. I know you're upset, too, but you need to really sit down with my daughters and make sure they understand you aren't leaving because of them."

I'm offended. I pull my head back so I can look at Aunt Nora straight on. "I'd never leave them. I love them."

"I know that, but they've dealt with way too much

abandonment in their short lives. You need to go in there and tell them you love them. Then you need to call, not just on birthdays, all the time. You can't show up and duck out. When you started helping Tammy with math and taking them trick-or-treating and playing with them every night, you took on a lifetime responsibility."

She's kind of trying to scare me, but instead she's making me glow with importance.

And I get it now: Rule 8. She wasn't afraid I would mess them up. She was afraid of how they would love me.

I go back into the living room and sit between my cousins, letting each of them nuzzle into one of my sides.

"Celie says you aren't really leaving," Tammy says, and my heart squeezes into my throat with the sudden realization of how hard this is going to be, and how sad this really is. How do I even do it? How do I give them a real good-bye like Aunt Nora just explained?

I take Tammy's chin in my palm and point her face to mine. "I love you," I say.

Then I turn and do the same to Cecelia. "And I love you."

She brightens immediately. "So you aren't leaving?"

I take her hands in mine. "I'm not leaving your life. But I am leaving Chicago."

"That's not fair!" Celie screams in my face. She yanks her hands out of mine and storms up the stairs. "That's not fair, Evie! I hate this," she screams when she gets to the top. Even though I'm not pregnant anymore, I feel like crying.

I look at Tammy. Giant tears fall off her face and dot her jeans. "Why?" she asks.

I put my arm around her. "I just need to go back and live

with my own mommy for a little longer. But I'm going to miss you every day. Every minute of every day. And believe me, you'll hear from me so much, you'll be sick of your cousin Evie."

I win a small smile, and Tammy throws her little arms around my neck, her little body onto my lap. "I love you, Evie," she says.

When my mom pulls out of the driveway, I'm wondering how the list of kids I've abandoned recently just jumped from one to three.

But the second we pull on the highway, about five minutes after we left the house, I dial Aunt Linda's number.

"Can you put Celie and Tammy on?" I ask.

"How'd you get so clever, little niece?" she says, before running to get her daughters.

When I hear Cecelia's little voice I say, "So how are you, Medium? I miss you."

"You're silly, Evie." I can hear her relief already.

"Maybe. But I love you. And I do miss you already. Listen to me, cousins. I'm going to call you every day. Every day," I say. And I will.

Homecoming

Nothing can really go back to normal until I get to Jacksonville. Or until I start school. Until I start running races. Until I win a race. Until I get a progress report. Until I drink and smoke and screw around again. Until Lizzie and I make another plan to go dad hunting. Normal never comes.

The Evelyn that comes back is not Bad or Good or any Evelyn anyone from Jacksonville has ever met. Somehow, I drag Talkative Evelyn back across the country. My throat gets sore.

Bean talk, Bean talk, Bean talk. To Lizzie at her house. To Lizzie at Sean's party. To Mom at our house one night. To Aunt Linda on the phone.

I hear everyone telling me how proud they are that I'm talking, that I'm studying, that I'm running, that I'm painting. They use words to describe me: brave, strong, capable. Words that seem as far away as the stars. I distract myself like an ant—carrying more than my weight on my back. My mind is still rooted to my belly, even though it's empty and concave again.

My brain is solidly in Never-Never Land with Bean.

After practice, my Jeep rolls into Mary's parking lot. My skinny butt lands back on her couch. And even though I'm not pregnant, I let myself sob while her tiny hands make ovals on my shoulders.

"It was stupid," I say. "I should have found out about them. I should have made it so I can see him, or so I can see if he's okay."

Mary strokes my back like she's been doing for the past week, like she's basically been doing over the phone since April.

"Nothing is ever going to be back to normal."

"Oh, Evelyn," she says, "I'm so sorry. You did a selfless thing. You gave him a good life."

But it hurts like she's stabbing me with each word because I did it for myself.

Mary asks, "What scares you the most?"

"What if he is always looking for me, like Lizzie?"

"Lizzie?"

"Yeah, she's always looking for her father, and she can never find him. She thought he was in Chicago last March but it turned out to be someone else. She's always looking and she'll never find him. And it's like this big hole in her heart—and what if that hole is always in Bean's heart?"

"Why don't you register on the adoption or lost parents websites so he can find you one day if he wants to?"

And it's not perfect, but it might be enough to let me drag myself through my senior year.

Single Dad

I go to my dad's new apartment for dinner. He greets me with a spoonful of delicious soup and a song. He's Daddy.

When I walk into his living room, my face is everywhere, redheaded little girls smiling out of a million frames—on the coffee table, on the divider to the kitchen, on the hearth, on the windowsills.

I pull a deck of cards out of my pocket. "How about a game of War after dinner, Dad?"

His smile beams into the living room all the way from the kitchen stove. "You got it, Pumpkin. Get ready to do the dishes."

And suddenly I realize it's actually easier to forgive him after all.

When he brings the soup out to the table, I open my mouth to try on him what I've been trying on everyone else in my life. "I miss him, Dad," I say.

He puts his arm around me. He says these words: "I do too, Pumpkin. I miss him too."

Something releases in my chest. Those are the words I've been waiting for someone—anyone—to say. Those are the words I needed to hear. I didn't even know it.

Being a Mother

Everything I do, I do it for Bean. If he finds me one day, I can tell him I did it for him. I study to get into a good school for him. I run my heart out and collect blue ribbons so I can give them to him. I paint little green-eyed boys smiling on a swing set, playing with a truck in a sandbox, making a snowman in as many layers as Celie used to wear.

I pray, just in case there is a God, that he is as happy as Celie and Tammy.

I'm praying and painting after school, my iPod cranking hip-hop into my ears, my brush flying across the top of the canvas so the leaves in the tallest trees add texture to the blue sky the way I know they're starting to in Chicago right now, and someone taps me on the shoulder.

I swing around and I don't feel bad when a streak of red covers the space where his heart should be.

"I know you hate me now," Todd says, and I do. I hate how his eyes are green, exactly like the little boy's on the canvas. But I never have to see him. He avoids me. He doesn't go to parties. He doesn't hang out at practice after school.

"You should leave," I say.

"No, I—"

"Okay. I will." I start packing up my paints but I'm pissed because that tree had me completely sucked in a minute ago.

"Evelyn, I'm a jerk." I freeze, paintbrushes in hand, halfway to the sink to wash them out. I'll listen. This is not a bug, it's a person. I'll listen, then I can keep hating him. "I had no idea what I was doing. I was so scared. It's not that I didn't care about you. I did. I thought about you every day last year. I missed you. I just . . . sucked at it."

I nod, still not facing him. Some of the hatred disappears through the top of my head, my blood slowing to normal. I kind of want to keep hating him—for putting me through that alone, for saying he wouldn't help—but letting it go does seem easier.

He keeps talking. "Once I saw him, he was real. I don't know . . . he was in you, so maybe he was, like, real to you the whole time. But once I saw him, I loved him. I love him. I, like, don't know what else to do, so I pray for him . . . sometimes."

Shit, don't cry. Not now.

"I just want you to know I would have helped. I was a stupid kid when I told you I wouldn't."

Don't cry. Don't cry.

"And . . . also, thank you. For, you know, having him. For taking care of him while he was with you."

"You need to go now," I say, failing to keep my voice steady.

"No, I need to tell you. Lizzie told me that I need to tell you that they are good. I talked to them. A lot. You were just wrapped up with him and all that so you couldn't, but I talked to them, and I just want you to know that I love him and I think your aunt Linda made a good choice."

A thank-you climbs up my throat but I don't want to give it to him. "It's good you talked to me," I say. "But you need to go now."

I feel his body turn behind me as if we're still connected and, I realize, we always will be, even though Bean's gone. He says, "I'm sorry, E," and goes out the door.

And it's enough. It's enough to pull me through my senior year. I have no choice but to believe him. Bean will be okay.

Being a Teenager

Everything I do, I do it for Bean. Except when I don't.

When I'm running the last hundred meters of the county championship cross-country race and I'm matching step for step with Lindsey Ehardt from the Bolles School and I can tell just how much she wants to beat me, I find the speed in my legs and push past her by half a step, hurtling my torso through the tape. I do it for me. And I feel happy. But is that bad?

When Aunt Nora starts copying Tammy's homework into a PDF file and e-mailing it to me so I can help her over the phone every night, I do it for Tammy. And me. And I'm proud. I'm proud.

When Lizzie, my date to the senior prom, raps into the mirror, dancing in her bright-pink dress while Mom flattens my hair into shiny, rolling curls, I'm laughing. Gut-squelching, tear-producing laughing and so are they. And I'm doing it for all of us.

But I'm not sure if I should be allowed to enjoy any of these things. Because, if Bean were in my life, I wouldn't get them.

And I don't want to be glad that Bean's not in my life.

Moving Back, Moving On

I wasn't the valedictorian. I didn't get into any of the Ivies. I spent the year marveling at everything I gained—Mary, Aunt Nora, Maryellie, Mom's and Dad's voices, Talkative Evelyn with Lizzie, a backbone with Todd—and how none of that matters next to what I lost: Bean.

But I got into Northwestern, so my mom and I are driving me back across the country. A weekend at Aunt Linda and Aunt Nora's house before starting college. Endless weekends with Celie and Tammy. It's more family than I ever dreamed. It should be enough. But a phantom car seat haunts me from the back.

I still have nightmares that he's crying.

We pull into their driveway and my eyes fill, remembering how painful and wonderful it was to live here last year. I hear squealing yells—"She's here!"—coming from inside the house like I'm a magical fairy like Aunt Linda.

A much-larger Cecelia bounces out the front door and

jumps directly into my arms, her legs wrapped around my waist. "You're so little!" she says.

I laugh. "You're so big!"

"There's a surprise inside. I'm not supposed to tell you, though."

"Celie!" Tammy squeals, wrapping her arms around my skinny middle, putting her little fingers in my hair.

I carry Celie into the kitchen, hand in hand with Tammy, hoping the surprise is a drawing or something that I can hang in my dorm room.

But it's him.

Babbling in his mother's arms. Pulling on her necklace. His father stands slightly behind them in the kitchen and Mom and Aunt Linda and Aunt Nora stare at me while Celie slips off my hip and my jaw drops to my chin and my tears fall on the floor. It's him. And he's smiling and drooling. And he's okay.

Green eyes meet mine and his hands stretch toward me. His hair is red.

"It's a closed adoption, but you needed to see him, just this once. Maria understood," Aunt Linda says. I look at Maria. She's short and plump with huge chubby cheeks creating parentheses for her smile.

"Do you want to hold him?" She puts him in my arms and he immediately pulls my red hair and his is the same color but his eyes are green just like Todd's and this is Bean and he's okay.

"Bean," I say finally, through tears.

His dad laughs. "We call him Brandon."

"Brandon-Bean," I say. "You're okay. You're okay."

"He's great," his dad says. "We love him so much."

But he's looking at me like he loves me so much, and now I know he's okay and I'm always going to be empty and I'm never going to be normal, but I'm going to college and Bean and I are going to be okay.

Or, maybe, we'll be happy.

Acknowledgments

Recently, I wake up every day riding a huge wave of joy. It first swept me away when I started writing this book, so I humbly offer abundant thanks:

To Michelle Nagler, Caroline Abbey, and everyone at Bloomsbury for their brilliant insights and their much-needed support and enthusiasm.

To Kate McKean, Always-Awesome Agent, for her editing prowess and for advocating for me and for Evelyn (and for Tammy).

To The New School class of 2012, especially to Monday Group—Dhonielle Clayton, Corey Haydu, Sona Charaipotra, and Amy Ewing—for priceless help with early drafts . . . and for telling me to keep writing!

To my teachers, especially Matt Benedict at Notre Dame and Hettie Jones and David Levithan at The New School—and especially-especially you, Patricia McCormick.

To the alumni of Chicago Jesuit Academy. By being who you are you nourish my soul. Special thanks to the class of

2012 for your continued pestering: "Ms. Carter, where is your book already?"

To my aunts, uncles, my slew of amazing cousins (Ali, Greg, Richie, Brittany, John, Bridget, Danny, Jamie, Kelly, Kelly, Dan, Sarah, Bill, Christopher—this means you!), and my new siblings (that's you, Erin, Tommy, Eric, and Eileen!) for providing countless moments of support, encouragement, and, most importantly, fun.

To my friends for your enthusiasm and excitement—this is really nerve-wracking but you're making it fun—especially Linda, Nestor, Katie, Megan, Melissa, Chemagne, Caitlin, Molly, Betsy, Jenn, Katherine, Kristin, Anna . . . and oh so many more I wish I could name.

To my brand-spankin'-new parents-in-law, Ronnie and Eric Larsson, for welcoming me with open arms and for saying you're proud of me. That means more than you probably know.

To my brilliant, hilarious, and bomb-diggity brother, Dan Carter, for always making me laugh and for being my best friend in toddler-hood. Much love to you, Fratre!

And of course, to the love of my life, Greg Larsson. As this book went from idea to hard-covered, you went from friend to boyfriend to fiancé to husband. Thank you for your unwavering support at every step, and for treating my dream like it's part of your own. I am so lucky.

Finally, to my parents, Bill and Beth Carter. I always said I wanted to write a book. Thank you for never telling me it's too hard. Thank you for always telling me to just do it. And thank you for the innumerable things I can't write in this space. This world would be a better place if every kid (Evelyn, for example) had parents like you.

Read on for a sneak peek of **CAELA CARTER**'s latest **breathtaking**, intensely **honest** tale,

My Best Friend, Maybe

Έκπληξη

(Surprise)

"So, you wanna go?"

That's how she asks me. Like she's talking about a party. Or a chick flick. Or lounging around in her basement during a thunderstorm making ants-on-a-log by scraping the peanut butter out of the middle of peanut-butter crackers because everyone knows that's the best kind.

It's been three years since we last did that, or anything, together.

I raise my eyebrows.

"It's on my mom if you do, the whole eight days. We'll fly into Athens from Newark," Sadie is saying, and I'm wondering if this is real or some bizarre dream. "Then we have to transfer planes for Santorini. That's where my cousin's getting married. Then we'll take a boat to Crete for the party with his family. He's Greek." She adds the last two words like they explain everything. Like my biggest confusion in this jumbled invitation is why Andrea is getting married in Greece.

I slump back in my chair to put a few more inches between us, and I watch her push her white-blond hair out of her eyes. It's streaked with red these days—a new look that blossomed for our junior AP exams last week.

"Charlie's bringing his girlfriend. I don't know about Sam," she's saying.

Her brothers. Who used to feel like my own brothers. It's been ages since I've seen any of them. *Do they miss me? Does her mom?*

"I thought about asking someone else . . ." Sadie trails off.

After a second she says, "I ended up buying you a ticket. So let me know either way, Colette. Okay?"

She actually bought me a ticket?

I shake my head to clear the fog. She takes that as a no, and for a moment I see disappointment clash with triumph across her delicate features.

Then I open my mouth. "Sure."

Sadie's dark-blue eyes grow huge in shock, and I force my own not to mirror them.

"Sure?" she asks, her casual attitude flickering. "That's all?"

"Yup, sure." I slam shut my French notebook and shove it into my backpack. Technically the bell hasn't rung signaling that we can pack up and talk, but everyone has finished their finals. Madame isn't even in the room. She walked out twenty minutes ago. I was the only one with a book open when Sadie plopped down on my desk, her beautiful and intimidating face looming over me as she started babbling about a trip to her cousin's wedding in a few days.

She didn't even say *hello*.

She didn't even look like *sorry*.

"Don't you have questions? Don't you need to think it over?" She leans into me, an amused lilt to her voice, and I remember how she always got most aggressive right before she lost a board game or a race in the pool.

I shake my head, not taking my eyes off my backpack. Of course I have questions. A million questions foaming in my lungs, but they aren't the ones she thinks I'll ask. And to ask them is to lose.

The tension is as thick as the heat in the classroom, the morning sun knifing through the window and drawing a harsh edge across Sadie's profile so that half her face is cast in shadow.

"You aren't going to ask your parents? Run it by Mark?"

Now I look at her.

"What's the problem?" I say, still not sure whose words I'm speaking. I want to say *Why, Sadie? Why now? If you're going to break the silence and invite me somewhere, why couldn't you ask me to hang out at the mall or go swimming?*

Why is everything so big and complicated with you?

She shrugs, but she's staring at me.

"What?" I say. "Do you think you have a monopoly on spontaneity and adventure?"

She raises her eyebrows, her face caught between emotions again: this time, amusement and mortification.

"Okay, I'll see you in Greece, Coley." She pats my brown hair like I'm a little kid. But she always used to do that. But then again, we always were little kids.

Coley. It's still repeating in my ears when the bell rings. No one has called me that in years. Three years.

Ω

"Come on, Coley, wake up!" Sadie said.

The words had barely wiggled their way through my hazy sleepiness before something soft but sharp crashed into my body, forcing me out of my slumber.

Ten-year-old Sadie stood next to my bottom bunk in our tiny beach bedroom. She was holding my purple Speedo, air-dried from our swim the previous evening, right after my family first arrived in Ocean City. She was already dressed in her own red racing suit. She smiled at me and whipped my suit across my middle once more for good measure. My four-year-old twin brothers breathed deeply in the bunks next to ours. "The sun is out," she whispered. "Let's go!"

I smiled and rolled out of the bed, grabbing for my suit. I knew my parents wouldn't let us go down to the beach without them—the shore was a few blocks away and Dad was always saying how dangerous the ocean was—but I didn't argue. I was still nervous about how it would feel to have Sadie on this vacation. This was the first time she'd been invited on my family's beach week, and in the year we'd gone from nine to ten, I'd begun to realize all of the ways Sadie and I were different. Sadie's house was big and extravagantly decorated; her family vacations were to places like France and Hawaii, places that required an airplane. What would she think of this typical beach vacation? What would she think of my mother's skirted bathing suits, my father's corny jokes? Would she get annoyed by Peter's constant whining? Would she be embarrassed by the tiny apartment we rented each year? The outdoor shower? The small room we had to share with my brothers?

But the thing about Sadie is, except for the ways we're

different, we're exactly the same. Or that's the way it used to be. Two brothers (but hers are older), skin so tanned it looked like we'd rolled in the mud pits by the bay, a love of peanut butter, and an ache to be in water whenever we were forced onto dry land.

In the water, all of the differences washed away.

Wearing our suits, we tiptoed down the short hallway and into the little yellow-tiled kitchen of our beach apartment. My mom was sitting at the kitchen table in her faded pink robe, a coffee mug in one hand, her book of morning meditations in the other.

"Good morning, girls!" she whispered. "Looks like you're all set to go."

"Can we?" Sadie asked as my mom handed each of us a granola bar. "Can we put our feet in, at least? The lifeguards are already on duty." Sadie was always the brave one.

My mom glanced at her watch and, to my surprise, seemed to consider the request.

"You won't go in past your knees until we get down there?" she asked.

"Oh, no, Mrs. Jacobs," Sadie said through a mouthful of granola. "We'll just play trip tag until you get there. Colette has been 'It' since last summer. I have to give her some chance to catch me."

I nodded enthusiastically beside my best friend. I loved trip tag. It was better played in deep water, but we could play it in the shallow part. It was a game we'd invented with Sadie's brothers the summer before. When you were It, you had to dive for someone else's ankle and yank it so that he or she tilted into the water. If the tripee got her hair wet, she became the next It until we played again. And Sadie was right—I'd been It for a good nine months now.

"We'll be safe until you get there, Mom," I promised.

Mom chuckled. "Well, I hope you'll be safe even after we get there," she said. And I knew we had won.

Minutes later we were sprinting down the few short blocks between us and the water, flip-flops clapping against the pavement, towels streaking behind us. By the time my parents finally got to the beach, I was no longer It.

That's how things went all week. Trip tag in the early morning. Jumping waves, body surfing, and making up imaginary games in the ocean all day. It was the best week of summer. My long hair turned to straw and my brown eyes were constantly ringed with an edge of red from hours and hours spent in salt water. Being in the ocean with Sadie was like being in another world, one without rules or gravity.

My dad called us mermaids, but I knew we were more than that. We were fish. We were best friends.

Sadie was mine and I was hers. I knew it the way I knew my backbone held me up.

I was wrong.

Ω

I dart out of the classroom the minute the bell finally buzzes. I need to beat Sadie out of here. I need to get out the door without looking in her eyes, without her seeing that I'm confused. Maybe terrified.

I dodge the start-of-summer celebrations in the hallway, hurrying through crowds of students to get to my locker. Was it a real invitation or a challenge? The tight knot of our friendship had been loosened by time and then frayed by all the ways she ignored me, all the times when we passed in the hall and I didn't even get a small wave. It's over. I've dealt with it. I've moved on.

Why did I say I would go?

I stop dead when I see my locker, and a train of squealing freshman girls crashes into my back. I wasn't even thinking that he'd be there.

It's a Friday, and even if it is only noon, it's technically the end of the school day, so of course Mark is leaning against my locker with a pink paper cone in his hands. I try not to roll my eyes as I resume walking down the hallway. It's peonies this week. It was just peonies, like, three weeks ago.

I used to love the Flower Routine. Back when we first started going out at the beginning of my sophomore year, it was so exciting to have this hot junior standing by my locker every Friday morning with a different bouquet. I counted the weeks we'd been dating by numbering the displays in my head: 1. White roses. 2. Purple orchids. 3. Pink carnations. 4. Red roses . . .

As a senior Mark has been able to leave the campus during his free periods, so he switched it up about halfway through the year and started bringing me flowers at the end of the day instead of the beginning. Living dangerously! The first Friday morning that he wasn't leaning on my locker, I was shocked at the relief I felt seeing its empty surface. Maybe we were done with the charade. Maybe we could be a real couple now. Maybe he'd start acting the way guys are supposed to: like he was into me—my lips, my hair, my chest—more than our relationship. But there he was at the end of the day, with sunflowers. That was a new one.

I'm not supposed to want those other things anyway. I have to be the girl who wants flowers.

"Here you go, beautiful," he chirps when I get to my locker. "Happy week-versary."

I make myself smell the purple buds. I make myself say "Thank you."

He puts his hands on my shoulders, and I bend my neck

back to look at him before he can give me a kiss. His chestnut hair falls across his forehead, into his hazel eyes. His smile makes his cheeks puff out and rearranges his freckles. I love how I never know quite where to look for them. His one front tooth is slightly crooked, something I'd never be able to see if I wasn't standing this close to him. It makes me think about running my tongue over it. It makes me imagine crushing my body into his, jamming him against the locker and feeling his pectoral muscles stiffen as he squeezes me tighter.

He brushes his lips lightly against mine. That's all I'm supposed to want.

"So, what's new?" he asks.

I blink hard to make the body-crushing fantasy go away. It fades but it's always there, buzzing on the edges of my being like a siren.

"I was talking to Sadie Pepper," I say.

His eyes go wide. "Seriously?"

Yes, seriously. She was my best friend.

I nod, then put the flowers down so I can finish cleaning out my locker.

"What did she want?" he asks carefully, and my heart melts. He tries so hard to never say anything bad about anyone. He won't admit he hates Sadie, even though I know he does. Even though he hates her for hurting me. He's so good.

"She wants me to go on her family vacation this summer. To Greece. For her cousin's wedding." I see him wince despite the fact that I left out the part about this Sadie-trip starting only one day before Mark and I are supposed to leave for Costa Rica for our service trip. The one we've been planning all year. The one that I raised thousands of dollars to go on. The one that took months of pleading and persuading and petitioning my parents before Mom granted permission.

I crouch, concentrating on cleaning the few remaining notebooks out of the bottom of my locker, stacking them neatly to put into my backpack. But everything should go in the trash at this point. Another school year mastered. Another check in the box indicating another 365 days of doing everything right. Perfectly.

"Really?" he asks, picking up the peonies from where I left them next to my knee.

I suck in air. He's staring at the flowers, chewing his bottom lip. Scared. Adorable. Maybe we'll get to make out again after his graduation tomorrow.

"I'm not going."

"'Course not," he says, but I feel his relief. He squeezes my shoulder and slides down to the floor, his back against the lockers, his long sweeper-legs sprawled out in front of him.

"Why would you give up the summer with me right before

I leave for college? Why would you give up Costa Rica for Greece?" He smiles a goofy smile. "Who does Sadie Pepper think she is?" He chuckles.

My best friend, I answer in my head. *Maybe.*

"That girl," Mark concludes, shaking his head.

I miss her.

It never does any good to tell him that.

"I know, right?" I say, rolling my eyes.

Maybe she misses me. Maybe she still thinks about the milk shake, the promise.

Guilt bites at my heart. I try not to lie to him. Unless it's about flowers.

CAELA CARTER is the author of *Me, Him, Them, and It* and *My Best Friend, Maybe*. She spent eight years working in middle and high schools as a teacher and a librarian. A graduate of The New School's MFA program, she also writes for Teen Writers Bloc, a blog on children's literature. She lives in New York with her husband.

www.caelacarter.com
@CaelaCarter